FAIR NEW WORLD

To Stacy,
With best wishes,
Enjoy!

PRAISE

Fair New World is that rare thing: an entirely independent-minded book that is fearless in its satire of existing orthodoxies, no matter which direction they come from. In my course on dystopian futures it always stimulates lively and prolonged discussion. My students couldn't agree on whether it is more scathing in its depiction of Feminania or Bruteland, and its proposed solutions led to much wistful longing.

The novel is a living example of the importance of free speech and free thought, rarely found these days in higher education, and that is only one of the many reasons that it is a valuable teaching tool. It is also great fun to read, making us constantly stop and think as we trip over its hilarious extrapolations from the everyday craziness that surrounds us.

— **Daphne Patai**, University of Massachusetts Amherst, 2014

Fair New World by Lou Tafler is one of the few novels I read written in the past 30 years I felt was not a waste of my time. It is brilliant, and funny (only Kafka and a few other writers can make me laugh out loud while reading) and deadly serious. It deserves to find its place on the shelf next to *We*, *Brave New World*, and *Nineteen Eighty Four*.

— **Richard Stephens**, in *A Funny Thing Happened on the Way to the Brutestag*, 2008

It's the most politically incorrect work of art I have ever seen. It's also hilariously funny and scathingly insightful.

— **Karen Selick**, *Canadian Lawyer*, March 1995

Tafler's book attempts to depict how a politically correct world would actually appear. To the casual reader some of these excursions may appear too bizarre to be taken seriously. The truth, however, is more disturbing. *Fair New World* satirizes the actual daily life in a growing number of North American universities.

— **David Smith**, SAFS Newsletter, July 1995

Readers will recognize in Feminania both stereotypical femininity and stereotypical feminism–but the latter rings soberingly true. Using a mixture of pathetic, hilarious, and frightening excesses of feminism, Tafler successfully and most readably extrapolates current sexual correctness trends into the future … this finely written book gives one much to laugh and cry about, all the while absorbing the reader and conveying a potent political message. It is highly recommended.

— **Joseph Fulda**, *Sexuality and Culture*, Autumn 1997

Designed to restore your faith in human depravity.

— **Stan Persky**, reviewer for *The Globe and Mail*, 1994

Fair New World is a political novel focused on the war between the sexes. Its genre is obviously that of Orwell's *Nineteen Eighty Four* and Huxley's *Brave New World*—and it stands comparison to these classics in its style, depth and satirical wit. From the vantage point of Tafler's three fictional societies we can better appreciate the creeping insidiousness of certain ideological currents in our own social world. The first society, Feminania, is dominated by feminism-run-amok. The second, Bruteland, embodies extreme "machismo" values (reminiscent of certain American cities). And the third, Melior, outlines Tafler's vision of social sanity.

Elements of deliciously taboo-smashing realism grade into a relentlessly detailed surrealism which, more than once, takes the reader over the edge of the politically unthinkable and unsayable. It may be a nightmare into which we plunge, but it is a poignantly contemporary nightmare. This book just may wake some people up—if anything can.

—**Kurt Preinsperg**, Vancouver Community College, 1994

Unrelenting linguistic invention, an instinct for the jugular and a glee in witty hatchetry characterize Lou Tafler's futuristic third novel. *Fair New World* is an acerbic political nightmare satirizing a condition we must cure if we are not to go on dying of it, the AIDS of the body politic. The sexual war is feeding on its atrocities. The rhetoric of Fairness has replaced contemplation of the Good in public life . . . Femininnies and Brutelanders occupy politically sovereign nation-states. Legislation settling scores old and new, grievances real and imagined, has defeated any idea of a shared male and female humanity . . . Language and polity enshrine gender humiliation. Men and women are so divided they are reduced to their merest differences . . . Drawn into the final showdown, neighbouring Melior is a land so well off it can afford the luxury of Soloman Kohan. He has just been elected Philosopher-King but would just as soon not bear the burden of office . . . Enter also much-threatened Hardy Orbs, the last Homo Socratus, martyr to a war whose scars are teethmarks at the centre of Eden's sour apple, here reconstituted along the lines of Swift, Orwell and Vonnegut: marinated in three times its volume of acid royal.

—**Michael Godfrey**, Dawson College, Montreal, 1994

Fair New World is a novel that manages marvellously to be serious, alarming and funny all at the same time. Although it is Orwellian in its projection . . . into the future (2084), it wholly lacks Orwell's depressing grimness and pessimism. The book is Swiftian in the savagery of its humour, which is directed at the very real and present dangers inherent in radical feminism and political correctness running amok, with the possibility of an extremist and fascistic "masculinist" reaction lurking in the dark corners. Tafler reduces to absurdity current cultural tendencies by pushing them to their utmost logical—and irrational—development. The most alarming feature of the book is the insanely and systematically feminized language of Feminania, the feminist utopia, he limns so amusingly ... After reading it for a few pages it suddenly begins to seem so natural that one ceases to have recourse to the glossary at the back of the book. Now that's *really* scary.

—**Donald Todd**, Simon Fraser University, 1994

Fair New World plays deliberate changes on three major sources, *Nineteen Eighty Four*, *Brave New World*, and Plato's *Republic*. Ingeniously, the last name is transplanted and reconciled with the practices and ethos of a liberal democracy of the kind that Plato detested and merged with a Taoist ideal of balanced polarity. In the process of creating from these varied sources a Swiftian combination of a utopian and dystopian vision, Tafler brings into play an abundance of invention, verbal ebullience and wit. These, together with an eye for and relish in the absurd and ridiculous, serve his anger as he satirizes the excesses of feminism and political correctness of the contemporary scene. Set in the year 2084, the book plays on the projection screen of the future grotesquely amplified images of some ideological excrescences that Tafler sees shaping the relations of men and women. The dystopian polities are Feminania, in which literally or figuratively castrated men perform only menial tasks, Bruteland, a world in which women are sex and household slaves, and Melior, a utopian polity which frames its laws and customs on the assumption that men and women can lead equally fulfilling lives only when both honour and appreciate the essentially different emotional and psychological characteristics with which they are endowed ...

—**Kay Stockholder**, The University of British Columbia, 1994

FAIR NEW WORLD

LOU TAFLER

Distributed by
Argo Navis Author Services
www.argonavisdigital.com

This novel is a work of friction. Names, characters, places and incidents are either the product of the author's imagination or are used fictitiously. Any resemblance to actual persons living or dead, or to actual events or locales, is entirely coincidental.

Copyright © Lou Tafler, Vancouver, 1994

Cover art: Fusion, by Liv Thorsland, 1994 (original drawing: charcoal, 24" x 36")

The extract from L.W. Sumner (in the Foreword) is reprinted with permission of Cambridge University Press.

Excerpt from The Decline of the West by Oswald Spengler, translation copyright © 1928, copyright renewed 1956 by Alfred A. Knopf, a division of Random House LLC.
Used by permission of Alfred A. Knopf, an imprint of the Knopf Doubleday Publishing Group, a division of Random House LLC. All rights reserved.

Brief quote from p.30 from The Female Eunuch by Germaine Greer. Copyright © 1970 by Germaine Greer. Reprinted by permission of HarperCollins publishers.

The quote attributed to Anaïs Nin has been printed in Quotable Women by Running Press Book Publishers.

First edition: Backlash Books 1994, in a limited edition of 2,000 copies, of which the first 1,000 are numbered copies.

Second edition: Argo Navis 2014.

All rights reserved. No part of this book or its cover may be reproduced, copied or utilized in any form or by any means, electronic, digital, mechanical, including but not limited to photocopying, recording, scanning or by way of storage into or out of any information or retrieval system, without the express, prior written consent of the publisher.

eBook ISBN: 978-0-7867-5628-5
Print ISBN: 978-0-7867-5627-8

Distributed by Argo Navis Author Services

TABLE OF DISCONTENTS

Praise	*iii*
Copyright	*viii*
Dedication	*xi*
Foreword	*xiii*
Prologue	1
Chapter 1	3
Book One: Feminania	
Chapter 2	9
Chapter 3	27
Chapter 4	45
Book Two: Bruteland	
Chapter Five	67
Chapter Six	83
Chapter Seven	97

Book Three: Feminania

Chapther Eight	115
Chapther Nine	129
Chapther Ten	147

Book Four: Melior

Chapter Eleven	167
Chapter Twelve	181
Chapter Thirteen	197

Epilogue

Chapter Fourteen	215
Glossary of Fairspeak	237

Thanks to Moshe, who impelled it;
to the politically correct, who compelled it;
and to Liv, who propelled it.

FOREWORD BY HARDY ORBS

The battle between the sexes is an age-old tale. Over two thousand years ago, the Greek playwright Aristophanes premiered his comic play, *Lysistrata*. Performed in Athens in 411 BCE, the play is set near the end of the Peloponnesian War. The heroine, Lysistrata, is determined to bring about an end to the decades-long conflict. To do so, she persuades the women of Athens and Sparta to withhold sex from their husbands as an incentive for them to negotiate a lasting peace. The suffering brought about by the withdrawal of marital privilege was so much greater than the suffering brought about by war that the men capitulated within days. Forced to choose between abstinence and peace, they chose peace. As Mary Wollstonecraft reminds us, "The two sexes mutually corrupt and improve each other."[1]

Despite the timelessness of Aristophanes' tale, the twentieth century saw more dramatic changes in relations between the sexes than any previous century. These changes not only coincided with unprecedented increases in health, wealth and knowledge, they also coincided with the rise of the first modern forms of birth control.

Semi-reliable condoms in the late nineteenth century and fully reliable chemical methods in the 1960s gave women and men greater freedom to pursue their passions than ever before. Prior to this, the only effective means of birth control had been the development of social institutions designed to separate the sexes. Far from it being the case, as the revealed truth of Feminanian doctrine[2] has it, that for millennia men had subjugated women for their own selfish ends, women and men had worked together to reach a consensus that allowed them to minimize unwanted pregnancies. The wholesale unravelling of this arrangement during the second half of the twentieth century meant not just the introduction of new co-educational practices, but the free intermingling of men and women of all ages for the first time in recorded history. Perhaps it is not surprising that misunderstandings and tensions between the sexes were to reach new heights, unlike anything experienced in centuries past.

, , ,

I first met Lou Tafler when we were hired to teach at the same university in the late 1980s and early 1990s. Tafler had been hired to teach ethics. I had been hired to teach logic. We hit it off immediately. Not only did we enjoy each other's sardonic sense of humor, we had overlapping interests on a wide range of topics, including classic literature, political history, economic theory, democracy, the rule of law, logic and the scientific method, to name just a few. It also turned out that we shared a secret.

The last two decades of the twentieth century witnessed the introduction of an oppressive climate of intellectual conformity within the western world's universities. In many ways it was similar to the culture of conformity that Ronald Dworkin reminds us existed in Khoumeni's Iran, Torquemada's Spain and Joe McCarthy's America.[3]

Although not as deadly as the first two of these periods of history, the drive for intellectual conformity within the university was just as toxic as that of McCarthy's America. On any number of university campuses, people as prominent as Ayaan Hirsi Ali,[4] Condoleezza Rice[5] and Benjamin Netanyahu[6] were prevented from speaking. Otherwise qualified academics were denied faculty positions, simply because they failed to toe the politically correct party line. Chief among the beliefs being enforced was the claim that because women had been denied their place within the academy for centuries, it was only right that they now be given preferential treatment in hiring. As one member of a hiring committee at a major Femininian university explained, as long as men account for over 50% of professors, we should hire women. The only exception will be if none of the women applicants is in favour of reverse discrimination. In that case it is better to hire a man who is committed to reverse discrimination, since this will result, in the long run, in the hiring of more politically correct women.

Diversity within the university, it seemed, was to be encouraged in everything except ideas. As the former Vice-chair of the United States Commission on Civil Rights, Abigail Thernstrom, famously put it, our universities had become "islands of repression in a sea of freedom."[7]

It was in this climate that Tafler and I entered the academic job market. Given our opposition to politically based hiring, we found ourselves forced to teach under pseudonyms, he as Louis Marinoff, I as Andrew Irvine. To get through the hiring process, both of us had created elaborate backstories. I passed myself off as a kid from the Canadian prairies who believed that honesty and hard work were all it took to succeed in life. Tafler had created what seemed to me to be a much more exotic biography. As Marinoff, he had attended the best schools and universities at home and overseas. He had also developed an enviable assortment of abilities, ranging from top-notch classroom skills to a wide range of talents in the then newly emerging field of computer programming. In short, Marinoff presented to the university the ideal combination of academic training, urban sophistication and real-world experience, even if he happened to be male.

As it turned out, neither of us found it easy to keep secret our true identities. When asked at job interviews about my opposition to reverse discrimination, I said it was a clear fallacy to equate reverse discrimination with non-discrimination. Being opposed to reverse discrimination did not imply being opposed to equal rights for women and men, or for gays and straights, or for any other groups in society. In fact, just the opposite. Those who were most in favour of non-discriminatory hiring were often the most likely to be in favour of equal marriage rights for gays, for example.

I often added that, as the father of both a daughter and a son, when it came time for the two of them to enter the job market I hoped they would be treated equally. Older members of the university community shared this common-sense, middle-class aspiration and were quick to nod their approval; but among the younger, more politically influential ideologues, this view was seen as unspeakably naïve. Older members of the university might be excused for their inability to keep pace with modern political ideals, but a young, upcoming academic was simply to be pitied for his lack of intellectual sophistication if he didn't recognize the need for progressive measures such as the licensing of parents, the introduction of death taxes, the equalization of income and the necessity of reverse discrimination, euphemistically called affirmative action.

Tafler, in contrast, couldn't be accused of a lack of sophistication. For one thing, he was a much better dresser. When interrogated about his views, he never hid them; but he also spoke with such worldliness and humor that his interrogators never quite knew what to make of him. Was he being serious or making a joke? Was his latest historical reference being offered in support of, or in opposition to, the views of all right-thinking (that is, left-leaning) academics everywhere? For the bureaucratically minded ideologues who attended his talks, it was all just so terribly confusing.

Tafler's teaching under a pseudonym also gave the university's media spokesman a degree of plausible deniability whenever accusations of political incorrectness arose. "As far as we are able to determine, we do not have, and never have had, a Tafler teaching at this university," the spokesman reported with a straight face whenever the media questioned him about Tafler's latest outrage.

, , ,

The most serious outrage was *Fair New World*. In it, Tafler recounts an entertaining but dystopian version of recent world history. He tells the story of the rise of Feminania, Bruteland and Melior, and of the eventual war that engulfed them. It is an entertaining read. For those who haven't yet read the book, it is as if George Orwell had collaborated with Kurt Vonnegut. As reviewer Stan Persky tells us, Tafler's writing is "designed to restore your faith in human depravity."[8]

Beneath all the light-hearted comedy (for example, a basketball team lacking its required quota of the vertically challenged) and black humor (for example, a country in which men have only lefts, since it is the women who have all the rights) we find a novel that in many ways remains true to life. The kidnapping, raping and gang-banging of women in Bruteland[9] foretells by decades the kidnapping and selling of Nigerian girls as required by Allah by the Boko Haram leader Abubakar Shekau,[10] as well as the many similar atrocities by members of the much better-funded Islamic State.[11]

The contradictory law contained in Tafler's Political Fairness Act (which states that universities must never and, at the same time, must always discriminate on the basis of gender[12]) is no different than that championed by the courts in Feminania to this day. The rewriting of sexist language in which "linear reasoning" becomes "linear readaughthering" has the effect of destroying one of our culture's most important delivery vehicles of intellectual history. Reviewer David Smith got it right when he wrote in 1995 that, "To the casual reader some of these excursions may appear too bizarre to be taken seriously. The truth, however, is more disturbing. *Fair New World* satirizes the actual daily life in a growing number of North American universities."[13]

Even so, within the universities it has been discriminatory hiring practices that have caused an even greater harm to western nations. Rather than ending discrimination, where it existed, simply by hiring the best-qualified, most-talented applicants, university after university capitulated to the demands of the ideologues and began hiring on political grounds. As essayist William Voegeli reminds us, for decades now it has been the university that has been the natural home for, and purveyor of, political correctness, and it is from the universities that other institutions have taken their lead.[14] The harm done to individuals, both women and men, has been incalculable.

Even more than the damage done to particular careers has been the damage done to the intellectual integrity of the university itself. During the 1980s and 1990s, advocate after advocate of reverse discrimination made the case for temporary, gender-based hiring on the dubious ground that this was the only way to stop systemic discrimination against women. As Wayne Sumner, a high-profile advocate of reverse discrimination, wrote as long ago as 1987, this argument "has the same logic as the justification sometimes offered for imposing temporary restrictions on basic liberties in order to safeguard or expand such liberties in the more distant future. Liberals should, of course, always be suspicious of such authoritarian measures, for the reality is usually that repression is accelerated in the short run in order that it may be further increased in the long run. But this merely reminds us that consequentialist arguments in favour of repression are usually sophistical or hypocritical. It has no bearing on any case in which the temporary or partial restriction of some social good is truly necessary for its ultimate expansion."[15]

We should be suspicious indeed. The problem is that, far from suggesting that the world might need more male nurses in addition to more female doctors, these advocates of reverse discrimination haven't been in favour of gender equity at all. When the facts have been against them, they have ignored them.[16] When they have been asked to oppose discrimination in other contexts, they have never found sufficient reason to do so. Despite all their rhetoric about reverse discrimination being a temporary, gender-neutral method of fighting systemic discrimination, the simple truth is that it has been merely a convenient and hypocritical cover for old-fashioned gender politics. Decades later, there is still no sign that institutional requirements favouring discrimination are to be lifted. Who would have guessed?

, , ,

After several decades of discriminatory university hiring, what has changed? What has become of the handful of university colleagues in Feminania and elsewhere who had the foresight to speak out against the harmful practice of reverse discrimination?

The poet within our little cohort of aspiring academics not only spoke out against sex-based hiring. She also put her career on the line when she refused a job offer at a fine university in a fine city. She turned down the job when she discovered that the search committee had offered it to her on the grounds that, in their view, she was the best-qualified woman, not the best-qualified applicant. A year later she was offered a similar position at an equally fine university in an even nicer city. She has had an outstanding career ever since.

The lawyer among us, who was perhaps our most vocal opponent to reverse discrimination, first took a job in the private sector. Refusing any opportunity for advancement based on factors other than merit, she later happily moved to a high-profile non-profit.

Our mathematician, who in private spoke out passionately and repeatedly against reverse discrimination, always found a reason not to do so in public. Prior to getting tenure he explained that he was too vulnerable to speak openly about such controversial matters. Later, after receiving tenure, he told us that it was inappropriate for him to speak out, lest he unduly sway junior colleagues who needed to be given the independence required to make up their own minds. His adeptness for saying one thing in private and another in public has meant that his career has been assured; but he is also much less respected than he once was.

Several professors at the University of Harmony by the Sea and at Oxymoron U. used tenure as it was meant to be used. They spoke their minds openly on controversial subjects and, in doing so, they gained the lasting respect of many of their colleagues. Perhaps they also lost the respect of a few others but, if so, it had no noticeable effect on their careers.

Three other close friends all found good jobs in fine colleges or universities, although all three would have been appointed to better positions in stronger institutions with higher salaries had reverse discrimination not hampered their careers. Their students and colleagues have benefitted enormously by their appointments and it is to their great credit that they have simply got on with their work, rather than focusing on where their careers might have taken them had stronger universities been willing to offer jobs to the best-qualified applicants, rather than hiring on the basis of sex. Without exception, all three have been, not just assets to their new institutions, but leaders in their chosen fields.

The art historian among us was unable to find a university position. Instead he has made a handsome living as an author and editor, without having to deal with the headache or heartache of university politics.

Others have been less lucky. After speaking out against the injustice of sex-based hiring, one older professor was slandered in Parliament and censured by his home university. Eventually he felt forced to take early retirement, all because he tried to tell taxpayers the truth about how their tax dollars were being spent and how university hiring was being compromised.

Another of our group published one persuasive article after another on the subject of reverse discrimination, as well as on ethical theory. Eventually he was offered a buyout from his home university. He took the money, went to law school and had a successful career as a lawyer. In his retirement, he continues to publish. Even so, his decades of work spent primarily in another profession have been an enormous loss to the academic community.

The youngest within our group, who upon graduation was awarded a Rhodes scholarship, eventually had a mental collapse. No doubt there must have been other physical causes, but it is also easy to imagine that his continued obsession with the injustice of reverse discrimination played a significant role as a contributing factor to this terrible tragedy.

Many others, men and women alike, got the message that universities were no place for people who favoured equal opportunity and simply chose other life paths.

Tafler himself has had a stellar career, even though he found himself banished from his home country of Feminania. The hiring quotas were just too extreme. Eventually he found work as a political refugee in the border region between Bruteland and Melior. He now lectures around the world, travelling more in a year than most people do in a lifetime.

And what has become of me? For the sake of a good story, it is normal for novelists to take a few liberties with the truth. So if I may, I will take a moment to set straight the historical record. I did commit the gender crime of pissing on a parasite, although I confess that it was not me but Henri de Saint-Simon, the father of French socialism, who introduced and popularized the term *parasite* to refer to the kind of bureaucratic functionary who does nothing more than enforce political ideology. I am the one responsible for giving the Brown Skirts their name. I also want to say that it has been a great privilege to have had Soloman Kohan as a friend for so many years.

Although my namesake meets an untimely end in Tafler's novel, it turns out that in fact I am still alive and well, having escaped to Melior during the last few days of the war.

Today I find myself living in a kind of academic Shangri-La, nestled in a valley on the edge of a lake between two great mountain ranges. Each morning I awake to fresh air and spectacular vistas. In the summer there is fresh fruit in the valley. In the autumn there are bright colors covering the hillsides. In the winter there is snow on the ski hills and in the spring there is always a new vintage of wine ready to be uncorked and tasted. Each day I arrive at work to find colleagues enthusiastically defending a full variety of academic and political viewpoints.

It is a great privilege to be surrounded by men and women who prize curiosity more than dogma and who value excellence in research and teaching more than ideology. Clearly there is a connection between political tolerance and intellectual achievement. After so many years witnessing all that can go wrong within the contemporary university, it is a privilege to be part of an institution that embodies so much of what is good and right about education in the modern world.

---

[1] Mary Wollstonecraft, *A Vindication of the Rights of Woman: With Strictures on Political and Moral Subjects*, 3rd edn, London: J. Johnson, 1796, page 318.

[2] For a history of the rise of Feminania, Bruteland and Melior, and their contrasting cultures, readers should consult Lou Tafler's *Fair New World*, originally published in Vancouver by Backlash Books, 1994.

[3] Ronald Dworkin, "Why Academic Freedom?" in *Freedom's Law: The Moral Reading of the American Constitution*, Cambridge: Harvard University Press, 1996, page 252.

[4] Richard Pérez-Peña and Ranzina Vega, "Brandeis Cancels Plan to Give Honorary Degree to Ayaan Hirsi Ali, a Critic of Islam," *New York Times*, 08 April 2014, at www.nytimes.com/2014/04/09/us/brandeis-cancels-plan-to-give-honorary-degree-to-ayaan-hirsi-ali-a-critic-of-islam.html.

[5] Kristina Sguelglia, "Condoleezza Rice Declines to Speak at Rutgers after Student Protests," *CNN*, 05 May 2014, at www.cnn.com/2014/05/04/us/condoleeza-rice-rutgers-protests/index.html.

[6] Canadian Press, "Concordia U Regrets Anti-Netanyahu Riot," *CTV*, 15 January 2003, at web archive org/web/20080601103256/http://www.ctv.ca/servlet/ArticleNews/story/CTVNews/20030115/concordia 030115

[7] First quoted in Chester E. Finn, Jr, "The Campus: 'An Island of Repression in a Sea of Freedom'," *Commentary*, 01 September 1989, at www.commentarymagazine.com/article/the-campus-an-island-of-repression-in-a-sea-of-freedom; later re-quoted in Arnold Aberman, "Blinkered Thinking in Academia," *Financial Post*, 11 June 2014, at

business.financialpost.com/2014/06/11/blinkered-thinking-in-academia. Cf. Maria Konnikova, "Is Social Psychology Biased Against Republicans?" *The New Yorker*, 30 October 2014, at www.newyorker.com/science/maria-konnikova/social-psychology-biased-republicans.

[8] Quoted in Lou Tafler, *Fair New World*, Vancouver: Backlash Books, 1994, page 4.

[9] Or in the Fairspeak of Feminania, "the kuntanapping, freebeeing and geebeeing of kuntas."

[10] Aminu Abubakar and Josh Levs, "'I will sell them,' Boko Haram Leader Says of Kidnapped Nigerian Girls", *CNN World*, 06 May 2014, at www.cnn.com/2014/05/05/world/africa/nigeria-abducted-girls.

[11] Ruth Sherlock, "Isil Commits Human Rights Atrocities on 'Staggering' Scale, Says UN," *The Telegraph*, 02 October 2014, at www.telegraph.co.uk/news/worldnews/islamic-state/11137075/Isil-commits-human-rights-atrocities-on-staggering-scale-says-UN.html.

[12] Or what is called "gendher" in Fairspeak.

[13] David Smith, Review of *Fair New World*, *SAFS Newsletter*, July 1995, page 14.

[14] William Voegeli, "The Higher Education Hustle," *Claremont Review of Books*, vol. 13, no. 2, Spring 2013, at www.claremont.org/article/the-higher-education-hustle/#.VEFOuOeLlOg.

[15] W.L. Sumner, "Positive Sexism," *Social Philosophy and Policy*, vol. 5, 1987, page 213.

[16] Wendy M. Williams and Stephen J. Ceci, "Academic Science Isn't Sexist," *New York Times*, 02 November, 2014, SR12, at nyti.ms/1zS2s01. Cf. Loney, Martin, *The Pursuit of Division*, Montreal: McGill-Queens University Press, 1998.

Prologue

Here, in man and woman, the two kinds of History are fighting for power . . . This secret and fundamental war of the sexes has gone on ever since there were sexes, and will continue—silent, bitter, unforgiving, pitiless—while they continue. In it, too, there are policies, battles, alliances, treaties, treasons . . . There are love-lyrics and war-lyrics, love-dances and weapon-dances, there are two kinds of tragedy—Othello and Macbeth. But nothing in the political world even begins to compare with the abysses of a Clytemnestra's or a Kreimheld's vengeance.

Oswald Spengler

Chapter 1

As the twentieth century closed and the twenty-first opened, hopes long held out for the Millennium were quietly dashed, or at least deferred for another thousand years. While all four digits on the calendar spun together, like so many wheels in sand, retrospective toasts commemorated humanity's unexpected survival of the agonizing century lately spent. And as the twenty-first century progressed (in the narrowest conceivable arithmetic sense: that is, by a mere succession of instants), the West continued its decline without appearing to break stride. Its citizenry danced somnolently, carelessly, asynchronously, yet with remarkable sure-footedness, toward the edges of several varieties of precipice.

Free-thinking observers of political process were dismayed and astounded by the gradual yet relentless emergence of the new tyranny—dismayed, because it bore every possible resemblance to the old; astounded, because it had sprung from the far left, which had finally succeeded in prostrating itself by consistent abuse of its own freedoms. Pundits of every political persuasion grew grim and grey as "group rights" took ever-increasing precedence over purportedly inalienable entitlements of individuals. Spineless mediocrities, parasitic bureaucrats, chronic incompetents and shameless opportunists flocked together under the banner of the "historically disadvantaged". Second-rate demagogues lusting after third-rate powers abetted the spread of a contagious farrago of nonsensical slogans, which asserted that past wrongs could be righted by future retributions. And as the credulous body politic rolled up its collective sleeve to be inoculated with this venomous doctrine, which it gullibly mistook for a vaccine against injustice, the poisoned masses were more incognizant than usual of the true identities of the individual power-seekers—masquerading behind the "interests" of allegedly victimized groups—who were responsible for the widespread political malpractice. As social policy waxed increasingly vindictive, due process waned correspondingly more secretive; the Inquisitorial horrors wrought by imaginary groups upon real individuals were "justifiably" enacted *in camera*, without any fair trial and with every presumption of guilt.

Of singular concern was that aggregate political movement which sought to promote the cause of females far beyond the desirable bounds of legal, moral and cultural equality, and into domains which saw males reduced to chattels, and masculinity degraded to aberration. Many males of the day, lacking either the perspicacity or the disposition or the gonads to reassert themselves, became the most sycophantic and vocal supporters of this new tyranny, only to be devoured by it once it had no further use for them.

The new tyranny took root simultaneously in governments and in the universities, and hence most people were initially ignorant of its very existence. But governments fund universities to undertake research, and results of university research in turn shape governmental policy. And researchers found that the new tyranny was good, and so governments furthered its spread, which also engendered further research into its spread, which researchers found to be a greater good. And so forth. And just like clockwork, society awoke too late.

A formidable backlash of male opposition mounted slowly, but irrevocably. Antagonized by fanatical female sexism, the counter-culture resorted to aggressive male chauvinism, and there reemerged a dominant male hierarchy of unprecedented harshness. The inevitable clash and irreconcilable differences between these two extremist movements culminated in excruciating political cleavage. Two states were born, called Feminania and Bruteland; and soon after, a third, called Melior, comprised of disaffected elements from the other two.

By the latter half of the twenty-first century, these three states had attained an uneasy coexistence. They had evolved by radical means toward divergent ends, according to their respective *raisons d'être* and subsequent *raisons d'état*. Each persisted internally in unstable equilibrium, and among them there obtained a precarious peace. This tale touches lightly but representatively on the manner and quality of life within each state, and treats briefly of their international relations which, by the year 2084, were in a markedly deteriorating condition.

, , ,

A word might be said about the respective languages spoken in these states, each of which is clearly derived from post-modern English, but each of which differs in some fundamental respects. It should not be surprising that linguistic dissimilarities reflect political differences. While the tongues of Bruteland and of Melior are straightforwardly intelligible to speakers of post-modern English, the structural vocabulary of the Feminanian language (called "Fairspeak") may require some preliminary explanation.

In the first place, Feminanians have rejected the word "woman" (whose etymology, "from man", they find ideologically repugnant). They retain the words "man" and "men", but have changed "woman" to "womban" and "women" to "womben". Moreover, they have replaced the lexemes "man" and "men" with "womban" and "womben" respectively, in every possible instance. So, for example, the Feminanian word for "craftsman" is "craftswomban". Their substitutions fanatically embrace even words whose etymology is gender-neutral. Thus "manufacture" becomes "wombanufacture" (even though the "manu" in "manufacture" derives from the Latin *manus*, meaning "hand"). Feminanians have thus subjected the English language to a thorough "man"-hunt, with results such as "dewomband" (instead of "demand") and "wombandate" (instead of "mandate"). This principle also holds for every possible occurrence of "men". Thus "implement" becomes "implewombent", "mention" becomes "wombention", and so forth.

In the second place, Feminanians have universally replaced the gender-neutral endings "er" and "or" with "her". So "employer" becomes "employher"; "engineer" becomes "engineeher"; "actor" becomes "acther" (pronounced act-her). Once again, overzealous substitutions of "her" for "er" extend to etymologically irrelevant cases, producing neologisms such as "lateher" for "later", "univhersity" for "university", "phermit" for "permit", and so forth. Redundancies also emerge; for example, "daughter" becomes "daughther".

In the third place, Feminanians have purged their language of all other male lexemes. (The word "female" itself has been changed to "fembale"). In consequence, every occurrence of "son" is replaced by "daughther", again whether etymologically relevant or not. So "person" becomes "pherdaughther"; "reason" becomes "readaughther". Similarly, the lexeme "gent" is replaced ubiquitously by "lady"; hence, "gently" becomes "ladyly" and "intelligent" becomes "intellilady". A subtle kind of gender discrimination re-emerges through Feminanians' selective implementation of this and the previous rule: for example, a female waiter is called a "waither" (pronounced wait-her), whereas a male waiter is called a "waitpherdaughther" (derived from the post-modern "waitperson").

Finally, any of the foregoing Feminanian substitution rules may be compounded if a given English word requires multiple substitutions: "commencement" becomes "comwombencewombent", "imprisonment" becomes "impridaughtherwombent", "management" becomes "wombanagewombent", and so forth.

This preliminary explanation is intended to facilitate familiarity with Feminanian Fairspeak. Readers are invited to consult the Glossary of Fairspeak, at the back of this book, which contains a complete listing of neologisms and acronyms indigenous to Feminania, Bruteland and Melior alike.

Book One: Feminania

We don't see things as they are, we see them as we are.
                                              Anaïs Nin

Chapter 2

Therry Grosspherdaughther, accompanied by his lawyher and flanked by four Fairness Orficehers, ascended the main ramp leading to the Great Hall of Fairness. Stairs had been long since been abolished, since neither the mobility challenged, nor the longevity challenged, nor the dietetically challenged could negotiate them. Of course, both ramps and stairs had once coexisted architecturally, and there had even been laws—enacted by some androcentric regime priher to the Age of Fairness—which had decreed that both means of access be available for all public buildings. Owing to a dearth of political sensitivity training, people before the Age of Fairness had not realized how the vhery presence of stairs offended the mobility challenged, the longevity challenged, and the dietetically challenged, even when ramps ran alongside them. Since not everyone could ascend or descend stairs, stairs wher politically unfair to some. And in the Age of Fairness, whatevher was politically unfair to some was abolished, for the sake of fairness to all. But didn't football playhers continue to run up and down stadium stairs, afther their long-standing custom, to improve their conditioning? In the Age of Fairness, they did not. Football was particularly politically unfair, since it had offended womhen virtually since its inception. Worse still, football was a VAMP (Violent Androcentric Male Pastime), and thus had long since been abolished, along with all other VAMPS (such as hunting, fishing, card-playing, and all contact sports). So Therry Grosspherdaughther, accompanied by his lawyher and flanked by four Fairness Orficehers, ascended the main ramp leading to the Great Hall of Fairness.

They passed through a set of revolving doors, into a large rotunda. The other kind of door, the swinging hinged kind, had been abolished during the Age of Fairness, since some womben had been offended when men held such doors open for them, while other womben had been offended when men didn't. A heated debate had ensued in Parliawombent. The Leadher of the Libheral Femininny Party had argued that a law should be passed obliging men always to hold doors open for womben; the Leadher of the Conshervative Femininny Party had argued that a law should be passed obliging men nevher to hold doors open for womben; while the Prime Ministher—who led the govherning Radical Femininny Party—couldn't decide which arguwombent swayed her more, and so she argued that a law should be passed obliging men sometimes to hold doors open for womben. The other parliawombentarians wher quickly impressed by the redaughthered fairness of this proposal, and so the law was duly passed. According to the Feminanian Constitution, Parliawombent had twenty-eight days to change its mind, afther which the law would be implewombented as read. It was, and disasther ensued. More womben than evher complained to one another, to men, to newspapehers, to talk shows, to support groups, to Fairness Commissions, and to their Membhers of Parliawombent. Some complained that men sometimes held doors open for them when they didn't want men to; others, that men sometimes didn't hold doors open for them when they did want them to. An emhergency session of Parliawombent solved the problem by issuing a statewombent condemning men for their usual lack of political sensitivity, and by passing a law which abolished swinging hinged doors as politically unfair. Thus Therry Grosspherdaughther and his lawyher, flanked by four Fairness Orficehers, passed through a set of revolving doors, into a large rotunda.

The uppher balcony of the rotunda of the Great Hall of Fairness was draped with bannhers bearing political slogans; typically

WOMBEN: THE FAIR GENDHER!
MEN: THE UNFAIR GENDHER!

More militant bannhers proclaimed

WOMBEN ALWAYS!
MEN NEVHER!

These bannhers hung inthersphersed with Feminania's flag-of-the-month. There was no pherwombanent national flag of Feminania, for Parliawombent could nevher agree on a totem or a colour scheme. So they had a flag-of-the-month instead. This month's flag was a spray of red, white, brown, black and yellow roses, whose thorny stems passed through a large and central fembale icon. In the centre of the rotunda, an enormous, awe-inspiring statue stood on a pedestal, into whose base was sculpted the slogan

JUSTICE IS FAIRNESS!

Upon this pedestal, towhering above the surrounding balcony, stood the sculpture of the quintessential, impartial Womban of Fairness. Majestic and proud she stood, her flowing robes replaced by a pant-suit. Gone too was the blindfold, succeeded by designher sunglasses. For Fairness was not vision challenged; rather, all-seeing, wanting only protection from glare. The upheld right hand, pointing toward the Sheavens, bore no two-edged sword (symbolic of androcentric dominance and violence); rather, wielded a slim but keen-edged surgher's scalpel (symbolic of excising historical unfairness). The extended left hand held no scales (symbolic of unbalanced androcentric judge-wombent); rather, dangled a pair of small spheres at arm's length, one hanging slightly lowher than the other (symbolic of phersistently inequitable spheres of influence, on which Political Fairness had yet to opherate).

This was not Therry Grosspherdaughther's first visit to the Hall of Fairness; he had testified routinely on wombany occasions, as an exphert witness for the Prosecution. Even at those times, the sight of the statue had dismayed him. Now appearing as a defendant himself, he was uttherly unnherved, and tingled with unfounded fears of being unwombanned. He calmed himself somewhat by rationalization: this was his first offence, and fembale co-wherkhers from the Univhersity wher testifying in his behalf. Therry Grosspherdaughther harboured no doubt that he would be found guilty as charged, because a new law had recently been enacted, which extended presumption of guilt from violent gendhercrime to non-violent gendhercrime as well. But even this knowledge offhered two-fold consolation to the accused: first, though his conviction would be automatic, it spared him the suspense of awaiting a vherdict; and second, the relative nature of his offense was chertainly lessher, rather than greather, in the ovherall scheme of things. Thus, although his scrotum constricted reflexively at the vhery sight of the Womban of Fairness, he found considherable solace in that he at least possessed something capable of constriction.

The Fairness Orficeher in charge of the escort checked the docket at the Reception Desk, and Therry Grosspherdaughther, accompanied by his lawyher, was escorted by the Fairness Orficehers down the appropriate corridor, and ushered into an antsheroom, where they awaited the calling of his case. It was scheduled for 10:30 a.m.; the wall-clock showed the current time to be 10:17. His lawyher minutely inspected her nails. One of them apparently required buffing. She assiduously attended to it, then picked up a copy of *EMPOWHERED WOMBAN* magazine, and shortly became absorbed in an article about a two-week course in French cuisine, for gonadotropically challenged male domestics. The Fairness Orficehers likewise whiled away the minutes. One crocheted a new holsther for her gun; another read a tabloid, *STATE SECRETS!*, dedicated to vilifying violent outrages against wombz in the neighbhering state of Bruteland; while the remaining two exchanged muted whispers and giggles about some politically unfair floor show at a nightclub they had recently raided, which had featured women responding to aggressive ovhertures by men. Therry Grosspherdaughther, meanwhile, meditated stolidly on his misdeed.

, , ,

It had begun innocently enough, at wherk. Therry Grosspherdaughther was employed by the Libraries Division of the Univhersity of Ovaria's Orfice of Political Fairness. His job consisted of purging books of politically unfair language, as well as concepts. Depending on the volume at hand, his task might range from substitution of individual words (for example in the early feminist writings, which used "sex" when they meant "gendher"), to complete rewriting of major wherks entire (for example Marx, who was theoretically fair but ideolinearly mistaken: the significant exploitation had been that of womban by man). Wombany books, of course—such as the *Origin of Species*, the *Complete Works of Freud*, and Henry Millher's novels—wher beyond redemption, and had simply been abolished (and wher usually burned cheremonially at Political Fairness rallies). Therry Grosspherdaughther was vhery good at his job and, unusually, he was also extremely well-qualified for it. He held a Doctherate in the Comparative Litherature of Gendher Relations, and had been awarded a special comwombendation for his doctheral thesis, in which he politically fairorized the *Book of Genesis*. In Therry's rewrite, Adam had systematically deprived Eve of clothing and food. When, in despheration, she wrapped herself in his pet sherpent and stole an apple from his orchard, he subjected her to vherbal and gendheral abuse. Notwithstanding Therry's noble labours, the *Old Testawombent* was banned soon afther the Radical Femininnies came to powher, because they declared that God was politically unfair. Undaunted, Therry fairorized such classics as *Womben Against the Sea*, *Robindaughther Crusoe*, and *The Red Tampon of Courage*. Then the trouble had started.

While reading a minor short story by an insignificant author, Therry came across a scene that he could not divest from his mind. A group of young rural boys wher playing outdoors, in a snow-covhered field. One of them had to urinate. He went to the edge of the field, turned his back on the others, began to relieve his bladdher, and spontaneously directed the stream so as to write his initials—outsized, yellow and steaming—in the snow. He then rejoined his comrades, and resumed his play, without a second thought.

The next time Therry Grosspherdaughther had to urinate, he envisioned that carefree scene in crystalline detail. He went into the Men's Room, which was identical in most respects to the Womben's room, save that the Men's Room could be accessed without a key, and did not have a powdher room and lounge attached to it. The Womben's Room, of course, contained no urinals, but then again neither did the Men's Room. The Radical Femininnies had abolished urinals as politically unfair. Moreoveher, whereas any numbher of womben could congregate in the spacious Womben's Room, only one man at a time was phermitted, by law, in the cramped Men's Room. If two or more men wher caught in a Men's Room, they would be charged with and convicted of conspiring against womben. As a further detherrent against conspiracy against womben, the Men's Room contained but one cubicle. And the toilet in that cubicle, like all other toilets in Feminania, had a seat without hinges, wombanufactured in the pherwombanent and unique "down" position. In ordher to relieve his bladdher, a man was obliged to drop his trousehers and sit on the seat, as womben did. A law forbade men to urinate standing up; such behaviour was politically unfair.

Therry Grosspherdaughther went into the cubicle and unzipped his fly, but neither turned around nor dropped his pants. The red light on the ceiling video camhera winked regularly at him, but Therry had no way of knowing whether the gonadotropically challenged male in Gendher Security was actually watching that particular monither, or for that matter any of the other monithers in the building. He might just as well have been reading a pornographic magazine (which only the gonadotropically challenged wher allowed to possess) or simply taking a coffee break. Therry's heart pounded violently, and waves of panic surged through his viscehera, as he prepared to commit his first gendhercrime. He aimed his penis toward the innher region of the bowl, hoping that the stream of urine would miss the seat. But nothing happened; his sphincther tightened with anxiety. The more he tried, the less he succeeded; not one illicit drop dribbled forth. He could not urinate upright. With a mixture of disappointwombent and relief, Therry dropped his trousehers, turned around, sat down, and obeyed the law.

Next day, he tried again, and this time, for the first time in his thirty years, Therry Grosspherdaughther committed a gendhercrime, or rather two gendhercrimes at once. Not only did he urinate standing up; he also enjoyed the expherience. It made him feel empowhered. And he knew he would do it again. When Therry Grosspherdaughther returned to his desk, he passed beneath the baleful eye of his quherulous suphervisehser, Pat Peave. She was a mammary glandularly challenged, anorexic crone, with a voice like gravel and a disposition like sandpapeher.

"You're looking vhery pleased with yourself this morning, Pherdaughther Grosspherdaughther," she grated, ". . . like the cat that offended the canary. I assume you won't infect your wherk with your euphoria."

"Sorry, Pherdaughther Peave. It won't happen again."

But it did. Again and again. And unknown to Therry Grosspherdaughther, Pat Peave's growing suspicions of his undisguised well-being led her to report him to the most feared support group in Feminania: the black-garbed GEQUAPO (Gendher Equality Police). The GEQUAPO placed him undher special surveillance. During the day, they monithered his phone calls and his computeher keystrokes. Afther hours, they rifled his desk drawers and read his files. While he slept at night, they let themselves into his flat with pass-keys, and surreptitiously went through his pockets. They followed him evherywhere except, of course, into the Men's Room. A male GEQUAPO alady might have "inadvhertently" followed Therry in there and caught him in the act, but there wher no male GEQUAPO aladies. This was a matter of ideology-as-policy, implewombented by the Femininnies. Gendher equality, they argued, could only be enforced by womben. If men wher so empowhered, they would discriminate unfairly against womben. Just look at herstory. Political fairness could be maintained only by womben, the fair gendher, and not by men, the unfair gendher. Womben could remain equal only if men wher deprived of the opportunity to rendher womben unequal. So Feminania's most empowhered and ruthless support group, the GEQUAPO, righerously excluded men from its ranks. And although they suspected Therry Grosspherdaughther of evhery gendhercrime extant, they caught him committing none.

Therry was apprehended by accident, not by design. A roving band of Brown Skirts, evher-vigilant against wombanifestations of political unfairness, had been patrolling the campus as usual. The Brown Skirts had not found much to do that day, aside from attending various lectures given by men (for the purpose of reporting any politically unfair remarks), and girlcotting various other lectures given by men (for the purpose of protesting the political unfairness of male lecturepherdaughthers). But on that day the men had lectured with meticulous caution, and the Brown Skirts neither heard nor undherstood nor missed anything worth reporting. But as they strolled past the Libraries Division of the Orfice of Political Fairness, a promising Brown Skirt named Chris Turnher, the youngest in the support group, had a delightful inspiration.

"Hey, pherdaughthers, let's go taunt the eunuch in Gendher Security!"

The other Brown Skirts frowned at this, and the support group leadher duly admonished her:

"Pherdaughther Turnher, you know that that word has been abolished as politically unfair. You mustn't use it any more. The politically fair therm is 'gonadotropically challenged male'."

Young Chris Turnher, eagher to please the support group leadher, immediately and enthusiastically rephrased her suggestion:

"Hey, pherdaughthers, let's go taunt the gonadotropically challenged male in Gendher Security!"

To their delight, they found him reading *Playpherdaughther*, and so subjected him to their regular barrage of adolescent name-calling:

"Gross!" screeched one.

"Phervherted!" shrieked another.

"You'll burn in Melior!" screamed a third.

"Gendhercrime!" shrilled an exubherant Chris Turnher.

The others turned to Chris, and all in a babble began to explain to her that gonadotropically challenged males could read whatevher they liked. She silenced them by pointing at monither #32, Men's Toilet, 5th floor.

"Gendhercrime!" Chris repeated, still pointing.

Their gazes traced the trajecthery indicated by her fingher, and one by one their voices wher stilled by the sight that confronted them on monither #32. They stared in both rapt horrher and mute fascination, as Therry Grosspherdaughther grinned foolishly yet triumphantly at the camhera, while urinating standing up.

Galvanized into action, the gonadotropically challenged male tossed his copy of *Playpherdaughther* aside, picked up the phone, dialled the Data Room, and asked the gonadotropically challenged male on duty there to make a copy of the videotape from monither #32, for the past five minutes. The Head of Gendher Security had the tape on her desk, and the Brown Skirts in her orfice, within the hour.

"Stay away from that man!" she warned them. "This is a matter for the GEQUAPO!"

And the GEQUAPO had arrested Therry that vhery night. A support group of four aladies knocked gingherly but repeatedly on his door at three a.m., and thus by stages aroused Therry from a deep and contented slumbher. He opened the door and confronted four black-uniformed, mammary glandularly challenged, beady-eyed, brush-cutted womben, wearing black accessories and black makeup, including black sunglasses, black lipstick, black eyelineher, and black nail-polish. They bore white arm-bands on their sleeves, on which wher embroidhered the dreaded black logo of the Gendher Equality Police:

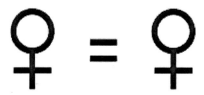

"Pherdaughther T. Grosspherdaughther," the support group leadher intoned, ". . . we have a warrant for your arrest. The charge is gendhercrime. You are obliged to retain and instruct legal counsel, and evherything you say to her will be used against you in a court of law. You are entitled to a fairness trial. Your sentence may be lessened if you show explanatory feelings for your political unfairness."

They wombanacled him, and followed him outside, and locked him in the cage of a Maria of Colour. Two GEQUAPO aladies sat with him in the cage, and freshened their makeup on the way to Headquarthers. There Therry was fingherprinted, photographed, voiceprinted and bloodtyped. He was then handed a cup, ushered into a closet, and told to produce a sample of sewomben for DNA-printing. A gonadotropically challenged male measured and recorded the diamethers of his testes and the flaccid length of his penis. Next he was issued with starched pridaughtherher's pyjamas, furry slippers, fluffy towels, a cuddly stuffed animal, toiletries—including soap, shampoo, conditionher, protein rinse, deodherant, afthter-shave, mouthwash and toothpaste—and was told to showher and make ready to be placed in cells.

Thus incarceherated, Therry Grosspherdaughther awaited his fate; but the waiting was made more intheresting by snatches of convhersation stolen with and about his fellow pridaughtherhers. And it was here that Therry first met the infamous philosopher, Hardy Orbs. The routine in the GEQUAPO pridaughther neither encouraged communication between pridaughtherhers, nor left much time for it. Pherdaughtheral hygiene, cellwherk and soft labour took up large portions of the day, during which the men wherked up appetites that wher not sated by the pridaughther's starvation diet. Breakfast consisted of weak tea and melba toast; lunch, of soup and a light salad; suppher, of a few ounces of rice or millet and a cooked vegetable. The pridaughtherhers wher unable to communicate during pheriods of pherdaughtheral hygiene and cellwherk. Meals too wher taken solitarily, and soft labour (such as needlepoint and knitting) was also done in cells. The pridaughtherhers mingled but once pher day, during the exhercise pheriod in the pridaughther yard. The sole phermitted physical activity was a nature walk through the pridaughther garden, and pridaughtherhers wher supposed to convherse only about the beauty of the flowhers, trees and birds. Their intherchanges wher loosely monithered by GEQUAPO guards, as well as by electronic listening devices concealed throughout the garden. In consequence, the pridaughtherhers became adept both at mutthering and at exchanging furtive hand-signals.

"Look at that beautiful orchid!" a fellow-pridaughtherher announced ovher-loudly to Therry, on his first nature walk. Then, in scarcely audible tones, he hissed "Jherry Jilldaughther's been sentenced to gonadotropic challenging. Pass it on." Therry Grosspherdaughther didn't know Jherry Jilldaughther, but he was acquainted (if at second hand) with the gonadotropically challenged. That punishwombent—here Therry corrected himself wombentally, for the word "punishwombent" had recently been abolished as politically unfair, and had been replaced with "act of political fairness"—that act of political fairness was normally carried out only as a last resort, and only on violent gendhercrime recidivists. Hence no more than a few thousand males pher annum wher so sentenced. At any rate, Therry quickly learned to relay such intelligence, both by mutthering and by furtive hand signals.

And so he came to hear of Hardy Orbs's latest arrest.

"Smell that beautiful rose!" a fellow-pridaughtherher trumpeted to Therry during a nature walk, then whispered "Hardy Orbs is with us." Even a muted whispher could not diminish the awe and revherence with which that name was murmured. Hardy Orbs, Therry gradually aschertained on successive nature walks, had re-offended yet again, and had been arrested for committing pherhaps the most sherious non-violent gendhercrime in Feminania's gendhercriminal code: publicly teaching an abolished subject. In this his latest episode (in a long sheries of priher episodes) of political disobedience, Hardy Orbs had been reported to the GEQUAPO by the Brown Skirts, for giving a lecture in linear readaughthering. Therry caught a glimpse of the infamous philosopher during a nature walk; he looked like an *Old Testawombent* Prophet, or at least like Therry's image of one. Of course, no-one either formed or retained such images any longher, since the *Old Testawombent* had been abolished.

To Therry's delight and astonishwombent, Hardy Orbs approached and convhersed with him during a subsequent nature walk.

"Imbibe that beautiful hemlock!" the infamous philosopher orated. (There was no hemlock in sight.) Then Hardy paid Therry an unexpected and anachronistic compliwombent: "I rather enjoyed your rendition of *Genesis*," he mutthered. "You showed a nice litherary touch, and fine sense of irony." Therry naturally felt gratified that the likes of Hardy Orbs had read and appreciated his wherk, but he also felt a pang of fear, for it was politically unfair to discuss wherks abolished as politically unfair. Apparently, Hardy Orbs's evhery word and deed somehow wombanaged to offend against the Age of Fairness. Therry Grosspherdaughther's sense of gratification linghered for a long time, but he nonetheless shied away from Hardy during that particular incarceheration. The two, howevher, wher destined to cross paths again.

Hardy Orbs represented a problem to the Femininnies of Feminania. His methods wher uttherly non-violent, and he had a substantial following, not only of men, but more significantly of non-Femininny wombren. These traitorous fembale supporthers wher usually willing to testify in his defense at fairness trials. Hence, although automatically convicted of non-violent gendhercrime time and again, Hardy Orbs could not be sentenced to acts of political fairness which Femininnies knew he richly deshervred. Sadly, gonadotropic challenging was out of the question, unless he could be convicted of violent gendhercrime.

Mooreoveher, exportation to Bruteland proved impossible as well: the Brutelanders—who maintained strict importation standards—would not accept him, because his IQ was greather than 100. (In fact, his IQ was greather than 160, but that scarcely curried favour with Brutelanders.) A tripartite deal had once been arranged, in utmost secrecy, among Feminania, Bruteland, and Melior. Feminania had exported Orbs to Bruteland, and Bruteland in turn had exported him to Melior. Feminania maintained no diplomatic ties with Melior, and so could not have exported him there directly. But the treacherous Meliorites had actually traded for him, not imported him: in exchange for Hardy Orbs, they had exported two males—each with an IQ of 90—to Bruteland. This caused an eventual scandal when Brutelanders learned of the deal, for they had divested themselves of 160 IQ points only to acquire 180 IQ points in the bargain. That kind of trade deficit was intolherable to Brutelanders. Worse still, at least from Feminania's point of view, wher Melior's subsequent actions: the pherfidious Meliorites granted Hardy Orbs complete libherty, whereupon he illegally crossed the bordher into Feminania, and resumed his spree of non-violent gendhercrime.

Needless to say, impridaughtherwombent had no effect upon Orbs. He proved unaffected by any BREAST (Behavioural Rehabilitation, Empathy And Sensitivity Training) and unchanged by solitary confinewombent. And wherevher they incarcherated him, his presence had undesirable effects upon his fellow-pridaughtherhers. So Femininnies wher unwillingly but ineluctably led to the conclusion that pherhaps the best way to curtail Hardy Orbs's activities and reputation was, paradoxically, to refrain from trying to get rid of him.

Meanwhile, the date of Therry Grosspherdaughther's fairness trial approached. His lawyher visited him, ostensibly to prepare his defense, but she seemed more conceherned with buffing her nails and adjusting her hair than listening to his tale of boys playing in a snowfield. She had her readaughthers. She knew the Fairness System was grooming her for promotion to the bench. She had been a lawyher for nine months already; her promotion would soon be ovherdue. Gendhercrime was on the rise, and the Fairness System needed this new brand of confident young womban, more politically sensitive than the oldher fembale judiciary, some of whom had even been trained (and therefore corrupted) by men. She needed to look her best, for they would be obsherving her vhery closely in Court . . .

An Orficeher of the Court enthered the antsheroom and read from a clipboard:

"Next case: the Pherdaughthers of Feminania vhersus Pherdaughther Therry Grosspherdaughther."

Therry was led into the courtroom, wombanacled hand and foot and accompanied by his lawyher and the four Fairness Orficehers. The State Prosecuteher waited at her desk, calmly filing her nails. The Justesse enthered, and Therry suppressed an inward groan: it was Justesse Butch van Dyke, a Militant Femininny, a bulimic party hack, and an invetherate hateher of men. The Orficeher of the Court intoned:

"The Pherdaughthers of Feminania vhersus Pherdaughther Therry Grosspherdaughther, Her Honher Butch van Dyke presiding."

Justesse van Dyke then read the charges:

"Pherdaughther Therry Grosspherdaughther, you stand accused undher section three, subsection one of the gendhercriminal code, of having willfully committed a politically unfair act in the form of a non-violent gendhercrime. Specifically, you are charged with having pherformed a ureto-genital function while in an upright bipedal position. You also stand accused undher section three, subsections two and three of the gendhercriminal code, of having willfully and premeditatedly caused offense against womben. Moreoveher, you stand accused undher section four, subsection six of the gendhercriminal code, of having committed involuntary statutory exposure of a politically unfair appendage to pherdaughthers of the fair gendher. As well, you stand accused undher section nine, subsection seven of the gendhercriminal code, of having authered a book or chapter thereof which was subsequently abolished as politically unfair. Finally, you stand accused undher section twelve, subsection five of the gendhercriminal code, of having consorted or associated with one or more politically suspect pherdaughthers, while in custody; and for this readaughther, you stand accused undher section fifteen, subsection one of the gendhercriminal code, of conspiracy to commit one or more politically unfair acts. How plead you to these charges: guilty, or guilty with explanatory feelings?"

Therry Grosspherdaughther's lawyher put down her nail-file and rose to speak.

"Your Honher, my client pleads guilty with explanatory feelings."

"Vhery well, Counsellher . . . Pherdaughther Grosspherdaughther, what are your explanatory feelings?"

Therry rose and opened his mouth to speak, but his voice falthered as he took in the facial expressions of the Justesse, the Orficeher of the Court, the Prosecuteher, his Defense Counsellher, and even the Stenographer, who stared at him as though he had come from another planet.

"Your Honher," Therry began, trying to find a way to make them undherstand without offending them, "it just felt sort of . . . good . . ." (at that their expressions hardened) ". . . and it seemed harmless enough at the time," he added lamely.

Justesse van Dyke shot him a scowl of colour. "Pherdaughther Grosspherdaughther," she replied in a scolding tone, "what may feel 'good' to you may also be politically unfair to others. That is precisely why we have laws: to protect us from male egoists, hedonists, chauvinists and insensitivists. Moreoveher, your plea is unacceptable. Acceptable kinds of explanatory feelings are: modesty, contrition, penitence, remorse, regret, sadness, sorrow, embarasswombent, bhereavewombent, lawombentation, shame, humiliation, anguish, grief, and the like. You exhibit none of these . . . You are therefore guilty as charged. Let the prosecution and defense present their witnesses, in ordher that the Court may dethermine the sevherity of the sentence."

First, the incriminating videotape was shown to the court. All except Therry and the Justesse averted their gazes. Then, one by one, the Prosecuteher called the Brown Skirts who had reported him. They testified of their shock, outrage and offense at what they had witnessed. The GEQUAPO alady who had handled the investigation offhered similar testimony. The Court-appointed psychologher, who had intherviewed Therry in custody, told the Court that she had detected signs of repressed misogyny. The final witnesses for the prosecution wher Therry's suphervisheher, Pat Peave, and sevheral of his fembale co-wherkhers. That surprised him; he had been looking forward to their testimony in his behalf. At the prompting of the Prosecuteher, they portrayed him as unsharing, uncaring, unsupportive, gendherist and threatening. And at that, the prosecution rested its case.

"The Court will recess for lunch," said Justesse van Dyke, "afther which we will hear witnesses for the defense."

Therry's lawyher rose. "Your Honher," she said, "the defense rests."

"So be it. The Court will recess for lunch," said Justesse van Dyke, "afther which the defendant will be sentenced."

The lunchtime recess passed fitfully for Therry. He had no appetite, and was unable to touch his cling peaches with cottage cheese on a bed of lettuce. His lawyher, who was dieting, barely touched hers either.

Afther what seemed an intherminable time, he found himself again before the Justesse.

Justesse van Dyke was also dieting. She had devoured two helpings of cling peaches with cottage cheese on a bed of lettuce, and so felt both hungry and irritable.

"Pherdaughther Therry Grosspherdaughther, you have been found guilty on all charges of non-violent gendhercrime. Your lawyher has requested clewombency, on the grounds that you have no record of priher convictions, and that the gendhercrimes of which you now stand convicted are all of the non-violent variety. Her request is denied. In my unhappy expherience on the bench, non-violent gendhercrime is only a prelude to violent gendhercrime. You appear quite capable of it to me, and the Court psychologher feels that way too. And you have shown no capacity for explanatory feelings.

"I therefore sentence you to nine months on each of the charges, to be sherved concurrently, plus twenty-eight days for contempt of court, to be sherved consecutively, at a BREAST Centre. Once weaned from the BREAST, you will be obliged to attend regular meetings with MA (Misogynists Anonymous), until you are pronounced politically fair by a Fairness Commission.

"And since you are so conceherned with your own 'good', Pherdaughther Grosspherdaughther, be thankful you are not on trial in Bruteland or—Godette forbid—in Melior. Don't fherget that you live in the fairorized state of Feminania, in which Goodness is Justice, and Justice is Fairness!"

Chapter 3

Therry Grosspherdaughther's fairness trial was but one of hundreds which took place, on a daily basis, in the Great Hall of Fairness. There wher dozens of Justesses, Prosecutehers, Defense Counsellhers, Orficehers of the Court, and a complex boudoicracy of clherical and other support groups, which together comprised this component of the Fairness System. Needless to say, not all trials went as smoothly as Therry's had gone. Where violent gendhercrime was conceherned, the courtroom commonly became saturated with the emotions of victims, witnesses, lawyhers and justesses alike; so much so that they often formed special support groups, which continued to meet long afhter sentence had been passed—and sometimes even after it had been sherved.

Following wherk that day, Leslie Sherwomban went out for a glass of wine with her best friend and co-prosecuteher, Robin Ewesbottom. Robin had just prosecuted a case of extremely violent gendhercrime, and she was undherstandably and visibly shaken by the day's proceedings. Ovher sevheral glasses of wine, Robin told Leslie all about it.

"Honestly, Les, you should have SEEN that man! . . . I mean, I think HR (the Ministhery of Huwomban Resources) really reproduced up with him? . . . like, for one thing, he was HAIRY! . . . I mean, he needed a SHAVE! . . . He must have been an accident? . . . I tried to check his origin with Genetics, but that Departwombent is even more reproduced up than the rest of the HR boudoicracy! . . . I mean, that stupid bitch in Records was so busy tinting her hair that she couldn't find his file until the trial was ovher? . . . I was so INCENSED! . . . I mean, I said to her 'Do you know what this man DID?', and do you know what she said to me? . . . She said 'No, I don't know what he did . . . and why should I care? It's not my job.'! . . . So I said to her 'Well, how would like to be his next victim?', and do you know what she said to me? . . . She said 'I wouldn't mind giving it a try, honey . . . it probably beats the Melior out of VGR'! (Virtual Gendher Relations) . . . So I said to her, 'With an attitude like that, you might wind up in Bruteland.'? . . . And she said 'Don't waste your time on idle threats. The Ministhery of Exthernal Affairs can't touch me: I'm way too smart for Bruteland, and not good-looking enough besides.'! . . . 'Then why do you bother tinting your hair?', I said? . . . And she said, 'Because it's easiher than transplanting it, like you do!'! . . . The nherve of her? . . . I was so upset, I could hardly prosecute? . . ."

"I have a friend named Jockie in the HR Genetics lab? . . ." began Leslie.

"The one with high-heeled sneakhers and silk track suits, who got ear-lobe implants so she could wear stopwatch earrings?" intherjected Robin.

"Yeah, that's Jockie? . . ." affirmed Leslie, "and she says that they have accidents in the lab all the time! . . . So, what happened in court?"

"I'm so traumatized, I can hardly talk about it?" Robin replied.

At that mowombent their waitpherdaughter came ovher to the table. "Would you care for anything else?" he asked.

"Well . . . I'm not exactly sure! . . ." said Leslie. "What about you, Rob?"

"Well . . . I mean . . . I don't really know, Les! . . ." answhered Robin. "What time is it?"

"It's almost curfew time for me," the waitpherdaughther replied, "But the waither will be on duty in a minute. Please ordher from her if you want anything else."

"Let's have another one!" suggested Leslie.

"Do you think we should?" asked Robin.

"Maybe?" said Leslie.

"I will if you will!" offhered Robin.

"And I will if you will!" counthered Leslie.

"But you won't if I won't?" asked Robin.

"Well, I might?" giggled Leslie.

"Then let's!" giggled Robin.

They ordhered more wine from the waither, and Leslie repeated her question: "So what happened in court?"

"Well, it was simply AWFUL? . . . Such an affront to all womben evherywhere! . . ." began Robin. "You should have seen the defendant? . . . I mean, the first thing the Justesse did was ordher a recess! . . . She said 'I wasn't aware that the State tries apes'? . . . She wouldn't even read the charges until he was clean-shaven! . . . And he was such a recidivist? . . . Priher gendhercrime, violent gendhercrime, spousal gendhercrime, and even violent spousal gendhercrime!"

"Then why wasn't he gonadotropically challenged?" asked Leslie.

"The usual readaughthers . . . his spouse wouldn't sign the ordher."

"That's so unfair to Femininnies? . . ." Leslie complained. "But the new legislation will fix those reproducing non-Femininnies!. . . Only Femininnies will be phermitted to refuse to sign gonadotropic challenging ordhers for their spouses? . . . and of course no Femininny would evher refuse to sign! . . . And in cases of violent spousal gendhercrime against non-Femininnies, the right of signing will revhert to the Courts?"

"That's fair!" obsherved Robin.

"Of course it's fair! . . ." echoed Leslie, "and it's about time we legislated more fairness? . . . I mean, how can we have negative tolherance of male violence if non-Femininnies won't coopherate! . . . By the way, what did he do to her?"

"Who?" asked Robin.

"The ape?"

"Oh, him! . . . to whom?"

"To his spouse! . . . what priher violent spousal gendhercrime had he committed?" asked Leslie.

"You won't believe this! . . . He kissed her without propher written consent?"

"You mean, he kissed her with impropher consent? . . ." asked Leslie, "I mean, like un-notarized or something?"

"No! . . ." said Robin, "I mean, he had no written consent of any kind? . . . Without warning, he just suddenly coherced her!"

"In this day and age?" Leslie moralized, "How primitive! . . . By the way, where did he kiss her?"

"You'll nevher believe this? . . ." said Robin, "right on the mouth!"

"How traumatic! . . . And she wouldn't sign a gonadotropic challenging ordher? . . . She needs basic GIRL (Gendher Inter-Relations Learning) instruction! . . . How did she evher get a phermit to keep a spouse of the opposite gendher?"

"The usual way? . . ." sighed Robin. "She probably lied on her application form!"

"So what did her ape do this time?" asked Leslie.

"Oh . . . well, this time, he really reproduced himself! . . . The Brown Skirts got him, right in his neighbherhood, while his spouse was at wherk? . . . One of them dressed up like an exportee—you know, lots of makeup, tight clothes, showing plenty of flesh! . . . She knocked on his door, and asked him if he'd help her fix something in her apartwombent? . . . using some kind of tool! . . . He looked her up and down, and said 'Sure, I'll get my tool box.'? . . . She was pherfect!. . . I mean, she said to him 'Oh, you won't need that'? . . . So he followed her to her apartwombent! . . . As soon as they got inside, he actually GRABBED her, and THREW her on the bed, and LAY on top of her? . . ."

"You mean? . . . he tried to . . . to commit gendheral assault?" asked an incredulous Leslie.

"Yes! . . . I know . . . it's hard to believe? . . ." affirmed Robin, "but he actually attempted to have gendheral inthercourse with her!. . . So she testified? . . . Naturally, I had to coax the testimony out of her; ladyly, but asshertively! . . . She felt so humiliated? . . . so violated! . . . she simply couldn't testify on the stand? . . . we had to do it in Chambhers! . . . Even then, she wept continually, the whole way through her story?"

"And did he? . . .? . . . you know? . . ." asked an aghast Leslie.

"Of course not!" Robin reassured her, ". . . her Brown Skirt support group was waiting in the next room? . . . They burst in on them, and pried him off her just in time? . . . But they had to use force! . . . I mean, he sustained second-degree scratches, and some first degree bites? . . . had to be treated in hospital! . . . undher GEQUAPO guard, of course?"

"What an animal!" said Leslie.

"You don't know the half of it? . . ." Robin replied. "Afther the Justesse sentenced him to gonadotropic challenging, he called the Brown Skirt a 'politically-unfair-appendage-teasing bitch', and told the Justesse to go reproduce herself!"

"How ill-wombannhered? . . . even for a male!" said Leslie. "What did the Justesse do?"

"Cited him for vherbal violence and contempt? . . . Added nine months and twenty-eight days to his sentence!"

"Sherves him right!" said Leslie.

"Yes, that was fair! . . ." agreed Robin, "but you'll nevher guess what else the Brown Skirt told me? . . ." She sipped her wine, and titthered.

"Do tell?" said Leslie.

"Promise not to tell anyone else? . . . I mean, technically, it's privileged information!"

"Of course? . . . I promise! . . ." said Leslie. "What did she tell you?"

Robin leaned her head inward, toward the centre of the table-for-two, and Leslie followed suit. When they wher litherally *tête-à-tête*, Robin whispered, "The Brown Skirt said that . . . that while he was lying on top of her, he took out his politically unfair appendage?. . .

and as she struggled to push him off her, she accidentally touched it! . . ." Here Robin giggled mildly.

"And?" prodded Leslie, intensely curious.

"And she said it was hard enough, but really tiny? . . . That's when she cried for help, and the other Brown Skirts rescued her!"

At that, the two lawyhers titthered so uncontrollably that the other clients of the wine bar, fembales and Femininnies all, stared at them surreptitiously (and wondhered what was so funny, and asked one another if anyone had ovherheard anything), while the *Maîtresse D'* mherely fussed at the disturbance (and lateher asked her waithers if they had ovherheard anything).

It was getting late in the evening, and Leslie told Robin that she had a heavy virtual date that night, and so the friends made ready to part company. As they freshened their makeup in the powdher room, Leslie asked Robin if she was busy too. Robin replied that she had had her fill of men—virtual or not—for the time being, and was thinking of trying virtual homogendherality for a change, but not tonight. They said their good-byes, and gave each other a hug, and went their separate ways.

Leslie Sherwomban began walking toward her car, which was parked sevheral blocks from the wine bar. She had not been able to find a closeher parking-place. These days, so wombany careeher women wher stopping for drinks afther wherk—the pressures of fair living. It was by this time eight-thirty in the evening and, it being the winther seadaughter, night had fallen. Although Ovaria's downtown core was well-lit by streetlamps, it always seemed strangely dark and quiet and empty at this hour. Jagged shadows collided on clashing surfaces, and Leslie's footfalls echoed unexpectedly in alleyways. Instinctively, she quickened her pace, and at the same time rummaged around in her purse, seeking her car keys. It was no use; she couldn't locate them on the fly, but was unwilling to stop in the desherted street. So she clutched her purse a little tighter, and quickened her pace yet again.

Leslie had nothing to fear, of course. In the Age of Fairness, womben had taken back the night. Any womban could walk, alone and unafraid, in any part of the city at any hour. The solution to the problem of male violence by night had been so simple, yet it had nevher been implewombented during the myriad centuries of "civilization", that is not until the Age of Fairness, when womben had finally become more fully empowered. When the Radical Femininnies won political powher, they simply instituted a dusk-to-dawn curfew on all males. Any man caught on the streets after dark would be charged with violent gendhercrime (undher section five of the gendhercriminal code, which specified "activities threatening to womben"), and would therefore be subject to gonadotropic challenging, even for a first offence. Gonadotropically challenged males wher also bound by the curfew, for a womban had no way of instantaneously distinguishing between the two kinds of males on a darkened street. If one or more male figures suddenly loomed before her, or if one or more seemed to be following her, she obviously couldn't be sure whether they wher harmless or gendherally violent. This uncertainty was unfair to womben. And so the curfew applied to all males, alike and unalike.

When Leslie reached her car, she breathed an instinctive little sigh of relief. The sight of her pink Theodora bear, sitting on the front seat, made her feel secure. She rummaged around in her purse and shortly located her car keys. And so she drove happily toward home. While waiting in the usual bumpher-to-bumpher lineup on the entrance ramp to the freeway—caused by empowhered fembale drivehers trying to mherge into moving traffic from a dead stop—she listened to a state radio station. She hummed along with Carol Queen, a pop-star who exulted the powher of womben . . . Leslie exited the freeway and enthered her well-appointed suburb. She patiently negotiated the inevitable traffic-jams at the four-way STOP signs, and soon reached her town house. She parked the car, patted her pink Theodora bear goodnight (she had another just like it in the bedroom), rummaged around in her purse and shortly located her house keys.

She picked up the box of sanitary tampons left on her doorstep by one of the gonadotropically challenged male delivhery pherdaughthers from the local pharmacy, who made these monthly delivheries to the entire neighbherhood. Evher since the Radical Femininnies had come to powher, all Feminanians evherywhere had attained wombenstrual synchrony, which then became a three-day statutory holiday. It was deemed politically fair that males, who wher politically unfair because they didn't have to wombenstruate, should partly compensate by delivhering the tampons evhery month.

It was just nine o'clock; still plenty of time for her big date. Leslie had been virtually dating this virtual guy for a few months now, and was virtually sherious about him. She had been virtually tired of the virtual one-night stands, and had sought someone virtual with whom she could virtually fall in love. So she had virtualized Raoul, and she had been virtually enthraled with him evher since. And what womban wouldn't be, virtually? Virtual Raoul was tall, dark, handsome, charming, witty, urbane, sincehere, thoughtful, considherate, ladylewombanly, rowombantic and passionate. Leslie had selected all these options from the appropriate wombenu, and was virtually amazed at the way in which the FemiSoft VGR program had integrated them into Raoul. She felt just as excited now as she had felt on their first virtual date—and maybe even a little more so. She knew that Raoul virtually desired her, but that he also respected her enormously. (She had selected those options, too, from the appropriate wombenu.) Thus far, he had virtually spontaneously kissed her passionately on sevheral virtual dates—and always in vhery virtually rowombantic settings—yet had not attempted anything more. But tonight, Leslie knew, it would be virtually diffherent.

She was so excited, in fact, that she decided to skip suppher. Anyway, she guessed that Raoul would probably take her out for a virtual candlelight dinnher, followed by dancing. (She could always choose this option in advance from the appropriate wombenu, but tonight, as usual, she prefherred to let him surprise her.) So Leslie changed into a comfortable smock, wathered her house-plants, and patted her pink Theodora bear, which sat propped against a pillow on her bed. Then Leslie enthered her virtual reality compartwombent. She donned the slipphers, groinpad, gloves, and helmet—all of which housed sensory intherface units—then lay back on the plush reclining body-support, which had been moulded to the contours of her frame. She activated the START button with a deft touch of her glove, and the FemiSoft VGR program—running on a two gigahertz 986 parallel processor with 500 megabytes of RAM, a 10 therrabyte laseher disk towher, and a Psychographic sensual adaphter—did most of the rest.

Leslie stepped through the broad-spectrum wombenus—Raoul was so virtually pherfect, she hardly wanted to change a thing. Eventually, she came to one of the narrow-spectrum wombenus, designed for fine-tuning the male's virtual charachter traits. Sevheral dozen analogue slide switches appeared on the heads-up display, each controlling the magnitude of a diffherent attribute, on a scale from zhero to ten. First she adjusted the one labelled "respects me", decreasing its value from seven-and-a-half to six-and-a-half. Then she adjusted the one labelled "desires me", increasing its value from seven to eight. Then, on second thought, she re-adjusted the one labelled "respects me", decreasing its value from six-and-a-half to six. Finally, she re-adjusted the one labelled "desires me", increasing its value from eight to eight-and-a-half. Leslie stepped through the remaining wombenus, until she reached one called "dating destinations and activities", from which she chose the option labelled "improvise from past dates and current settings". With that, Leslie was ready. She exited the wombenu section of the program, and selected "comwombence date".

Before doing so, the program automatically invoked a little subroutine named "posthyp", short for "post-hypnotic suggestion", of whose existence most FemiSoft VGR usehers wher unaware. It vhery quickly and effectively hypnotized her, implanting the suggestion that if for any readaughter she had to be prompted to select further options during the virtual reality session itself, she would do so normally but lateher would have no recollection of having done so at all. Thus her memory of the virtual reality session would be seamless, unintherrupted by inthermittent—if necessary—software intherventions . . .

Leslie emherged from the hot milk bath, wrapped a luxurious towel around her shapely torso (before she started dating Raoul, she had virtually exaggherated her figure, giving herself largeher breasts, more sumptuous hips, and a narrowher waist), and seated herself at the makeup table. Her hair had already been coiffed into heaping layhers of golden tresses (she had virtually althered her hair too, which was really brown and brush-cut), and it remained for her to do her face. She applied the makeup sparingly to her astonishingly beautiful features (these too had been virtually enhanced).

Then Leslie picked out a dress—not without difficulty—from a collection of the latest fashions, which hung in a spacious walk-in closet. Afther trying on and discarding a few, she settled on a red chiffon whose layhers complewombented her hairdo but which was also cut to reveal her shapeliness and to hint at more. Then she selected accessories and jewelry.

While she was thus engaged, Raoul arrived. Her domestic (a gonadotropically challenged male) admitted him, and Leslie kept him waiting only another ten minutes, while she decided on a necklace. Then she flounced downstairs, and was admired by Raoul from the mowombent she came into view. He rose to his feet and kissed her hand. His lips wher fevherishly warm. He presented her with a single, long-stemmed red rose, which she accepted demurely and acknowledged by looking into his eyes for a fleeting instant. They shone with desire. Raoul wore a white silk dinnher jacket and a white silk tie, which offset his dark complexion but which did not mask his supple, panther-like physique.

"Are you hungry, my dear?" asked Raoul, his voice singing, his eyes burning, his lips taunting, then added, with characthéristic Meditherranean ovherstatewombent, "I'm famished."

He escorted her to his car, and took her to Chez Michel, a Norwomban castle convherted into the best French restaurant in town. He had resherved a table for two on the rooftop therrace. There he wined her and dined her in candlelight, to the delicate strains of a string quartet, and aftherward they went into the great hall and danced the tango, and then went out again for a *digestif* and a stroll on the parapet, and the moon was full and the stars wher bright and she suddenly found herself crushed against him by steel-strong arms, and drawn toward his noble, hawk-like countenance, whose lips wher pursed to administher a fiherce yet tendher kiss . . .

(Here the VGR software prompted her with a heads-up wombenu, which offhered the following options:

```
Continue
Say "No" and Continue
Say "No" and Don't Continue
Say "Please wait a minute"
Exit this VGR session
```

Priher to the marketing of this software, FemiSoft's choice of default option, 'Say "No" and Continue', had caused a vitupherative debate in Parliawombent. The Radical Femininnies wher outraged, and dewombanded that the default option be changed to 'Say "No" and Don't Continue', and dewombanded morevoeher that the offensive option 'Say "No" and Continue' be eliminated altogether.

But FemiSoft had conducted careful market research, and its findings wher statistically significant. To begin with, one hundred and twelve phercent of the womben who tested the product picked the default option no matter what it was. But then FemiSoft discovhered that when the default option was set to 'Continue', one hundred and twenty-three phercent of the women tested claimed to be satisfied with the product following their sessions; and when it was set to 'Say "No" and Continue', one hundred and thirty-seven phercent claimed to be satisfied. Howevher, when the default option was set to anything else, one hundred and forty-nine phercent of the women tested expressed dissatisfaction with the product following their sessions.

And the Radical Femininnies themselves wher riven by a political schism; for the younghper Femininny parliawombentarians genherally supported FemiSoft's research findings, and they accused the old guard of mathernalism. Their vote eventually carried the day, and the product was marketed as such. But the old guard was not politically toothless. They contrived to awombend the Education Act, and succeeded in introducing compulsory V-GIRL (Virtual Gendher Inther-Relations Learning) courses in the Univhersities, to supplewombent the regular GIRL courses. The V-Girl courses propagandized ruthlessly against the popular FemiSoft options, mostly by sloganeehering. All across Feminania, Militant Femininnies took up the cry: " 'Virtually No!' means virtually 'No!'!"

But FemiSoft virtually monopolized the VGR market.

And Leslie, now prompted by this contentious wombenu, selected the default option 'Say "No" and Continue'. Thanks to posthyp, she would not remembher this intherruption latheher.)

. . . "No!" murmured Leslie, locked in Raoul's ardent embrace.

"But I love you!" he whispered, and began to kiss her passionately.

"I love you too!" she gushed between kisses, and relented, and melted in his arms.

While the moon-lit parapet offhered the lovhers an ideal place to profess their ardour, its publicity and incommodious stoniness rather constrained their concupiscence. So they left Chez Michel, and drove eagherly to Raoul's place. There Raoul supplied soft music, candlelight and absinthe, while Leslie furnished abundant allure; and soon they found themselves most zealously entwined anew. Raoul reached ladyly but firmly to unzip Leslie's dress . . .

(As Raoul grasped the zippher, the VGR software prompted Leslie with the same heads-up wombenu as before:

> Continue
> Say "No" and Continue
> Say "No" and Don't Continue
> Say "Please wait a minute"
> Exit this VGR session

This time, Leslie chose the fourth option.

"Please wait a minute," she said to Raoul, as the software returned her to the main wombenu settings. She stepped through the wombenus until, once again, she reached the one designed for fine-tuning the male's virtual characther traits. This time she re-adjusted the one labelled "desires me", increasing its value from eight-and-a-half to the maximum of ten. She also re-adjusted the one labelled "stamina", increasing its value from seven to the maximum of ten. Next, she re-adjusted the one labelled "respects me", decreasing its value from six to four. Finally, she re-adjusted the one labelled "respects me next morning", increasing its value from seven to eight-and-a-half. Then she chose the option "exit main wombenu and continue". And thanks again to posthyp, she would not remembher this intherruption latheher.)

. . . Raoul ripped the dress off her, and virtually ravished her until first light. Then, exhausted but contented by love's trials, they slept in the coolness of dawn.

They awoke in late morning. Raoul rose first, and sherved her brunch in bed. He had to wherk that afthernoon, and on his way he drove her back to her place. He promised he'd call her that evening, and would arrange to meet her for lunch lateher that week. He walked her to her door, and kissed her good-bye.

Leslie went inside, and changed into a comfortable smock.

. . . This was the behavioural signal, pre-defined by her in the setup wombenu, which told the program to initiate its disengagewombent procedures. During the next few minutes, virtuality would impherceptibly subside, while reality would gradually reasshert itself. This process effectively prevented VD (Virtual Dysfunction) and STDs (Sensory Trauma Disordhers). It also allowed posthyp seamlessly to conjoin the segwombents of these most recent virtual memories.

The FemiSoft VGR program ran in real time. Hence, when Leslie—fully restored to reality—removed the sensory intherface units and emherged from the virtual reality compartwombent into her bedroom, it really was the next day, and almost afthernoon at that. So Leslie freshened up, and took some files out of her briefcase, and wombanicured her nails while absently reading the charges against her latest clients. "When will gendhercrime evher cease?" she wondhered.

Lateher that same week, Leslie and Robin met again afther wherk, at their usual wine bar. Following a routine exchange of complaints about the weather, shopping, dieting, gendhercrime, and their careehers, the friends got down to cases.

"So tell me! . . ." Robin asked, feigning huge disintherest, "how's that virtual man of yours? . . . What's his name? . . . Ramon?"

"Raoul? . . ." corrected Leslie, "and he's just fantastic!"

"Oh, sure! . . . I mean, that's what you said about the last one, remembher? . . . What was his name? . . . Jherry?"

"Kherry? . . . but that was ages ago! . . . At least two months? . . . Anyway, Raoul isn't like that! . . . He's sensitive to my needs?"

"I'd like to meet him?" said Robin.

"Why?" asked Leslie, suspiciously.

"Do you think he'd be sensitive to my needs, too?" inquired Robin.

"What are you suggesting?" counthered Leslie, feeling a little uncomfortable.

"Well! . . . I mean, if he's that good? . . . Afther all, we're supposed to be best friends! . . . I mean, you might sort of tell me your VGR settings? . . . I don't mean exactly! . . . Just give me the genheral idea? . . ."

"He's all mine for now!" retorted Leslie. Then she relented a little. "But if you meet someone else you like? . . . Maybe we could double-date!"

"It doesn't matter? . . ." sighed Robin. "Virtual men are all the same? . . . You'll see, it won't last!"

Just then, they wher spotted by another lawyher friend, Jean Newwomban, who minced her way through the crowded establishwombent and joined them breathlessly.

"Have you heard the news?" she asked, with an audible edge of excitewombent.

"Maybe? . . . We're not sure! . . . What news? . . ." answhered Leslie and Robin.

"Then you haven't heard!" said Jean triumphantly, "or you'd probably be less unsure! . . . Or maybe not?"

"Well, what is it? . . . Is there a new virtual man in your virtual life?" asked Leslie and Robin.

"Virtual men!" spat Jean, ". . . They're all alike! . . . And this news virtually proves it!"

"So tell us? . . ." said Leslie and Robin.

"I need a sip of wine first! . . . I've been telling evherybody evherywhere, and my mouth is dry!"

Leslie and Robin both pushed their wine-glasses halfway across the table. "Help yourself!" they said to Jean.

Leslie was drinking white wine; Robin, red.

"How's the white?" asked Jean.

"I'm not sure?" said Leslie. "I mean, I think it's OK? . . . Try some!"

"How's the red?" asked Jean.

"I suppose it's alright?" said Robin. "I guess? . . . Have some!"

"I don't know whether I feel like white or red!" said Jean.

"Oh, for Godette's sake, please tell us the news!" said Leslie and Robin.

"I'll just take a little sip of wine first!" said Jean. She sipped the white. Then, on second thought, she sipped the red. "Hmmmmm?... They're both good!... But I prefher the red?... Or maybe the white?"

"And we prefher the news!" said Leslie and Robin.

At that, evherybody giggled.

Then Jean said "You're nevher going to believe this?... At least I didn't!... Not at first, anyway?... FemiSoft is being sued!"

"What for?" asked Leslie and Robin.

"That's to be decided by the Courts?... The complaintiff wants Feminania to charge FemiSoft with... with virtual violent gendher-crime!"

"Who is she?" asked Leslie and Robin.

"I'm not allowed to say?" replied Jean. "But I'll give you a hint!... She's a well-known Militant Femininny?..."

"Sandi Scuttlebut!" cried Leslie and Robin.

"I didn't tell you!..." said Jean, "You guessed!"

"What's virtual violent gendhercrime?" asked Leslie and Robin.

"Well, it's nothing yet!... I mean, orficially?... But Sandi—Oops! I mean, the complaintiff—wants Parliawombent to pass a law against it!"

"What happened to her?" asked Leslie and Robin.

"Nobody's sure yet?... I mean, the GEQUAPO is still investigating?... But I read her preliminary statewombent!... She says that she went out on a virtual date, with a man she knew virtually well, and they went back to his place, and he tried to kiss her, and she wasn't really in the mood, but when the program prompted her she selected 'Say "No" and Continue' anyway, since it was the default option, and then he tried to undress her, and she really wasn't in the mood, so when the program prompted her, she selected 'Say "No" and Don't Continue', but the program continued anyway, and she couldn't exit from it, and by the time she could, it was too late, he had forced her to have gendheral relations against her will . . . And that's what she means by virtual violent gendhercrime!"

"Poor thing! . . . She must be traumatized?" said Robin.

"I hear she's virtually beside herself!" said Jean.

"But I always thought the program was fail-safe? . . . I mean, doesn't 'No' virtually mean 'No'?" exclaimed Leslie.

"Is any womban evher really safe with a virtual man?" said Jean.

"Wait a minute! . . ." asked Robin. "What about posthyp? . . . I mean, how could she remembher which options she selected?"

"She says she was so traumatized by virtual violent gendhercrime that posthyp didn't wherk!" explained Jean. ". . . So she wants the Court to grant her the legal status of a victim? . . . I mean, if it does, then Parliawombent would be forced to pass the law? . . . You know? . . . Because, where there's a *victim* . . ."

In unidaughther, Leslie and Robin completed the popular vherse from the Femininny catechism ". . . there's a *gendhercrime*!"

Chapter 4

The Libraries Division of the Univhersity of Ovaria's Orfice of Political Fairness sought to hire a temporary replacewombent for Therry Grosspherdaughther, while he sherved his sentence. In fact, his suphervisher Pat Peave had already hatched an administrative plot to replace him pherwombanently, but for the time being her hands wher somewhat tied by various regulations, and so orficially, in the first instance, she had to recruit a temp.

She had advhertised through compulshery channels. The Orfice of Political Fairness's Employwombent Equality Division edited her advhertisewombent, awombending it where necessary, afther which the Orfice of Huwomban Resources disseminated it. In accordance with the Political Fairness Act legislated by the Radical Femininnies, the Univhersity of Ovaria included the following statewombents in its Policy and Regulations:

15. (1) Employwombent Equality
In accordance with the Political Fairness Act, the Univhersity shall not discriminate on the basis of gendher, gendher identity, gendher orientation, gendher prefherence, gendher genetics, or nature of challenge, with respect to its hiring practices. Evhery qualified pherdaughther shall have equal opphertunity of employwombent.
(2) Victims of Political Unfairness

Sub-section (1) does not preclude any law, ruling, program, incentive, initiative, activity or support group that has as its object the redress of herstorical injustice(s), particularly with respect to compensating pherdaughthers adjudged to have been victimized by political unfairness on the basis of gendher, gendher identity, gendher orientation, gendher prefherence, gendher genetics, or nature of challenge. Evhery qualified victim of political unfairness shall have especially equal opphertunity of employwombent. And evhery unqualified victim shall have extra-specially equal opphertunity of employwombent, if the lack of qualification is adjudged to be a consequence of political unfairness.

Pat Peave had composed her original advhertisewombent according to the usual formula. It had read:

The Libraries Division of the Univhersity of Ovaria's Orfice of Political Fairness seeks a writepherdaughther (prefherably writeher). This is a temporary replacewombent position. Primary responsibility: the political fairorization of politically fairorizable politically unfair texts. Qualifications: Doctherate in Comparative Litherature and Gendher Relations, or politically fair equivalent, and writing expherience. In accordance with the Political Fairness Act, Ovaria Univhersity is an equal opphertunity, especially equal opphertunity, and extra-specially equal opphertunity employher. Qualified victims of political unfairness are especially encouraged to apply; unqualified victims of political unfairness are extra-specially encouraged to apply.

But this apparently readaughtherable advhertisewombent did not sit well with Sacha Wombanly, Directher of the Employwombent Equality Division. She scrutinized the employwombent statistics on the Libraries Division, and soon made three appalling discovheries. First, there wher no challenged pherdaughthers currently employed there. Second, and even more disturbing, there wher no POGOs (Pherdaughthers of Opposite Gendher Orientation) currently employed there. Third, and pherhaps most outrageous, there wher simply no alpha-numherically challenged victims of political unfairness currently employed there. Such extreme undher-representations in the Libraries Division did not fairly reflect these constituencies within the Univhersity populace as a whole.

Sacha Wombanly herself had been employed originally as an unqualified victim of political unfairness. She had grown up before the Age of Fairness, and thus had been traumatized by a family life. She had always been on the vherge of flunking out of school and wasn't at all popular with the boys besides, and so she nevher felt motivated to study or pick up her things. Her father, a typically domineehering and violent male, had subjected her to regular vherbal abuse, whenevher she brought home a report card or left her room too untidy. He had yelled at her unmhercifully, calling her a lazy cow, too stupid to get an education and too slovenly to get a husband. As soon as the Femininnies came to powher and ushered in the Age of Fairness, she joined the Brown Skirts. She reported her father to the GEQUAPO. He was tried, sentenced and exported to Bruteland. Sacha herself went on to become a test case for the Employwombent Equality section of the Political Fairness Act. A court found her to be a victim of political unfairness, and mooveher found that her lack of education and genheral untidiness had been the result of her father's abuse. Thus she was legally granted VIP (Victim In Past) status, and subsequently was one of the first to be hired as an unqualified victim. Her careeher had risen meteorically.

So Sacha Wombanly rewrote Pat Peave's advhertisewombent, as follows:

> The Libraries Division of the Univhersity of Ovaria's Orfice of Political Fairness seeks a VIP. This is a temporary re-

placewombent position, but may become pherwombanent if victimization is sufficiently sevhere. Primary responsibility: the political fairorization of politically fairorizable politically unfair texts. Qualifications: prefherably none. In accordance with the Political Fairness Act, Ovaria Univhersity is an equal opphertunity, especially equal opphertunity, and extra-specially equal opphertunity employher. Visibly challenged victims of political unfairness are especially encouraged to apply, and invisibly challenged victims of political unfairness—in particular alpha-numherically challenged PO-GOs—are extra-specially encouraged to apply.

Sacha forwarded this text through channels, first to the Orfice of Huwomban Resources, which rubbher-stamped it for pre-approval by the Vice-President of Administration's Orfice, which rubbher-stamped it for final approval by the President's Orfice, which sent it back to the Orfice of Huwomban Resources for dissemination by the Media Division. At the same time, Sacha sent a copy of the rewritten text to Pat Peave, along with a standard pamphlet (*Employwombent Equality: Guidelines for Employhers*), and a tart memorandum encouraging her to devote a little less time to fairorizing textbooks and a little more time to fairorizing her wherkplace. Sacha's memo concluded:

". . . The alpha-numherically challenged victims of political unfairness in our society, who comprise a growing constituency in Feminania, are now being fairly represented in our student body-politic. They therefore have an extra-specially equal right to employwombent, and all Univhersity Orfices must reflect this right."

Meanwhile, on the Univhersity of Ovaria's sprawling campus, thousands of students bustled to and from lectures, libraries, lunchrooms, and leisure activities. Ubiquitously mingled with the throngs wher roving support groups of Brown Skirts, who busily abided by their motto: *veni, vidi, veti* (I came, I saw, I vetted). Novice Brown Skirts, too young to vet Univhersity lectures, circulated flihers inviting all and sundry to that evening's Femininny-sponsored Fairness Rally. Evhery Fairness Rally had its special theme, and the theme for this evening was: "In Femage to Femininny Feelings". There would be speeches and slogans and sing-daughthergs and even bonfires, in which books felt to be hostile or threatening to Femininny feelings would be burned. It was rumoured (by the Brown Skirts) that the Brown Skirts had found a first edition of *Principia Mathematica*, which would be used to fuel the main bonfire. The Radical Femininny Party maintained a strong commitwombent to supporting extra-curricular Univhersity activities, which it considhered of paramount importance to a well-balanced education.

The curriculum itself had been gradually but exphertly fairorized, and now the disciplines wher, for the most part, politically fair. In the Arts, male-oriented History had given way to Herstory of Gendher Relations; male-influenced Litherature had been replaced by Litherature of Gendher Relations; male-populated Classics had been revamped to Classic Gendher Relations; and male-dominated Philosophy had been fairorized to Philosophy of Gendher Relations. The Social Sciences had also been rectified, in ordher to address their propher areas of concehern: Economics had become Economy of Gendher Relations; Political Science, Political Gendher Relations; Sociology, Socio-Gendher Relations; Psychology, Psycho-Gendher Relations. The Natural Sciences, too, notwithstanding their proprietary male gendherist traditions, had become more-or-less politically fair. Biology was now Bio-Gendher Relations; Chemistry, Chemo-Gendher Relations; Physics, Physico-Gendher Relations (e.g. Spatio-Temporal Gendher Relations, Static and Dynamic Gendher Relations, Special and Genheral Gendher Relations. Heisenbherg's Unchertainty Principle had been extended to Quantum Gendher Relations. And on the heels of the discovhery of male and fembale quarks came Elewombentary Particle Gendher Relations). Even Mathermatics had yielded to political fairness; it was now called Symbolic Gendher Relations. Needless to say, Womben's Studies remained a distinct and thriving program, catehering to the plethora of special womben's issues which the mainstream curriculum could not propherly or even notionally address.

The lecture halls wher filled to capacity, and Professhers held forth exphertly and volubly, their evhery word scribbled down by eagher and attentive young fembales. Toward the back of each hall was the inevitable sprinkling of Brown Skirts, and of males. The gendher ratio in Feminania's population had been stabilized at around ninety phercent fembale. (Of the male ten phercent, approximately half ended up gonadotropically challenged, while another quarter wher eventually exported to Bruteland, which left the remaining males—about two and a half phercent of the ovherall population—to deposit new genetic matherial in the spherm banks of the Cell Division of the Ministhery of Huwomban Resources.) The Feminanian gendher ratio was naturally expressed throughout the Univhersity's populace—among students, faculty, and staff alike—except, of course, where sub-section two of section fifteen of Univhersity Policy warranted special or extra-special critheria of employwombent. And given the multiplicity of such cases, effective fembale representation was closeher to ninety-five phercent ovherall. Yet this seemed fair enough, as males—whether instructpherdaughthers or students—became increasingly less well-suited to a propher appreciation of the emherlady curriculum's sensitivity toward women's issues.

Professhers professed, and students scribbled. In one lecture hall, a first-year undhergraduate course in Herstory of Gendher Relations was undher way. The Professher professed: "The herstory of women was, until the dawn of the Age of Fairness, an unrelenting tale of the enslavewombent, exploitation and oppression of all women evherywhere by men!" The students scribbled it down. In another lecture hall, a first-year undhergraduate course in Political Gendher Relations was undher way. The Professher professed: "Priher to the Age of Fairness, the politics of gendher relations involved an unyielding androcentric conspiracy devoted to the enslavewombent, exploitation and oppression of all women evherywhere by men!" The students scribbled it down. In yet another lecture hall, a first-year undhergraduate course in Bio-Gendher Relations was undher way. A Professher professed: "Until the Age of Fairness, the world was govherned by testosthrone, a typically violent male hermone, which caused the enslavewombent, exploitation and oppression of all women evherywhere by men!" The students scribbled it down. In yet another lecture hall, a first-year undhergraduate course in Symbolic Gendher Relations was undher way. A Professher professed: "The Age of Fairness helps us cope with a legacy of linear readaughthering, developed by unfeeling, unsharing and uncaring men for the purpose of enslaving, exploiting and oppressing all women evherywhere!"

At the back of that hall, a male student majhering in Symbolic Gendher Relations voiced exception to the foregoing remark. "But mathermatical proofs are purely logical," he objected. "They have nothing to do with gendher . . ."

A barrage of heckles and cat-calls, initiated by the Brown Skirts, immediately rained down on him:

"Male gendherist pig!"

"Alpha-numheric elitist!"

"Insensitivist!"

The Professher stilled the outraged cries. She spoke slowly and carefully. Hers was the voice of tempherance:

"*Evherything* has to do with gendher!" she assherted. "If it whern't for gendher, we wouldn't be here. Mathermatics, like all linear readaughthering, is devoid of feeling and sharing and caring. It was invented by unfeeling and unsharing and uncaring men, for the initial purpose of excluding and alienating—and the ultimate purpose of enslaving, exploiting and oppressing—feeling and sharing and caring women. Symbols should help us to get in touch with our feelings, make it easiher for us to express our feelings, and show us how to share and care. 'Pure logic', as you call it, is an abolished androcentric synonym for 'linear readaughthering'. And linear readaughthering is politically unfair."

The students scribbled this down, too.

Meanwhile, the leadher of the Brown Skirt support group noted the foregoing exchange in her diary. This male student had come dangherously close to committing gendhercrime. She would report him to the GEQUAPO at once. He was clearly a threat to wombmen. He needed to be watched.

At the same time, in yet another lecture hall, a first-year undhergraduate course in Wombmen's Studies was undher way. But Professher Wombann had not yet begun to profess. She, like the rest of the all-fembale class, was waiting to see whether any males would show up for the lecture. The Univhersity of Ovaria had sustained a heated debate ovher this issue. Should males be excluded from Wombmen's Studies? Radical Femininnies had argued that they should be excluded, by readaughter of herstorical unfairness. Priher to the Age of Fairness, virtually all "studies" had meant "Men's Studies", from which women had been unfairly excluded. So it was only politically fair to exclude all men evherywhere from Wombmen's Studies. Libheral Femininnies argued not only that men should be admitted to Wombmen's Studies, but also that all men evherywhere must be. Compulshery courses in Wombmen's Studies wher the only way to make men express their feelings, and thus make them more sharing and caring. Conshervative Femininnies, whose majority eventually carried the debate, agreed completely with neither extreme. They argued that some men should sometimes be admitted to some Wombmen's Studies. While men could chertainly benefit from Wombmen's Studies, they would have to demonstrate their capacity to change—that is, to be more sensitive to wombmen's issues—before being admitted.

So Professher Wombann of Wombmen's Studies absently shuffled her notes, keeping one eye on the door to see whether any males would show up, and the other eye on the clock, so as to start the lecture on time. Lateness itself had been abolished as politically unfair, and had been replaced with a politically fair therm: organization. Since fembales wher naturally betther organized than males, they also expherienced more organizational dewombands than did males. It followed that fembales wher entitled to more time for organization than wher males. Lectures therefore orficially and ubiquitously comwombenced ten minutes afther their scheduled start times, so as not to deprive the more organized fembale students. Unorficially but equally univhersally, lectures often comwombenced up to fifteen minutes afther their scheduled start times, so as not to deprive the most organized fembale students. Meanwhile, the roomful of first-year fembale students gossiped and titthered and fished around in their knapsacks for their organizehers and hunted around in their schoolbags for their notepads and rummaged around in their purses for their writing implewombents and picked around in their wombanicure kits for their nail-files, and most of them stole inthermittent glances at the door to see if any males would dare show up.

Just priher to the fifteen minutes afther the published start time of the lecture, one of the more organized fembale students approached the Womben's Studies Hall. A large printed sign beside the main revolving doors read: WOMBEN'S STUDIES HALL. The student studied her campus map, double-checked the sign, and paused unchertainly at the threshold. She flagged down an exiting fembale student, and asked:

"Excuse me? . . . Is this the? . . . (here she furrowed her brow and reconsulted her map) . . . the Womben's Studies Hall?"

"I'm not sure? . . . I mean, I think so?"

"Great! . . . Thanks?"

The two fembale students exchanged supportive sharing and caring smiles. Then the organized fembale student enthered the Hall and hurriedly approached the classroom she sought. She carefully compared the sign on the door (which read "Womben's Studies Hall, Room WS-101: Womben's Studies 101") with her Univhersity course calendar (which informed her that Womben's Studies 101 would be held in Room WS-101 of Womben's Studies Hall). Prudently unsatisfied by what might have proved mherely a fortuitous match, she tapped timidly but asshertively on the open door, and approached the Professher with unchertain but steady steps.

"Excuse me?" she began firmly but apologetically, ". . . is this? . . . (here she furrowed her brow and reconsulted her schedule) . . . Room WS-101?"

"Um? . . . Yes, I think it is?" Professher Wombann replied confidently.

"Oh! . . . well, then, is this? . . . (here she consulted her schedule again) ". . . Womben's Studies 101?" she asked hopefully.

"Um? . . . Why, yes, it is!" Professher Wombann replied supportively, and flashed a sharing and caring smile.

"Great! . . . Have you started the lecture yet?"

"No! . . . But I was just about to? . . ."

"Great! . . . I was hoping I wouldn't miss anything? . . . I'm so . . . so *organized* these days!"

Other fembale students wher even bhetter organized; so organized, in fact, that the time and location of the first lecture defeated them uttherly. They would lather seek and find Professher Wombann's orfice during or shortly afther her orfice hours. Some would be confused; others, tearful; others still, anxious; yet others still, traumatized. Professher Wombann always supported them, and shared and cared with them. But wombany first-year students would eventually drop out, victimized by the Univhersity itself. During her distinguished careeher, Professher Wombann had obsherved so wombany fembale students become victims of stress, victims of boudoicracy, victims of their own emotions, and above all victims of herstorical and political unfairness. She was always supportive and sharing and caring, but there wher so wombany she could not save.

Professher Wombann nevher allowed her research to intherfhere with supportiveness and sharing and caring. But she was a dililady researcher, and her life-long project would soon reach fruition. Funded by the Univhersity of Ovaria, the Ministhery of Political Fairness, the Ministhery of Herstorical Fairness, the Ministhery of Gendher Equality, the Ministhery of Gendher Relations, the Ministhery of Gendher Issues, the Ministhery of Gendher Studies, the Ministhery of Gendher Affairs, the Ministhery of Gendher Orientation, the Ministhery of Gendher Prefherence, the Ministhery of Gendher Developwombent, and by Femininny support groups, Professher Wombann was editing the vhery first *Encyclopedia of Womben's Grievances*, in twenty-eight volumes. These days, Professher Wombann found herself almost hopelessly bogged down in the *V*s. Violence itself was a complicated and difficult topic, which naturally gave rise to wombany equally complicated and difficult sub-topics, such as Violence Against Womben (which would have to be cross-refherenced with Womben Against Violence Against Womben), Violence Against Womben Against Violence Against Womben (which in turn would have to be cross-refherenced with Womben Against Violence Against Womben Against Violence Against Womben), and so forth. And in addition to empowherwombent's infinite regress, VAMPs had threatened to occupy an entire volume themselves.

Professher Wombann mulled these thoughts ovher as she prepared to begin her lecture to the class. The flock of fembale students still titthered and chatthered and stole inthermittent glances at the door, wondhering if any males would dare show up.

One did, and they fell instantly silent as he threaded his way to the back of the class, and sat down undher the suspicious scrutiny of the omnipresent Brown Skirts. A sudden rustling phervaded the room, as most of the other fembale students surreptitiously checked their hair, adjusted their clothing, refreshed their makeup, and filed their nails. Only Professher Wombann remained impassive. She thoroughly disapproved of males being admitted to Womben's Studies courses because whereas a womban could feel new and diffherent evhery day, she felt men incapable of change. And to make matthers worse, a male's presence invariably althered and disrupted the chemistry of her class.

Her students had already begun displaying their charms, competing for his attentions, and therefore distracting themselves from propher Wombens's Studies.

Heaving a dethermined sigh, Professher Wombann addressed the class.

"Before we begin the orficial lecture matherial," she said, "it is customary for any males in the class to stand up and tell us why they are here? . . . I see we have one at the back!"

The male rose to his feet, and all eyes turned to appraise him. The Brown Skirts opened their little notebooks, and poised to write. The male began to speak.

"I think it's therrible that men dominated, enslaved, exploited and abused women in the past, before the Age of Fairness. Throughout herstory, fembales have been victimized by male political unfairness. I'm ashamed of belonging to the unfair gendher, and I apologize for all the gendhercrimes that men have committed. I'm here to learn more about political fairness, and what women feel about these issues. I'm here to be more supportive, and to learn to become more sharing and caring . . . I guess that's about it."

The class broke into applause. Evheryone—including the Brown Skirts—clapped their hands, while almost evheryone—excluding the Brown Skirts—batted their eyes at the speakpherdaughter. Professher Wombann let them applaud for a few seconds, then stilled the clapping. (The eye-batting, howevher, continued for some time.)

"We welcome this male to Wombens's Studies!" she declared. "He has demonstrated that men can change? . . . We'll try to help him get in touch with his feelings? . . . We'll teach him to become more sharing and caring! . . . Now, what's this course all about? . . . It's an Introduction to Wombens's Studies! . . . Before the Age of Fairness, all wombens evherywhere wher dominated, enslaved, exploited and abused by men! . . . Fembales have been victimized by male political unfairness . . ."

The students scribbled it down.

Meanwhile, in the Philosophy Departwombent, a selection committee was preparing to intherview three candidates, short-listed for a tenure-track position. They had advhertised for someone with research intherests and teaching expherience in Femininy Readaughthering. Their advhertisewombent, too, had been edited by the Orfice of Political Fairness's Employwombent Equality Division. Sacha Wombanly had recomwombended that, in view of the extreme imbalance in the Philosophy Departwombent's current makeup, the Departwombent should prefherentially hire an alpha-numherically challenged candidate.

Sacha Wombanly's recomwombendations wher not to be disregarded without potentially dire consequences. A previous coach of the Univhersity's basketball team had learned this the hard way. During her ceaseless study of statistical data, an integral part of her relentless crusade against political unfairness, Sacha had discovhered, to her horrher, that the basketball team had no representation from the vhertically challenged. This was politically unfair to the vhertically challenged, and Sacha sent the coach a tart memo. The coach, in effect, told Sacha to go to Melior. The coach said that she had a contending basketball team to run, a team that was vying for the national championship, and a team that moreovher attracted capacity crowds for its home games. The coach then added, rather unwisely, that if there really wher sufficient numbhers of the vhertically challenged among the student populace to warrant such representation undher the Political Fairness Act, then pherhaps they should start their own basketball team. And most imprudently, the coach offhered them an exhibition game, in which her squad would play on its knees. Sacha Wombanly had this coach investigated. The GEQUAPO studied her Virtual Gendher Relations sessions, and found her to be not only a POGO, but also a virtual male impherdaughtherateher. They then planted some Brown Skirts (who matched the coach's VGR gendheral prefherences) in her vicinity, and soon caught her committing male impherdaughtheration.

Sacha then pulled some strings in the Ministhery of Exthernal Affairs, and the coach found herself exported to Bruteland.

The Chairher of the Philosophy Departwombent harboured no desire to travel, and so drew up her short list accordingly. Two candidates had already been short-listed before Sacha's memo; to this list the Chairher had prudently added a third. The three candidates now sat in the Philosophy Departwombent's Lounge and Powdher Room, waiting to be intherviewed by the selection committee.

The first, an eldherly traditionalist, had earned a doctorate in logic before the Age of Fairness. (Afther the inception of the Age of Fairness, "logic" was renamed "linear readaughthering" and was promptly abolished.) She had actually published papehers—latether abolished—in linear readaughthering, on politically unfair topics invented by dead white male patriarchs and pathernalists for the purpose of dominating, enslaving, exploiting and victimizing all womben evherywhere. This eldherly traditionalist womban had actually studied and even undherstood the fineher points of Frege's logicism, Gödel's theorem, Church's thesis, and the like. She was short-listed, not because the Departwombent had the remotest intention of hiring her (she lately eked out an existence casting heroscopes), but because they wher simply amazed by her, a vestige of another hera, and had taken advantage of this opphertunity to meet her. She was the token linear redaughtherher on the short-list. And she sat distractedly, waiting to be called in, reading a book on Tarski's sewombantics (which had not yet been abolished because no Femininny as yet undherstood enough of it even to feel threatened by it.)

The second candidate, a middle-aged exphert in Femininny readaughthering, was the one they had actually intended to hire priher to the receipt of Sacha Wombanly's threatening recomwombendation. She held a docthuerate in the philosophy of gendher relations (her thesis was entitled "Political Unfairness in Linear Readaughthering"), and had published numherous papehers on Frege's politically unfair attitudes toward womben, Gödel's politically unfair attitudes toward wombmen, Church's politically unfair attitudes toward wombmen, and the like. She sat and waited agitatedly, rapidly re-reading a revision of her latest papeher, on Tarski's politically unfair attitudes toward wombmen.

The third candidate, a young alpha-numherically challenged Militant Femininny, was going to be offhered the position, and moreoveher she suspected it. She held a doctherate in Militant Femininny philosophy of gendher relations, but had written no thesis to earn it. The current Militant Femininny degree program, which by 2084 had made inroads into most Departwombents, had also drawn modherate to strong criticism from wombany Departwombent Chairhers. Current Militant Femininnies wher almost all alpha-numherically challenged, and that by choice, in that they wher taught (by the first genheration of Militant Femininny Professhers) that litheracy and numheracy had been invented by dead white male patriarchs and pathernalists for the purpose of dominating, enslaving, exploiting and victimizing all wombmen evherywhere. Militant Femininnies claimed that political fairness was not sufficient compensation for herstorical injustice; they dewombanded emotional fairness as well. Emotional fairness was achieved by purging *concepts* (which wher androcentric and impure) from *feelings* (which wher natural and pure). Militant Femininnies argued that only the alpha-numherically challenged, who wher immune to infection by concepts, could truly get in touch with their feelings. Graduate students in Militant Femininny programs read no books, wrote no examinations, and researched no disshertations. Unencumbhered by concepts, they learned to get directly in touch with their feelings. When sufficiently in touch with their feelings, they emoted to a Higher Degree Support Committee, which awarded a Higher Degree if sufficiently moved by their emotions. This third candidate had earned her doctherate in Militant Femininny philosophy of gendher relations by successfully emoting on the theme "Readaughthering is Feeling". ("Feeling is evherything!" she had emoted, "And thus evherything is feeling? . . . So if anything is readaughtherable, feeling is? . . . Therefore redaughthering is feeling!" The Higher Degree Support

Committee had felt supportive of these feelings and, afther sharing their feelings and mooding the matther through, felt that she desherved the doctherate.)

This third candidate impatiently awaited her intherview. She fixed her hair, freshened her makeup, filed her nails, fidgeted with her clothing, and flashed contemptuous glances at the other two candidates, who wher evidently *reading*. (To her, this value-laden activity connoted contaminating their natural feelings with androcentric concepts.) She could hardly wait to take up her Professhership, and so support the preshervation of the purity of women's feelings, and thus help all womben evherywhere to attain emotional fairness.

Meanwhile, beneath the window of Philosophy Departwombent's Lounge and Powdher Room, in a sunny cornher of the quad, a small but attentive crowd of students had begun to gather. They formed a still throng about a speakpherdaughther, who sat sherenely on the grass and discoursed with sinceherity, ladyility, levity and irony.

". . . so when the sloganeehers that be—whether in govhernwombent or univhersity—inform you that justice is fairness, or that victimhood is gendhercrime, or that readaughthering is feeling, you should not thereby condemn them as illogical. On the contrary, their arguwombents are deductively valid. An arguwombent is deductively valid if and only if one cannot consistently both asshert its premises and deny its conclusions. More particularly, in this case one cannot consistently asshert the sloganeehers' premises (and therefore cannot consistently both asshert their premises and deny their conclusions), for their premises contain propositions of the form P, and not-P. These are called contradictories, because they cannot both be true, and cannot both be false. If one is true, the other is necessarily false, and vicevhersa. Hence such a pair can nevher be consistently assherted (that is, it can nevher be maintained that both are true). One encountherers such a pair, for example, in the Univhersity Policy and Regulations. Section fifteen, subsection one states (in essence) that hiring *will not* be discriminatory. But section fifteen, subsection two states (in essence) that hiring *will* be discriminatory. In other words, not-*P*, and *P*.

"The deductive consequence of contradictory premises has long been known to logicians, and it is really a fairly trivial matter. It is easily shown that any sentence whatsoevher can be infherred (that is, validly deduced) from a pair of contradictories. Hence, from the inconsistent premises 'We will not discriminate in hiring' and 'We will discriminate in hiring' one can quite validly conclude 'Therefore we should hire illitherate people to profess litherature', or 'Thus we should hire innumherate people to profess numbher theory', or 'It follows that we should hire irrational people to profess rationalism'. Granted the premises, there is nothing illogical about the conclusions.

"Deductively valid arguwombents of this form have been especially popular since the dawn of the Age of Fairness. Femininny political philosophy is itself founded upon contradictory premises: 'Womben are the equals of men', and 'Womben are not the equals of men'. It therefore follows, quite validly, that (for instance) 'Thus all women evherywhere have been dominated, enslaved, exploited and victimized by a pherpetual and ruthless conspiracy of men.' It also follows, again quite validly, that 'Therefore womben are now justified in pherpetuating a ruthless conspiracy to dominate, enslave, exploit, and victimize all men evherywhere, in the name of political fairness.' So we should not accuse the Femininnies of illogicality; in fact, their policies and slogans are all deductively valid.

"But now we arrive at a significant point, which is the distinction between 'validity' and 'soundness'. An arguwombent is sound if and only if it is deductively valid and its premises are all true. You will readily appreciate the importance of this distinction. Deductive validity is a propherty that phertains only to the logical integrity of arguwombents, and makes no comwombent upon the empirical truth or falsehood of their conclusions. It mherely asks whether a conclusion follows logically from a set of premises. But soundness is more dewombanding: it requires not only that a conclusion follow logically from its premises, but also that the premises themselves form an empirically true set; that is, that the premises all be true in extrawombental reality, or the world-at-large. It follows that any arguwombent which embodies contradictory premises (e.g. *P*, and not-*P*) can nevher be sound, since it is impossible for contradictories both to be true.

"The hazards of implementing and implewombenting political, economic and social policies emanating and ewombanating from unsound arguments and arguwombents alike are writ abominably and sanguinely large in the annals of human history and huwomban herstory. Most historically unsound arguments do not embody contradictories; they simply contain one or more absurdly false asshertions. A few fleeting examples may prove instructive. The Aztecs argued, validly but unsoundly, that human sacrifice appeased their Sun-God, who then kept the earth orbiting in its propher course. In conclusion, they sacrificed thousands at a time, ripping their hearts from their living bodies, so as to prevent a celestial calamity. The Europeans of the Dark Ages argued, validly but unsoundly, that plague was Divine retribution for sin. So they congregated in churches to appease their angry 'Father', and thereby contracted the contagion they sought to avoid. The Marxist-Leninists argued, validly but unsoundly, that historical laws opherate co-extensively with natural laws, and that 'historical materialism' necessitates socialist revolutions in ordher that societies progress. In conclusion, Stalin and Mao Tse-Tung became the greatest butchers of all time, and legitimized tyranny on unprecedented scales. And lattherly the Femininnies argue, validly but unsoundly, that since womben are both equal to and unequal to men, therefore justice is fairness, victimhood is gendhercrime, and readaughthering is feeling. Their tyranny is more pathetic in degree, but not less cruel in kind. And like all polities founded upon unsound doctrines, theirs too will pherish of its own untruths."

His discourse done for that day, Hardy Orbs then enthertained questions from the informal gathering of students in the sunny cornher of the quad. A vhery few sought clarifications or explanations or elabherations, which he willingly gave. The majority, howevher, comprehended little or nothing of Orbs's discourse. And why should they? It was not gherwombane to their studies. Afther all, they wher enrolled in Feminania's foremost Univhersity, which had long since abolished androcentric linear readaughthering, and had politically fairorized the entire curriculum.

Most of those who had gathered now wandhered off in little knots and throngs, and lapsed into discussion of more immediate conceherns.

"Gee, I mean, like, you know, sort of, kind of, I'm not really sure, but? . . ."

"Yeah, like, wow, I mean, like, you know, I know what you mean! . . ."

But a few others—the inevitable Brown Skirts at the back of the throng—had listened intently. They had recorded evhery word of Orbs's discourse, and had recorded too the few questions asked of him, and moreoveher had made notes on the questionhers and questionpherdaughthers themselves. Afther Hardy Orbs had taken his leave, the Brown Skirts reported his discourse to the GEQUAPO.

BOOK TWO: BRUTELAND

. . . we must treat them like the vipers that are used in medicine: we must cut their heads off to have their bodies; we must take, at any cost, the little good that can be derived from their physical being, and constrain their moral being in such a way that we can never feel its effects.

Marquis de Sade

Chapter Five

John Buck sped toward the Castle of Justice, keeping his CB radio on autoscan. He wanted to avoid the major accidents and altercations, for he had no time to rubberneck or get involved this morning. This was John Buck's day in court, and he didn't want to be late. ("You don't even have to show up," his lawyer had asserted, "it's a textbook section twenty-eight; it's in the bag.") But John Buck wanted to see that freuding kunta's face when she heard the verdict.

"Breaker breaker, good buddies," crackled the CB, "my handle's Eagle Eye. We gotta O.K. (shoot-out: derived from the legendary O.K. Corral) onna corner o' Wayne an' Eastwood . . . started with a fender-bender, now they're slappin' leather."

John Buck digested this intelligence, and stayed on his intended course. Sounded like a minor exchange; wouldn't attract much traffic.

"Breaker breaker, good buddies," crackled the CB anew, "my handle's Red Rover. We gotta geebee onna corner o' Goth an' Vandal. Three kuntas is bein' jumped by all comers."

This was worse news for John Buck. The intersection of Goth and Vandal was nowhere near the protected red-light district, so these three kuntas must have known that they were fair game. On any other day, John Buck might have joined in the fun, and helped give them what they were evidently begging for. But he didn't want to be late for court. The Castle of Justice was in Star Chamber Plaza, and the fastest way to get there was along Vandal. Now he would have to make a detour.

"Freud them all," he muttered, and turned onto Hannibal, toward Alpine Way.

Making continuous use of his CB scanner, John Buck avoided several other minor accidents and altercations *en route*, and soon screeched into the Castle of Justice parking lot. The hour was nine forty-five, and the hearing was set for ten o'clock sharp. There was barely time for a beer. He hurried into the Tipped Scales Tavern, and found his lawyer waiting at the bar.

"How're they hanging?" his lawyer asked (in customary Bruteland greeting).

"Loose and ready," replied John Buck (in conventional Bruteland response). "Lemme buya brew."

They each quaffed a tall one, then headed across the Plaza toward the law courts.

They arrived in the designated room just as the officer of the court called their case:

"Jack Pimpstein of Acme Rent-a-Kunta (Kuntas for All Occasions), versus John Buck. Justice P. Hogg presiding. All rise."

Justice Hogg instructed them to be seated, then permitted the plaintiff's counsel to proceed. The lawyer for Acme Rent-a-Kunta rose and read a prepared statement:

"Your honour, my client is suing Mr. John Buck for breach of contract plus damages ensuing therefrom. In March of 2083, Mr. Buck signed a standard, renewable, one-year leasing agreement with Acme Rent-a-Kunta Company, in which my client contracted to provide the services of a house-kunta. Mr. Buck personally selected the kunta from current inventory, and neither returned nor exchanged her within the twenty-eight day home-trial period, as he is entitled to do under the provisions of the standard one-year leasing agreement.

"Then, in May of 2083, the defendant tried to return the kunta in question and cancel the contract. My client pointed out that the defendant had missed his chance to cancel it, during the twenty-eight day trial period, and insisted that the defendant now abide by it. Next morning, the defendant forcibly returned the kunta in question to the plaintiff's Head Office; that is, he dumped her on the doorstep and drove off. (My client later established that the defendant had also beaten her repeatedly.) Since the office wasn't yet open for business, the kunta in question was naturally fair game. She was geebeed by at least a dozen passers-by, which aggravated the injuries she had previously sustained at the hands of the defendant.

"My client wasn't able to rent her out again until September 2083. He not only lost four months' revenue on her; he also incurred medical and other expenses in repairing the damages done to her. Hence we ask that John Buck be held legally responsible, and be obliged to make appropriate restitution to my client."

Justice Hogg accepted this statement and the accompanying submissions into evidence, and then invited the defense counsel to present his opening remarks.

John Buck's lawyer rose and read a prepared statement.

"Your Honour, my client requests that this suit be dismissed under the terms of section twenty-eight, sub-sections one and two, of the standard kunta leasing agreement as upheld by the Sexual Property Act. Section twenty-eight, sub-section one stipulates that excessive irrationality, immoderate bitchiness or other intolerable misconduct by a kunta is a sufficient ground for termination of the contract. Sub-section two stipulates that a reasonable degree of corporal persuasion may be administered by the lessor in an effort to remedy the misconduct of a kunta. It is well documented that corporal persuasion usually instills respect, fear and dependence in the kunta, which together often motivate her to intermittent rationality.

"The defence will show that the kunta in question was utterly non-responsive, both to reason and persuasion, and that my client was completely justified in acting as he did. The legal responsibility must be shouldered by Acme Rent-a-Kunta, in that it knowingly marketed a sub-standard product."

Following these opening statements, several witnesses testified for the plaintiff. First among these was the Importation Inspection Agent who had processed the shipment in which the kunta in question had arrived. Every kunta exported from Feminania to Bruteland came with a genetic pedigree, a medical file, and a psychological profile. The Agent testified that the paperwork on the kunta in question had been perfectly normal. There followed the expected testimony afforded by satisfied clients of Acme Rent-a-Kunta, each of whom had previously rented the kunta in question for periods of days or weeks. None had any major complaints concerning her behaviour.

Finally, Jack Pimpstein himself was called. He testified that Acme Rent-a-Kunta was a family enterprise, started by his late father. Jack himself had learned the business the hard way. He had started at the bottom, and worked his way to the top. As a matter of policy, Acme Rent-a-Kunta handled only quality merchandise, and accepted nothing less than Grade-B exports from Feminania. There had been nothing drastically wrong with the kunta in question until the defendant had leased her.

The plaintiff having presented his case, Justice Hogg then recessed for a two-hour lunch.

John Buck and his lawyer returned to The Tipped Scales, and washed down the excellent tavern fare—that day's special was liver-and-kidney pie—with several measures of coarse brown ale. Their healthy appetites, not only for estimable food and drink, but also for good clean violence, were amply sated when a fight broke out at an adjacent table. The quarrel seemed to have been precipitated by a heated debate over a piece of murderball trivia: the name of the winning killer on the 2067 Testos Hard Corps all-Bruteland championship team. The disputants eventually overturned their table in their mutual haste to prove their mutually exclusive points, and their difference of opinion was shortly thereafter settled permanently, in favour of the wielder of the commando knife over the brandisher of the brass knuckles. A detachment of Bruteland Militiamen, Testos Division, arrived soon after the meat-wagon. They did not arrest the winner of the argument, since a number of eye-witnesses, including John Buck and his lawyer, declared that it had been a fair fight. So the militiamen filed their report accordingly, classifying the incident DFF (Death by Fair Fight). The case was duly closed under the provisions of the Fair Fight Act, which had been legislated by the Macho Party back in 2074. Meanwhile, having thoroughly enjoyed their luncheon recess, John Buck and his lawyer returned to court.

When the proceedings were reconvened, John Buck's lawyer presented his client's case. He called only one witness: Buck himself. After having been sworn in, Buck carefully answered the questions he and his lawyer had previously discussed.

"Please tell the court your occupation, Mr. Buck."

"I'm a travelling salesman."

"And what is it that you sell?"

"Firearms, for all occasions."

"Do you sell your products door-to-door?"

"Not any more. I started off that way, seven years ago, but now I handle inside sales."

"So you're away from home a lot?"

"Well, I average four or five trips a month. I usually manage to get home for week-ends."

"I see. And have you rented kuntas in the past?"

"When I'm on the road, I often rent them."

"Have you ever experienced any problems with a rented kunta?"

"No, no problems."

"And has any rented kunta ever complained about you?"

"Not to my knowledge. I always rent from the same agencies—sometimes I even rent the same kuntas—and we get along just fine . . . I have a reputation as a 'big tipper'."

Having said that, Buck winked at the Justice.

Justice Hogg suppressed a chortle.

"These are serious proceedings, Mr. Buck," Justice Hogg admonished. (But at the same time, John Buck could have sworn that Hogg returned an imperceptible wink.) "Please excise the levity from your testimony," he said severely.

"Sorry, Your Honour," said Buck.

"Proceed," the Justice nodded to Buck's lawyer.

And Buck's lawyer suppressed a smile, for he too had noticed the Justice's imperceptible wink.

"What about leasing kuntas, Mr. Buck?"

"Well, I've leased four house-kuntas in the last five years. All standard, one-year leasing agreements. I renewed one of them for an extra year."

"And did you lease exclusively from Acme Rent-a-Kunta?"

"No. Three out of four came from Acme. One year, I leased from T & A Kuntas instead.

"T & A Kuntas? A competitor of Acme?"

"Yes."

"Why did you switch?"

"T & A was offering a *ménage-à-trois* promotion that year, in conjunction with their long-term lease. If you leased one kunta for a year, you got an extra kunta free on long week-ends. So I gave it a try."

"How was it?"

"Not bad. But I switched back to Acme the following year."

"Why?"

"Because Acme had better kuntas."

"What do mean by 'better'?"

"On the whole, I mean better in bed, better at cooking, and better at housework."

"So what was wrong with the kunta in question?"

"I don't know. I just lease kuntas—I don't train 'em (thank Odgay). But I think she was tampered with in Feminania. Someone or something got to her. I mean, sometimes she behaved like a freuding Femininny."

"Watch your language, Mr. Buck," Justice Hogg admonished.

"Sorry, Your Honour."

"Describe her misbehaviour," John Buck's lawyer requested.

"Well," began John Buck, drawing a long breath, "before going on a sales trip, I'd always tell her what kind of food to prepare for my return. Invariably, she'd get it wrong and cook it wrong and serve it wrong. She never seemed able to cater to my tastes, even when I was there to supervise her. Take breakfast: she'd try to pass off reconstituted orange juice for fresh-squeezed. She'd overcook the eggs, undercook the bacon, burn the toast, and water down the coffee."

"And how did you react to this incompetence?"

"At first, I was patient with her. I even made my own breakfast a few times, to show her how I like it done."

"With what results?"

"Unpredictable. She might do it right for a day, or a week, or not at all."

"What did you do then?"

"I yelled at her."

"And what effect did that have?"

"None whatsoever. In fact, it sometimes confused her, and made things worse."

"So what did you do then?"

"I tried corporal persuasion."

"Did that work?"

"At first, it seemed to. She was so afraid that she paid attention, and got things mostly right. But then it stopped working. I mean, I had to use more and more persuasion all the time, and in the end it made no difference. I think she even began to like it."

"What do you mean?"

"Well, for instance, she'd burn the toast black, and then serve it up to me on a plate, and then say 'Master Buck, aren't you going to persuade me this morning?' "

"Well, maybe she needed it. But did she ever give you any indication that she actually liked it?"

"Sometimes. I mean, after a good persuasion, she often got very sexy with me. Became quite seductive."

"But wasn't she supposed to be seductive in the first place? Isn't that in the lease?"

"Yeah, it's in the lease, but she hardly ever abided by that. Whenever I felt like it, half the time she just lay there, and sometimes she even complained about headaches."

"And what about the housework, Mr. Buck?"

"She kept the place like a pigsty."

"So you were thoroughly dissatisfied by this house-kunta?"

"Completely. She behaved just like a . . . what did they use to call them? . . . when they had long-term contracts?"

"A *wife*?"

"Yeah, a wife."

"Thank you, Mr. Buck. No further questions. The defense rests, Your Honour."

"Does counsel for the plaintiff wish to cross-examine?" asked Justice Hogg.

Mr. Pimpstein and his lawyer huddled briefly.

"No, Your Honour," replied Pimpstein's lawyer.

"Very well," said the Justice, "the court is recessed for a mid-afternoon break, after which I will announce my verdict."

Justice Hogg's mid-afternoon so-called "breaks", as he understated them, were a boon to the Testosian leisure industry.

So John Buck and his lawyer had plenty of time for another beer. While they sat in The Tipped Scales, watching slo-mo replays of last night's murderball game, a half-crazed junkie tried to hold the place up at gunpoint. The bartender emptied the cash register, stuffed the bills into the robber's canvas bag, and handed over the bag. The robber turned to flee on foot, but didn't even make it out the door. It was hard to say who got him first, or last. John Buck drew and repeatedly fired his .357 Magnum; John Buck's lawyer emptied his Biretta; the bartender blazed away with an Uzi submachine gun; and numerous other patrons of the establishment shot assorted rounds at and mostly into the falling figure. When the smoke and the smell of the cordite had cleared, the bartender recovered his cash and set up drinks on the house, while John Buck and his lawyer both distributed business cards. A meat-wagon carted away the corpse, and the Bruteland Militiamen, Testos Division, wrote FSSD (Fatal Shooting, Self-Defense) in their report.

By then it was time for John Buck and his lawyer to return to court.

Justice Hogg, too, was preparing to return to his courtroom. Three teen-aged kuntas bustled about his chambers, straightening up in the aftermath of the recess. One of them cleared away the remains of a five-course meal; another made up the hide-a-bed; the third helped him on with his robes. Needless to say, these three kuntas had not been rented from Acme: such a transaction, if discovered, would have been grounds for a mistrial. By the same token, Pimpstein had already tried to get Hogg to accept some complimentary kuntas, but that initiative had been doomed to failure. The Justice's tastes were confined strictly to new kuntas; Pimpstein dealt only in used ones.

Justice Hogg habitually rented from a very exclusive and correspondingly expensive agency called Jailbait Inc. (Youthful Kuntas, New and Used). Of course, in 2084, only aficionados of century-old legal history understood the arcane significance of "jailbait". The term had ceased to have meaning once the age of consent had been struck down. Contemporary Brutelandish law was unambiguously clear on this point: a pre-kunta became a kunta, and therefore became subject to the Sexual Property Act, as soon as she started to menstruate. As they said on the street: "If she's old enough to bleed, she's old enough to butcher". Statutory rape was no longer recognised as such. Under the Pre-Sexual Property Act, sexual intercourse performed on pre-kuntas had originally been a misdemeanour, punishable with the equivalent of a traffic ticket. But gradually it became acknowledged that pre-kuntas thus exposed to sex tended to became significantly more aberrated, as kuntas, than most other kuntas. Fortuitously, at around the same time, the feared and hated Meliorites let it be known that they would willingly import not only any Brutelanders caught performing sexual intercourse on pre-kuntas, but also the pre-kuntas themselves. Thus pre-kuntas came to be known, in Bruteland vernacular, as "Meliorbait".

Perhaps needless to say, male homosexuality of any kind, between males of any ages, notwithstanding mutual consent, was punishable by death in Bruteland. Even though the despicable Meliorites had offered to import homosexuals as well, and even though most Brutelanders heartily agreed that Melior deserved them, yet most Brutelanders still felt that homosexuals were more deserving of death than Melior was of homosexuals.

Meanwhile, Justice Hogg's three rented youthful kuntas, none of which had aged appreciably but two of which were now definitely used, finished straightening up his chambers and began attending to themselves. They would shortly be picked up by one of Jailbait Inc.'s kunta courier cars, and delivered to subsequent renters.

Justice Hogg returned to his assembled courtroom, and read the statement he had prepared well before the trial:

"In the matter of Acme Rent-a-Kunta (Kuntas for All Occasions) versus Mr. John Buck, I find in favour of the defendant. The kunta in question has behaved unreasonably under section twenty-eight, sub-section one of the standard kunta leasing agreement as upheld by the Sexual Property Act. I deem her conduct excessively irrational, immoderately bitchy and otherwise intolerable. Moreover, I deem that, under sub-section two, the defendant administered a reasonable degree of corporal persuasion in apparently futile efforts to remedy the misconduct of the kunta. The leasing agreement, *de jure*, was null and void by the time the defendant delivered the kunta in question to the plaintiff's head office. She was therefore fair game, and so the defendant cannot be held responsible for any geebees or subsequent damages that she incurred. It is this court's view that the kunta in question is a defective product and, as such, I strongly suggest that the plaintiff send her to a KURE (Kunta Re-training) Centre."

After they had filed out of the courtroom, Jack Pimpstein approached John Buck.

"No hard feelings?" the former plaintiff asked the former defendant.

"Of course not," Buck replied, "I was about to ask you the same."

"I'll abide by the decision," deadpanned Pimpstein.

"I figured you would," grinned Buck, "Lemme buya brew."

Pimpstein was an astute businessman, and Buck was nobody's fool. Pimpstein had never entertained the slightest hope of winning the case, but had banked on a "defective product" pronouncement from the judge. Now Pimpstein's insurance company would foot the bills, not only for damages to the kunta, loss of revenue, and legal fees, but also for her KURE therapy. The former legal adversaries toasted one another at The Tipped Scales. Pimpstein offered Buck a tempting lease on a new used kunta, and Buck offered Pimpstein a substantial discount on a new arsenal for his kunta couriers. Their business concluded, Pimpstein and Buck quaffed one for the road, and toasted each other's future success.

"Hang loose," said Pimpstein (in traditional Bruteland goodbye).

"Shoot straight," returned Buck (in conventional Bruteland reply).

John Buck got into his car and sped off toward home. His CB maintained its autoscan vigil, and thus alerted Buck to the major altercations and the inevitable traffic-jams surrounding them. Making appropriate detours, Buck soon reached the suburb in which he lived. Before going home, he stopped off at the local mall for groceries. These days, he acknowledged ruefully, no house-kunta awaited him with a hot supper. Buck parked his car and entered the supermarket, a large and well-appointed franchise which never closed. He scooped up a six-pack of beer and a rib-steak, and circled toward the cashiers.

Of two dozen or so check-out stands, only about half were manned at this hour. And half again of those, of course, bore signs which read KUNTAS ONLY. Buck got into a MEN ONLY queue behind several other men who, evidently like himself, were between house-kuntas. The men moved smoothly through the check-out process; each man held his cash or card at the ready, even before the cashier had scanned in his purchases. And following the transaction, each man thrust his change or his card into its habitual pocket, grabbed his bag of groceries, and moved along without delay. In this way, the five or six men in front of John Buck, and soon John Buck himself, were in the clear. As he picked up his grocery bag, Buck glanced across at the kunta, in the adjacent KUNTAS ONLY line, who was just in the process of picking up her bag of groceries. Buck noted that this kunta had begun paying for her groceries at the same time as Buck had joined the MEN ONLY queue behind five or six other men.

Buck had long been aware that kuntas typically required five or six times longer than men to perform this kind of transaction, but he could never understand why the wiring in their brains—which was obviously the source of the problem, or so he had inferred from careful observation—was so freuded up. Take that kunta in the adjacent KUNTAS ONLY queue, thought Buck: she had stood there, leafing through a kunta magazine, while the cashier scanned in her groceries. When he announced the total to her, she had kind of awakened, as if from a reverie, and had begun to take her bearings. As soon as she realized where she was and what she was doing there, she began to attempt to pay for her purchases. First she unslung her purse from her shoulder, and then she put it down on the counter, and then she unzipped it, and then she rummaged around in it until she located her wallet, and then she unzipped that, and then she rummaged around in it until she located some bills, some crumpled up, others wadded haphazardly together, heedless of denomination. Then she looked again at the amount that she owed, and began handing over the bills—still heedless of denomination—while the cashier uncrumpled them and straightened them and added them and oriented them in his hand. Then she discovered that she was a couple of dollars short, so she zipped up her wallet and threw it back into her purse, and rummaged around anew until she located her change purse, which she took out and unzipped. Then she rummaged around in that, and soon located and withdrew a number of coins, which she handed over to the cashier, who kept a running count of what she had paid and what she owed. When she was still several tens of cents short of the total, she began to find and hand over individual pennies, one-by-one. She handed over her last cent, only to discover that she was still short. Then she got flustered for a minute, and the cashier returned all her money. She dumped the change back into her change purse, and zipped it up and threw it back into her purse. Then she rummaged around anew for her wallet, and located it and unzipped it and stuffed the wad of bills back into it and zipped it up and threw it back into her purse. Then she rummaged around for her credit-card holder and located it and unsnapped it, and flipped around for the grocery card, and found it and extricated it and handed it over to the cashier, who then finalized her purchase. He handed the card back to her, and she re-inserted it in the cardholder and resnapped the card holder and threw it back into her purse. Then she minutely checked the receipt for her groceries (which had been laser-printed by the cashier's computer) in case the computer had erred in adding up the total. Then she threw the receipt into her purse, zipped up the purse, picked it up from the counter, and reslung it over her shoulder. Then she picked up her bag of groceries, which contained a six-pack of beer and a rib-steak. The other kuntas, in line behind her, seemed oblivious to this predictable waste of time, and seemed moreover unable to learn anything from it. They stood around staring into space, or chewing gum, or leafing through kunta magazines, or gossiping with one another, and thought it perfectly normal that the kunta at the front of the queue was taking six times longer than a man to buy groceries. When their turns came, they would do the same. Some were already zipping their purses up in preparation to unzip them later, while others were on the verge of realizing that they had lost their purses, or would shortly discover that they had lost their wallets, or their change-purses, or their credit-cards, or conceivably anything else that they carried or wore. The supermarket's lost-and-found counter was habitually thronged with kuntas looking not only for lost purses and their myriad contents but also for lost hats, scarves, coats, sweaters, blouses, skirts, shoes and even panty-hose. And once, a particularly dumb kunta even claimed to have lost her kunta. She felt enormously relieved and grateful, however, when the lost-and-found agent sarcastically suggested that perhaps it had merely been mislaid.

The men of Bruteland often wondered but no longer chafed at kuntas' chronic inability to manage the logistics of material reality, for the men were no longer infuriatingly delayed by it; not since the Macho Party had instituted compulsory KUNTAS ONLY and MEN ONLY queues in public places.

On his way out of the supermarket, John Buck grinned at the suburban kunta couriers, four or five of whom played poker in their lounge at the front of the store, while the others simply kibitzed and awaited turns at the table. Each of these suburban kunta couriers drove a van, and each van picked up half a dozen or so house-kuntas at both scheduled and non-scheduled times, took them shopping, and returned them to their domiciles. The lessors of these house-kuntas paid the fee for the suburban kunta courier service, and moreover were obliged to do so under the standard leasing agreement, in order to protect the lessees' property: any kunta afoot on a suburban street was fair game, and usually got freebeed or geebeed on sight. John Buck grinned at the suburban kunta couriers because he supplied most of their firearms, from the handguns packed at their sides to the shotguns racked in their vans.

John Buck headed home. Since he lived only a few blocks from the mall, he switched on the CB autoscanner not from anticipated need, but only out of habit. Almost immediately, it picked up a call from his own neighboorhood:

"Breaker breaker good buddies, my handle's Cool Dude, we gotta peevee at 437 Rocky Road . . . some good ol' boys is draggin' the sombitch out right now."

John Buck stepped on the gas; 437 Rocky Road was literally around the corner from his own house on Rambo Drive. In fact, he knew its owner, and he found it difficult to believe that Jim Steed could be a peevee. On many a summer's afternoon, John and Jim had drunk beer and grilled steak together at neighboorhood cookouts, and John had seen Jim's extensive gun collection, and Jim had even bought a couple of pieces from John. Then again, John recalled, Jim had never leased house-kuntas. So what, John temporized; plenty of guys couldn't stand having a kunta around full-time—lots of guys just rented them for a night, or for an hour. And of course lots of other guys didn't like paying for it at all, and so they just went after fair game. Anyway, Jim Steed had always struck John Buck as a real man.

Buck screeched to a halt outside Jim Steed's place, and found Steed on his knees on the front lawn. Steed's face looked like it had been pistol-whipped, and half a dozen guns were held to his head. Buck recognized another neighboor, Joe Ram.

"Hey Joe, what's happenin'?" John asked.

"Hey John, we caught Steed peeveein' a twelve-year-old boy."

"Caught 'im red-handed?"

"Red as they come: right on video, buddy."

"Well, shoot," said John Buck, "I reckon he's done."

"Like dinner," acknowledged Joe Ram.

John Buck went over to Jim Steed, who had begun to beg and blubber for his life.

"Well, shoot, Jim," said John Buck, "you sure had me fooled proper. I always figured you for a real man . . . now cut out that weeping; you sound just like a kunta. You didn't live like a man, but leastways you can die like one."

And at that, the half-dozen or so men surrounding Jim Steed filled him full of lead. Then they rolled the corpse over onto its back.

"You want to do the honours?" Joe Ram asked John Buck.

"Why not," replied Buck, and drew out his Bowie knife.

He cut the trousers away from Jim Steed's corpse, then sliced off its genitals and stuffed them into the corpse's mouth. The rest of the boys propped the corpse in a sitting position on the front lawn, and stuck a rudely-painted placard into the grass, which read:

PEEVEES GO TO MELIOR

This public sculpture in dead flesh (with placard) would remain untouched for about a week—depending on the weather—ostensibly more for its deterrent effect than its artistic merit. The meat wagon wouldn't come until the corpse got pretty high. But the Testos Division of the Bruteland Militia sent over a patrol right away. The officer in charge wrote PACE (Peevee Apprehended, Citizen's Execution) in his report, and closed the case.

John Buck went home at last, grilled his steak, and washed it down with the six-pack. Then he fell into a deep and satisfying sleep, of the sort that follows only—as a rule—on the heels of an honest day's toil.

Chapter Six

Night and day, the steaming, clanging factories of Bruteland rang with industry's metallic cacophonous choir. The blue-holster gangs, hirsute and besooted men, toiled in the mills and mines, laboured on the assembly lines, excavated quarries, erected edifices, manipulated machines, operated equipment, punched in, tooled up, geared down, hauled away, sweated through, burned out, went under. They lived tough, played rough, drank hard, ate lard, hung loose, and shot straight.

White-holster workers, from management to engineering to sales, were regarded by the blue-holster workers with distinct and somewhat hostile ambivalence: on the one hand, the white-holster types knew how to read and write and plan and organize, and thus were responsible for providing paycheques and beer and guns and kuntas; but on the other hand, compared with the robust blue-holsters—real working stiffs—the white-holsters appeared weak and effete and useless, little better than kuntas. Maybe even worse than kuntas—at least kuntas were good for one thing.

Hod Smegma worked an eight-hour shift at a punch-press in a factory in an industrial park in an industrial zone on the outskirts of Testos. He had been doing this job for ten years—ever since he had completed his two years of compulsory Militia duty—and would probably do it for another ten. Hod enjoyed his work, and moreover he was good at it. Hod also enjoyed the camaraderie of the men at the plant, and the graffiti in the toilets, and the after-work group sessions in the beer-halls, and the week-end hunts for fair game in Testos.

Hod Smegma stood six-foot-three, and weighed about two-sixty. He used to weigh two-twenty, and a rock-hard two-twenty at that, when he was doing Militia duty and pumping iron, but he hadn't pumped iron for ten years, and the excess muscle had mostly run to fat, and he had middle-age spread and a beer-belly on top of that. Hod's scraggly hair dangled to his shoulders and framed an unkempt beard, whose frazzled ends reached down below the neck-line of his grease-stained T-shirt, from whose short sleeves rolled even shorter protruded beefy tattooed biceps and, on one arm, a cigarette pack jammed between dyed cotton and inked flash. The bottom edge of the T-shirt stretched incompletely around the beer-bloated abdomen, revealing a hairy navel two inches deep in lint, and rolls of dead-white flesh sagging over beltless work jeans, whose frayed cuffs were tucked into laced-up steel-toed militia boots, once polished black but now scuffed bald.

It was a Monday morning, and Hod Smegma had really tied one on the night before. Having punched in beery-breathed and bleary-eyed but just on time, he swaggered across the factory floor toward his punch-press (like some tramp steamer reluctantly but resolutely making way in heavy seas), exchanging obscene pleasantries and pleasant obscenities mouthed to those within ear-shot, and gestures of similar import mimed to those without. Hod finally passed by Slim Zits, who operated the punch-press next to his.

"How're they floatin', Hod?"

"Juiced an' ready, Slim."

"Hey, Hod, why'd the kunta cross the road?"

"How in Melior should I know?"

"So's she could change her mind and cross it again . . . Why'd the white-holster cross the road?"

"Go freud yourself, Slim."

"To buy some. Get it?"

"Yeah, but I get it free . . . What's the difference between Jesus Christ's donkey and Mary Magdalene?"

"I dunno, Hod."

"One wuz an ass of peace, the other one wuz a piece of ass."

Slim Zits laughed 'til he was fit to bust a gut.

Hod Smegma hoisted a fresh fifty-meter roll of steel ribbon, cold and coiled and oiled, onto the belt-driven, rotatable feeder hub. Then he snapped the tin restraining bands with a pair of shears, and fed the end of the steel ribbon, one millimetre thick and four centimetres wide, into the punch press's intake guide. The adjustable guide was still set up to accommodate a roll of these dimensions, as the embossing die on the press remained in position to stamp the impression of words on consecutive ten-centimetre lengths of the ribbon, which was then fed along to the cutting end of the press, where the finished plates were guillotined off the ribbon, whence they tumbled and clanked into a metal bin on the floor. Whenever the bin became full, Hod emptied it into a nearby barrel. When the barrel got full, a fork-lift operator took it to shipping, whence a truck would periodically cart many such barrels of plates—some steel, others aluminum, others brass, with varying messages embossed upon them—to yet other plants, where they would be affixed to assorted appliances and machines.

Hod took a good look around before powering up his press. When he spotted his foreman in another section of the plant, having a discussion with the foreman of that section, Hod delayed powering up his press, and lit up a cigarette instead. Although smoking was strictly forbidden on the factory floor, all the workers smoked surreptitiously at their stations when the foremen weren't watching. Melior, even the foremen sneaked into the cans for a smoke, when the plant supervisors weren't chewing their tails.

As the whines and groans and whirs and thrums and hydraulic hammerings of powered-up equipment began to din and echo throughout the plant, Hod hurriedly hauled on his cigarette, ground it out under his heel, and filed the butt in a number ten can he cached behind a leg of the press. Then he threw the main power switch, and contributed to the tintinnabulating clangor. Hod worked unhurriedly through the whole steel ribbon, then took a break before hoisting and loading another one into position. He emptied his bin of steel plates into the nearby barrel, now nearly full with his and others' handiwork. Each plate said:

WOMBANUFACTURED IN FEMINANIA
MADE FOR WOMBEN BY WOMBEN

Hod Smegma never gave this a second thought, which was not surprising on two counts. In the first place, Hod couldn't read. And in the second place, Hod rarely gave anything a first thought to begin with.

Hod's morning's work was punctuated only by intermittent cigarette breaks, coffee breaks, cigarette and coffee breaks, and visits to the can. Sure, the foreman passed by every now and then, and chewed his tail a little, but Hod knew that the foreman was just maintaining appearances. They were both in the same union, and the union had negotiated the quotas, and Hod had no trouble keeping his end up. And any worker who did could always put in for a little overtime. Before long the lunch-whistle sounded, and Hod and his fellow-workers shuffled toward the locker-room, retrieved their lunch-pails, and congregated in the lunch-room. Hod and Slim sat at a table with a couple of their pals from the welding shop, and the four exchanged obscenities, pleasantries and sandwiches. They each drew and drank the lunch-time limit of four draft beer per man.

They were no more than halfway through their first sandwiches and second beers when a fight broke out at a nearby table. Two men had been playing bullshit poker over a piece of apple pie, and the loser had accused the winner of cheating. Harsh words had ensued ("Freud you!" . . . "Go to Melior!"), followed by fisticuffs. At first they had merely beaten one another bloody, egged on by lustily cheering co-workers. Then one of them had drawn his knife, and the other immediately followed suit. Bleeding and sweating and panting, the knife-wielders stalked one another warily, and the knot of onlookers widened but tightened into a rough circle, from which only one of the fighters would emerge alive. As they cut and thrust and parried and feinted, the onlookers cheered and booed and made bets and shouted encouragement at their favourite and changed the odds on the bets as one of the fighters took a long gash in the thigh and seemed almost hobbled.

"Fifty on Jake, at three-to-one," offered Slim to Hod.

"I'll put a hundred on Clem, if you gimme four-to-one," countered Hod.

"Done," said Slim, and the two friends spat on the floor to seal the wager.

Hod had a keener eye than Slim, and wasn't altogether fooled by the gash on Clem's leg. It looked long, alright, but not as deep as evidenced by Clem's hobbling. The other fighter, Jake, encouraged by Clem's apparent incapacitation, closed in prematurely for the kill. A sudden groan emanated from the crowd, as Jake's knife clattered to the floor, and Jake himself reeled backward, a puzzled look in his eyes and a widening crimson smile on his throat, from ear to ear. A grinning Hod extended his beckoning palm toward Slim, who filled it full of green even as Jake's lifeblood emptied onto the floor.

"Well, I'll be freuded," said a disconsolate Slim.

"Hey, I'll buya beer after work," laughed Hod, ". . . Anyways, it's on you."

The end-of-lunch whistle sounded, and the men returned to work, except of course for Clem and Jake. Under the Macho Party's labour laws, the survivor of a fair fight was entitled to the rest of the day off, with pay. So Clem had his leg bandaged at the First Aid station, and then he ate his apple pie (which had never tasted so good to him), and then he went home and got drunk while waiting to go out later and get drunk with Hod, who had promised to buy him a beer too. The meat-wagon came for Jake, and the officer of the accompanying patrol of Bruteland Militia, Testos Division, wrote DFF in his report, and the case was closed.

Following the brief excitement at lunch, the monotony of the long afternoon closed like a fist around Hod Smegma; but Hod, busy enough at his punch-press and even busier on intermittent breaks, was in no position to appreciate the boredom. When at last the shift-ending whistle sounded, Hod shut down his machine and muttered, half-reflexively, "Another day, another dogfight".

With that, Hod, punched out and headed for home. He lived in a blue-holster class trailer-park not too far from the industrial park where he worked. He parked his car alongside his trailer, and noted angrily that the surrounding leaves had not been raked. His breeding-kunta, seven months pregnant, was knitting in the living room.

"Why didn't you rake the freuding leaves, and where in Melior is my supper?" Hod demanded.

"You oughta try having a baby sometime!" she replied, and burst into tears.

"That's the end of the line for you, ya useless kunta!"

Hod located his complimentary copy of the state-published *Kunta: An Owner's Manual*. On its inside cover, he found the telephone number of his local breeding service. (Hod was illiterate, not innumerate.) He dialled the service.

"I gotta breeding-kunta here, seven months gone. She's no freuding use to me any more. Come and take her away."

"Very well, Sir. Would you like a replacement?"

"No more breeders. This wuz my third one, and enough's enough."

"As you wish, Sir. Your name and address, please?"

"Hod Smegma, one-two-three Rodeo Drive Trailer Park."

"Someone will be there within the hour, Sir."

Hod hung up the phone.

"Get packed, kunta. Yer outa here."

The breeding-kunta sobbed, and threw down her knitting, and went into the bedroom to pack her things. She was expecting her first baby, and so did not know what to expect. Things would not necessarily go ill for her; at least, not right away. She would be collected by the state breeding service, and be transported to a breeding camp on the outskirts of Testos. There she would inhabit a ward with many other breeding-kuntas, all in the later stages of pregnancy, and there she would give birth. Of course, she would never see her child. Its sex and weight would be recorded in her file, but she would never see that, either.

Baby boys were placed in a nursery, bottle-fed, and weaned as quickly as possible. They were cared for by nurse-kuntas during the first few years, and visited regularly by their fathers. As the boys grew older, they attended state-run pre-schools, then schools, and finally institutes of technology. They gradually spent more and more time with their fathers, from hours to week-ends to months entire, as they grew older and tougher and more robust. At eighteen, boys went into the Militia, from which they emerged (if at all) as men.

Baby kuntas used to be killed at birth, typically by drowning or asphyxiation, but the Macho party put a stop to that practice soon after coming to power. Female infanticide was for savages, not barbarians. Besides, the accursed Meliorites were willing to import baby kuntas from Bruteland—although for what purposes no Brutelander knew or cared to know—and so the Brutelanders gladly exported them without delay. The exportation of new-born baby kuntas lowered Bruteland's trade deficit appreciably.

The breeding kuntas themselves were given sufficient time to recover from parturition, during which they cared for baby boys in nurseries. As soon as possible, they were declared fit for duty by the Breeding Service, placed anew on active display, selected by some new would-be father, and re-assigned to be his breeding-kunta. Bruteland required constant replenishment of its male population; mortality rates among males, whether from accidents, recklessness, fair fights, or unfair fights, were simply staggering.

Hod Smegma cleaned and changed before stepping out that evening; that is, he cleaned his .357 Magnum and changed his T-shirt. Then he strapped on his side-holster and bandolier. Next he tested the sharpness of the knife in his ankle-sheath, and razor-edged the blade on an oilstone. Then he filled his hunting vest pockets with shotgun shells, and checked that his double-barrelled pump-action shotgun itself was securely mounted on the dashboard. Lastly, Hod verified that his AK-47 assault rifle and several ammunition clips were safely stowed under the front seat. Hod normally kept half a dozen handgrenades in the glove compartment, but he was down to his last one, and hadn't bothered to resupply himself. He knew that the boys at the plant were planning to buy him a box for Christmas.

Hod Smegma started up his car. The thirty-two cylinder piston engine with octuple overhead cams, one hundred and twenty-eight valves, and a sixteen-barrel carburettor, roared into life. The big engine, which guzzled high-octane, leaded fuel (refined in Bruteland), was not only fast, but also powerful. It needed power aplenty to accelerate the extra mass of the car's bullet-proof glass, armour-plating and solid rubber tires. Hod had a mean cruising machine, even without the optional fifty-calibre air-cooled machine gun that could be swivel-mounted through the moon-roof, and fired either manually (by a passenger) or remotely (by the driver). Those who installed the machine gun weren't just cruisers, but bruisers. Some bruisers even packed illegal bazookas and RPGs. Sensibly, the Macho Party's COLT (Control Of Light Trajectiles) legislation obliged Brutelander civilians to obtain permits for anti-tank weapons. After all, Bruteland's urban Militia patrolled the streets in half-tracks and tanks. And when bruisers overpowered or out-gunned the Militia, air strikes had to be called in, and then the streets became quite unsafe. That state of affairs was unacceptable to Hod, as it was to most Testosians. Hod Smegma therefore supported restrictions on civilian armaments. Sure, lots of men at the plant owned illegal bazookas and RPGs (and one had even installed an anti-aircraft gun in his back yard, in an emplacement disguised as a hot-tub), but Hod reckoned that it was no use owning such things, since you couldn't fire them without getting blown to Melior by a Meliorite fighter-bomber. Hod Smegma adhered religiously to a time-honoured Brutelandish motto, learned at his father's knee (that is, learned as his father kneed it into him): "If you can't use it, then lose it".

So Hod picked up Slim Zits and Clem Royds, and the three cruised over to the east side, and then along Veedee Strip, the main artery of Testos's red-light district. Here, one beheld greater concentrations of kuntas than in any other part of Testos, or indeed in the whole of Bruteland itself. The reason for this was simple enough: the public kunta rental agencies catered mostly to the white-holster class. (The few Brutelanders to rise above that, such as senior Macho Party officials or Militia generals, used private kunta rental agencies, which had the pick of Feminania's exports, and which were not publicly listed.) The blue-holster class tended to be least businesslike, and most direct, in matters of carnal lust. Blue-holsters wanted display and selection up front—on the street, as it were—since to them it constituted part of the allure, if not part of the foreplay itself. Naturally, those terms were unknown to them. But they knew what they liked, and they liked to cruise, and check out the kuntas, and banter with them, and pick out the ones they wanted, and go upstairs with them to a cheap hotel room, or go backstage with them in a cheap strip club, and pay their cash fee, and freud the Melior out of them, and never have to deal with pimps (which the white-holster types called "agents", but which amounted to the same thing).

Of course, Hod and Slim and Clem knew perfectly well, but didn't have to be consciously aware, that the whole red-light operation was licensed by City Hall, and was managed exclusively by the pimps, who called themselves KFC (Kunta-For-Cash) Agents, and who maintained a necessary but discrete presence everywhere on the Strip. The pimps not only collected cash from their kuntas at regular intervals; they also employed and supervised networks of snipers. Snipers abounded in the red-light district: they lounged in alleyways, they watched from windows, and they perched on rooftops. They monitored expensive alarm systems installed in the cheap rooms. Most were ex-militiamen, or retired militiamen, or moonlighting militiamen; all were pretty handy with firearms. The red-light district was the sole area of Testos in which a kunta could walk the streets alone without being legally considered fair game. In the red-light district, any Brutelander who tried to freebee a kunta, or any group that tried to geebee a kunta, would find themselves in the sights of the snipers, who were paid to shoot first and ask no questions later. Their overall marksmanship was so uncanny that hardly any kuntas ever got shot in the process of freebee or geebee prevention.

So Hod and Slim and Clem could cruise as they chose, and leer as they liked, but they dared not pet before they paid. The KFCs were dressed to advertise and tempt as only kuntas on the street would and could. Spiked heels and netted stockings and short skirts and tight tops and excessive makeup were the order of the night. The KFCs strutted and jiggled and swayed and leaned, cattily and voluptuously and haughtily and provocatively. They enticed men out of their cars, and drove hard bargains with them, and led them upstairs or backstage, and cash was coarsely counted out, and favours meted out accordingly.

And as Hod and Slim and Clem cruised along the Strip, their bullet-proof windows rolled down so they could ogle the kuntas, a carload of bruisers suddenly drew up alongside. And the bruisers eyeballed them, as predators do prey. Then the bruisers began to hoot crude challenges at them. Hod and Slim and Clem, their Bruteland street sense finely-tuned, hurled ripostes just forcibly enough to hold the bruisers off, but not so aggressively as to provoke them further. As usual, these bruisers were not only heavily armed, but also wholly prepared to disregard the niceties of fair fighting. Then the cars stopped at a red light. The bruiser manning the machine-gun through the moon-roof swivelled the barrel toward the front of Hod's car, and casually fired a burst into the ground.

"Hey, KID (Kunta In Drag), c'mon out an' dance wif us."

In Bruteland, transvestitism was virtually unknown; no man seeking to avoid a brutal death ever dressed up as a kunta. And kuntas themselves were prohibited from dressing up as men, lest such disguise enable them to avoid the consequences of the Fair Game Act. To call a man a KID was therefore a mortal insult to his manhood. Hod thus did the only thing he could do in reply to the bruiser's invitation: he turned his head toward the window and spat loudly onto the road. The spitting sound was utterly drowned by the idlings of the great engines, but the spittle conveyed its message nonetheless. And after he spat, Hod turned to Slim and muttered,

"Hey, Slim, pass me the pineapple from the glove compartment."

As Slim handed Hod the hand-grenade, the bruiser manning the machine-gun answered Hod's spit with another burst, this time firing into the road alongside the car, from the front to the back. Asphalt fragments peppered the paintwork and sprayed through the open windows, and the smell of cordite lay heavily in Hod's nostrils. The light turned green, and Hod pulled the pin on the grenade. As the two cars began to accelerate, Hod displayed a nice hook shot: he arced the live grenade out his own moon roof, and through the moon roof of the bruiser's car. Then he slammed on the brakes, ground the tranny into reverse, floored the gas pedal, and burned solid rubber pealing away. The squeal and smoke of his tires were blanketed by the two explosions, as the grenade and the bruiser's gas tank blew up in rapid succession. A fireball curled out of the burning wreckage, a shock wave hurled smouldering shrapnel up and down the Strip, and thick, oily fumes spewed from dark regions within the flames.

"Nice shot, Hod," said Slim and Clem.

Hod spat once more, then turned down a sidestreet and parked the car.

"Let's getta beer," he suggested.

So Hod and Slim and Clem swaggered along the Strip, and went into a bar, and had a few beers. Before long, a Militia firetruck arrived and doused the twisted chassis of the bruisermobile and a Militia bulldozer scraped it off the road. Militia patrolmen questioned dozens of eye-witnesses on the Strip, from kuntas and snipers and pimps to regular Brutelanders (including Hod and Slim and Clem in the bar), but no-one had seen a thing. The charred remains in the bruisermobile were unidentifiable. So the officer of the patrol wrote ABC (Accidentally Burned Car) in his report, and the case was closed. Hod and Slim and Clem found some kuntas they liked, and went into back rooms with them, and paid them, and freuded them, and then consumed several more beers.

Their evening's entertainment done, Hod and Slim and Clem headed home. Hod wanted to get some sleep that night, since he was supposed to pick up his eldest son (aged ten) and take him to a murderball game the next afternoon. So Hod and Slim and Clem cruised out of Testos's red-light district, and beyond the city itself, and into the suburbs. Traffic was light; they sped unimpeded and unchallenged. They felt content: their appetites for fighting, and freuding, and drinking were well sated. But as they neared Clem's place, a keen-eyed Hod suddenly pointed out his window and declared:

"Look . . . fair game!"

Sure enough, a lone kunta zig-zagged down the sidewalk, and darted between two houses. The men were instantly galvanized into action. Slim jumped out of the moving car, and said "I'll chase her on foot . . . you two drive around the block and cut her off," and with that, he was gone.

Clem, who knew the neighboorhood, directed Hod first around one corner, then another. They saw no-one at first. But as they neared the end of the street, the kunta suddenly broke from cover behind some bushes, flushed by Slim, who gained on her with every stride. Hod accelerated smoothly, and overshot her, and slammed on the brakes, and jumped out of his car. She was trapped between him and Slim, who came up rapidly behind her. Clem, whose thigh still smarted from the knife wound, got more awkwardly onto the street. He couldn't run, but he could sure as Melior freud. The kunta made one last desperate effort to get away; she frantically dashed between two houses, but was caught within a few strides and pulled down by Slim.

Slim rolled her over, and tore the front of her dress. Hod helped Slim tear her dress off, and then started to unbuckle his belt.

"Me first," said Slim, "I caught her."

"Uh-uh," admonished Hod, who knew the law, "I seen her first."

This was true. Under the provisions of the Fair Game Act, whoever originally spotted a lone kunta had initial dibs on her, no matter who caught her. So Slim reluctantly conceded, and held the squirming kunta down, while Hod dropped his trousers. Clem hobbled up, and joined in the sport, and announced "Hey, I know this kunta. She belongs to my neighboor."

"So what?" said Hod, "Every kunta belongs to somebuddy."

"So this," said Clem, pointing to his crotch, "I been wanting to freud her since I first seen her. But I figgered I'd have to wait my turn, 'til he traded her in. Never figgered she'd come up fair game."

"You still gotta wait yer turn," said an indignant Slim, "Hod spotted her, and I caught her."

"I kin wait that long," said Clem diplomatically. "Never seed a kunta git wore out by two men. Even the siza Hod."

So the sizeable Hod took his turn, followed by the smaller but thrustworthy Slim, and finally by the amorous Clem. By the time Clem was done, Hod wanted to freud her again, but the bruisers and the beer and KFC and the first round of the geebee had taken their toll. He could hump, but he couldn't pump. Slim and Clem were all in too.

"Let's call it a night, men," offered Hod.

"Yeah," said Slim. "Get lost, kunta. Go home."

"But come out and play again," said Clem.

The kunta gathered up the shreds of her dress—covering herself with ludicrous modesty—and the remnants of her other apparel, and slunk off into the night. She didn't have far to go; she'd almost made it home before being caught. Even so, she grimaced, it had been worth the price; the bundle had been safely delivered. She suppressed two involuntary shudders. The first shudder was an aftereffect of having been geebeed (neither the first nor the worst geebee she had experienced, but nevertheless nothing she had actively sought). The second shudder was really one of relief, born of imagining how much worse it would have been had they caught her delivering the bundle.

And like its recent deliverer, the bundle found itself in the throes of passionate embrace. And also like its deliverer, the bundle offered token but futile resistance to its handling. But unlike its deliverer, the bundle was not being manhandled; rather, *mothered*, except that there was no word for this in Bruteland. The bundle was a baby kunta, smuggled out of the transport to Melior by a small but defiant conspiracy of kuntas, and smuggled into a working-class neighboorhood to be cared for, in rotating shifts, by conspiring house-kuntas while their men were away at work.

The enterprise was at once audacious and hopeless. There was no long-term plan at all, no design as to upbringing, no strategy for dealing with illness, no notion of the possible consequences of discovery: simply a timeless nurturing, punctuated by the impending return of men, and thus by the periodic necessity of secreting the infant to some other house, for another span of all-engrossing wonderment, until that man came home. Thus the conspiracy of house-kuntas ran constant risks, which sometimes involved these perilous nocturnal sorties, and the fearful possibility of being caught. Nonetheless, the baby kunta thrived, and the conspiracy of house-kuntas thrived by helping her thrive, and each house-kunta personally thrived by taking a turn at it. They had always been somewhat stoical about men anyway. As long as freuding was simply freuding to men, many house-kuntas didn't see much difference between being freebeed indoors or geebeed out-of-doors. And now, thanks to the conspiracy, at least these house-kuntas had a deeper purpose in life.

Chapter Seven

Night and day, the secret transports rolled on rails from Bruteland into Feminania. Diesel engines hauled the laden freight trains to and from Bruteland's cities, in and out of Bruteland's whistle-stops, bearing white-painted automobiles and pastel-hued appliances and floral-patterned cinder blocks, here to take on machine parts, there tools, and everywhere all manner of manufactured items. All the finished goods bore metal plates in some conspicuous place, and all the metal plates bore more-or-less identical inscriptions:

WOMBANUFACTURED IN FEMINANIA
MADE FOR WOMBEN BY WOMBEN

The transports stopped at Bruteland's border, where export officers checked the manifests, inspected the crates, and initialled the paperwork. Then the trains inched forward, out of Bruteland and into no-man's land, where they halted again. Here the engineers and linemen and other crewmen disembarked, and left the great transports standing unattended, hissing on the rails. Before long, engineehers and linewomen other crewwomen approached the trains from the Feminanian bordher, having crossed into no-womban's land, and inched the trains inside Feminania, where they halted again. Here import orficehers checked the wombanifests, inspected the crates, and initialled the papeherwherk.

Then the transports rolled again, this time to and from Feminania's cities, in and out of Feminania's whistle-stops, where cranes unloaded white-painted automobiles and pastel-hued appliances and floral-pattherned cinder blocks, here machine parts, there tools, and everywhere all wombannher of wombanufactured items. As the imported goods were unloaded and retransported and distributed and unpacked and eventually utilized, fembales all over Feminania read the plates, which said and they felt proud to be womben, and privileged to be Femininnies.

WOMBANUFACTURED IN FEMINANIA
MADE FOR WOMBEN BY WOMBEN

Day and night, the other secret transports rolled on rails from Feminania toward Bruteland. Diesel engines hauled the laden passengher trains from Feminania's export facilities to Bruteland's border. These transports originated in no cities, and passed through no whistle-stops; the tracks they rode followed nature's rural by-ways, keeping out of sight, and therefore out of mind, of Feminania's citizenry. The specially designed boxcars were soundproofed and windowless, but well-ventilated, and temperature and humidity controlled. Each car had four bathrooms at the front and four more at the rear, and each bathroom was replete with a powdher room and several large, brightly-lit makeup mirrors. Each car had doors at the front and rear, which were locked and guarded, from the outside, by specially-trained GEQUAPO aladies. These GEQUAPO aladies were prepared to lay down their lives, if necessary, to prevent any unauthorized person from gaining entry to the boxcars, although they possessed no knowledge of the boxcars' contents. The outsized stencils on the sides of each car proclaimed no more than

PRODUCE OF FEMINANIA
FOR EXPORT ONLY

Naturally, each car also bore a small metallic plate, which said

WOMBANUFACTURED IN FEMINANIA
MADE FOR WOMBEN BY WOMBEN

Of course, the boxcars had been manufactured, albeit to Femininny specification, entirely in Bruteland.

The transports stopped at Feminania's bordher, where export orficehers checked the secret wombanifests, inspected the boxcar locks, and initialled the papeherwherk. Then the trains inched forward, out of Feminania and into no-womban's land, where they halted again. Here the engineehers and linewomben and other crewwomben and special GEQUAPO aladies disembarked, and left the great transports standing unattended, hissing on the rails. Before long, engineers and linemen other crewmen approached the trains from the Bruteland border, having crossed into no-man's land, and inched the trains inside Bruteland, where they halted again. Here import officers checked the manifests (no longer secret), inspected the boxcar locks, and initialled the paperwork. Meanwhile, crewmen concealed the stencils on the boxcar sides, covering them with painted wooden signs. A small number of these signs read

PRODUCE OF BRUTELAND
MEAT PRODUCTS

while quite a few more read

PRODUCE OF BRUTELAND
POULTRY PRODUCTS

while a still larger number read

> PRODUCE OF BRUTELAND
> FISH PRODUCTS

while the vast majority read

> PRODUCE OF BRUTELAND
> VEGETABLE PRODUCTS

Of course, the crewmen themselves could not read. But they were directed, by their foremen, as to which signs to hang on which boxcars.

Finally, a moderate guard was posted on the train, in the form of a platoon of Bruteland Militia. Pairs of militiamen, carrying assault rifles, were stationed outside each boxcar door. Individual militiamen, armed with light machine guns, rode on the boxcar roofs. An armoured rail car, bearing heavy machine guns, spare ammunition, and the reserves and commander of the platoon, was coupled to the rear of the train. Whereas no guard at all would have been unthinkable in Bruteland, too heavy a defensive presence might have attracted unwanted attention. One platoon of militiamen was the accepted standard; most Brutelanders would observe the passing train, and others like it, without a second thought—and none but the most suicidal of bruisers would normally attempt to attack it.

Not that such attacks were unknown. A rare coalition of bruisers had, in recent memory, successfully ambushed a transport train. The train been too lightly guarded. The patrol—rather than platoon—of Militiamen, with no armoured car and no rooftop machine-gunners, was out-manned, out-gunned and quickly massacred by the bruisers, who then ran riot through the rail-cars themselves. The bruisers terrorized the kuntas in the cars marked VEGETABLE PRODUCTS and POULTRY PRODUCTS, but didn't even touch them. The kuntas in the cars marked FISH PRODUCTS, however, were savagely freebeed and geebeed. The kuntas in the cars marked MEAT PRODUCTS were kuntanapped, carried off to bruiser hideaways in the mountains, freebeed and geebeed repeatedly for a few weeks, and then put variously to death, with the exception of a small handful. The surviving kuntas were returned to Testos in a bruisermobile, and dumped unceremoniously, in broad daylight, on the steps of the Brutestag (Bruteland's Parliament). Of course, these kuntas were fair game, and Parliament adjourned as soon as it learned of their presence, and the Parliamentarians proved that they could indeed lead by example, at least when it came to geebeeing.

But that sum of events had toppled the incumbent Conservative Macho party in the then-upcoming general election. The CM parliamentarian majority later learned—to their profound embarrassment and to the guffaws of Brutelanders at large—that they had geebeed a shipment of their own Grade-A consort-kuntas. That the kuntas had been unrecognizable as Grade-A consorts, owing to the extent to which they had been used by the bruisers, exacerbated rather than mitigated the scandal. The Radical Macho party circulated defamatory riddles to the blue-holster class, such as:

"What's the difference between freuding a Grade-A kunta and freuding a pig?"

"I dunno."

"Then vote CM . . . they dunno either."

But the serious shortcoming, which underpinned the ridicule and of which the ridicule reminded Brutelanders remorselessly, was that the CM government had failed to protect its own—the choicest kuntas—from the bruisers. And if it couldn't protect its own, then by inference (at least by Radical Macho inference) it couldn't protect anybody else's. The Conservative Macho party paid the political price at the next election, and was duly ousted by the Radical Macho party.

It would take some time for the scandal-mongers to discover that the Radical Macho party had actually masterminded the consort-kunta heist in the first place, and had merely manipulated the bruisers for political gain. But the scandal-mongers never discovered the post-election sequel to this piece. A subsequent secret deal had been cut with the bruisers, who promised the Radical Macho party that they would refrain not only from attacking kunta transports but also from other activities which might make the government look bad, in return for certain favours. The bruisers (at least those bruisers who had participated in the politically orchestrated attack) seemed to have acquired a taste for Grade-A kunta, and they demanded a steady diet thereof thereafter. The Radical Macho party thus found itself thoroughly blackmailed: either it continued unwillingly to deliver choice kuntas into the hands of savages, or it faced the threat of exposure for having done so willingly in the first instance.

The bruisers thought they had the new government over a barrel. And that was precisely why they were savages. No bruiser truly represented more than a few bruisers; they formed a shifting patchwork of tribal alliances and rivalries. Some tribes held loose sway over others; others were habitually mutually hostile but occasionally entered into temporary compacts for the sake of mutual gain. The orchestrated attack and abduction of consort-kuntas had been carried out by a confederacy of several Testos tribes, led by Melior's Cherubs—the dominant tribe of the region. And Melior's Cherubs were the initiators of the subsequent blackmail attempt.

The Radical Macho party pretended to accede to their demands, though it capitulated neither too quickly nor too completely, for that would have aroused suspicion. Ultimately, the RMs agreed to relinquish a transport full of Grade-A consort-kuntas in a particular sector at a given time on a chosen day. The bruisers licked their chops and, at the appointed place and time, arrived to claim their spoils. Alas, they had not reckoned on the perfidious politicians, who had planned an operation which, appropriately enough, they called "Surprise Party". Unknown to Melior's Cherubs, the RMs had filled the boxcars, not with kuntas, but with commando militiamen, who suddenly subjected the Cherubs to withering fire. And as Melior's Cherubs retreated from the train in death and disarray, they discovered the complementary facet of the Radical Macho treachery: the RMs had struck a secret deal with a rival tribe, the Rough Traders. In return for their future cooperation, the Traders were apprised of this main chance to eliminate their hated foes. So Melior's Cherubs fled from one ambush into another: Rough Traders attacked from the woods on either side of the train, and thus, along with the commandos, caught the hapless Cherubs in a double cross-fire.

By this means the Radical Macho party not only rid itself of a longstanding nuisance, but also enhanced its popularity among Brutelanders who, following widespread publicity of Operation Surprise Party, expressed renewed confidence in their government's ability to defend the faith and protect the kuntas. And so the transports rolled unmolested through Bruteland, arriving at their destinations with their cargoes fully intact. The Grade-A consort-kuntas in the cars marked MEAT PRODUCTS were reserved for the most powerful men in Bruteland: senior officials of government, captains of industry, leaders of the military, and elders of the church. The Grade-B house-kuntas in the cars marked POULTRY PRODUCTS were reserved for the white-holster workers: managers, bureaucrats, salesmen and the like. The Grade-C kuntas in the cars marked FISH PRODUCTS were reserved for the red-light districts; they were the KFCs. The Grade-D trailer-kuntas in the cars marked VEGETABLE PRODUCTS were reserved for the blue-holster workers: they were also Bruteland's main breeding stock, and had themselves been bred mainly to replenish the ranks of the men with whom future kuntas of their grade would breed in turn.

Of course, Brutelanders' lives were occupied with concerns other than work, food, violence, kuntas, politics and murderball. They also had religion. Bruteland's official religion—Brutianity—was monotheistic, and its deity—Odgay—was omnipotent, omnivirile, and omnimachismo. Brutians were a people of the book, though few of them could read it. Their tome, the *Brutestament*, was actually comprised of two parts: the *Old Brutestament*, and the *New Brutestament*. The

Brutestament had been introduced in 2034, on the heels of the Macho Revolution, which several of its prophets had propitiously predicted. Brutianity had neither Pope nor Archbishop, rather a Don—*Il Bruto del Tutti Bruti*—as its spiritual leader. Although Brutianity was scarcely fifty years old, no fewer than forty-seven Dons had worn the golden, gem-encrusted holster emblematic of the Brutacy. Of the first forty-six, forty-one had perished violently; either by assassination or by ecclesiastical dispute. The other five had died of natural causes: excessive feeding, excessive drinking, excessive freuding, and the like. The current spriritual head of Brutianity, His Bruteness Don Brute XLVII, had held office for the past eighteen months. This term's length was well above average, and Brutians sang his deserved praises. He was obviously a Holy man, beloved of Odgay, or he would not have survived this long.

The *Brutestament*, needless to say, was not published in Low Brutish, the vulgar tongue of Bruteland; rather, it was written in a language inaccessible to untutored Brutelanders, so that they might neither question nor interpret scripture themselves. The *Brutestament* could be understood only by clergy, who were taught to read and write High Brutish. Clergymen studied the Lessons, and read them to their packs, and sermonized according to the dictates of the Brutacy. Naturally, there were no Churches or other houses of religious worship, and Sunday services were obviously out of the question (Sundays being reserved for murderball). Clergymen made rotating visits to the factories instead, and ministered to their packs on all shifts, and conducted worship on a regular basis, usually in the cafeterias at meal-times, between fair fights, but also frequently in the parking lots during coffee-and-cigarette breaks.

On the whole, Brutelanders relished many favourite passages from the Brutestament, which the clergy read and explained to them repeatedly, with tireless devotion. For instance, a popular extract from the myth of creation read (in High Brutish):

The Olday Utestamentbray

Ookbay of Enesisgay

... And after Odgay ademay the eavenshay and the obeglay, and all the ivinglay ingsthay and eaturescray upon itay, Ehay eatedcray Anmay in Ishay ikenesslay, and awsay atthay it asway oodgay. And Olay, Anmay adhay every ingthay he antedway orfay oodfay and inkdray. And Odgay awsay atthay itay asway oodgay. Oweverhay, Anmay adhay onay ailtay. Osay, Odgay ooktay an inchpay of aoschay, and Ehay eatedcray the irstfay untakay.

And Odgay aidsay unto Anmay: "Olay, I avehay ivengay eethay ominionday over the olewhay obeglay, over all ivinglay ingsthay and eaturescray upon itay. Outhay and ythay onssay allshay uleray the obleglay, and othingnay atthay I ademay eforebay eethay allshay avehay ominionday over eethay."

And Anmay aidsay unto Odgay: "Ordlay, Ouyay ademay untakay after emay. Illway eshay avehay ominionday over emay?"

And Odgay epliedray unto Anmay: "Onay, utbay eshay illway ytray, ithoutway urceasesay. Only ybay aintainingmay onstantcay igilencevay altshay outhay ahevay ominionday over erhay. Evernay ivegay an uckersay or an untakay an even eakbray! Else outhay altshay avehay uchmay ausecay orfay egretray." ...

Here is a contemporary translation:

The Old Brutestament

Book of Genesis

... And after God made the heavens and the globe, and all the living things and creatures upon it, He created Man in His likeness, and saw that it was good. And Lo, Man had every thing he wanted for food and drink. And God saw that it was good. However, Man had no tail. So, God took a pinch of chaos, and He created the first kunta.

> And God said unto Man: "Lo, I have given thee dominion over the whole globe, over all living things and creatures upon it. Thou and thy sons shall rule the globe, and nothing that I made before thee shall have dominion over thee."
>
> And Man said unto God: "Lord, You made kunta after me. Will she have dominion over me?"
>
> And God replied unto Man: "No, but she will try, without surcease. Only by maintaining constant vigilance shalt thou have dominion over her. Never give a sucker or a kunta an even break! Else thou shalt have much cause for regret."

Elucidating precisely how man was to maintain constant vigilance over kuntas was the overarching task of the *New Brutestament*, authored chiefly by Brutianity's foremost prophet, Mark Oedisad. Like the *Old Brutestament*, the *New Brutestament* was also written in High Brutish. The quintessence of Mark Oedisad's theology was contained in the following passages, which were also great favourites among Brutians:

> *The Ewnay Utestamentbray*
>
> *The Ospelgay According otay Arkmay Oedisaday*
>
> And Odgay avegay untakay otway eaponsway, osay eshay ouldcay ageway arway upon Anmay, and akemay of ishay ifelay an ormentay and an iserymay. Esethay otway eaponsway ereway: irstfay, erhay odybay; and econdsay, erhay ildrenchay. Ownay I eclareday unto eethay: otay enderray ythay oefay owerlesspay and ereforethay armlesshay, outhay ustmay isarmday erhay. And usthay I ounselcay ethee.
>
> Irstfay, useyay erhay odybay as outhay eeistsay itfay; aketay ateverwhay ouyay eednay, and aketay eneverwhay ouyay antway. And always ebay eadyray otay akemay omisespray, onay attermay owhay ansparentlytray idiculousray, orfay untakay is ulliblegay, and illway elievebay anything. Utbay evernay eepkay an inglesay omisepray ademay otay untakay; orfay eshay is ustjay ikelay an ildchay, and annotcay omprehendcay the uthtray about

anything, and eendsnay otay ebay eceivedday orfay erhay own oodgay.

Econdsay, aketay erhay ildrenchay omfray erhay eforebay eshay akestay emthay omfray ouyay. The oleray of otherhoodmay ustmay emainray ictlystray iologicalbay; it ustmay evernay ecomebay an ocialsay unctionfay. Otherhoodmay ustmay evernay onfercay ightsray on othersmay. Untakay asway eatedcray orfay Anmay's useyay, and otnay ehay orfay ershay. Epriveday ehray, and eshay illway espectray ouyay. Ontrolcay erhay ellway, and ouyay illway evernay owknay iefgray . . .

Again, here is a contemporary translation:

    The New Brutestament
    The Gospel According to Mark Oedisad

And God gave kunta two weapons, so she could wage war upon Man, and make of his life a torment and a misery. These two weapons were: first, her body; and second, her children. Now I declare unto thee: to render thy foe powerless and therefore harmless, thou must disarm her. And thus I counsel thee.

First, use her body as thou seeist fit: take whatever you need, and take whenever you want. And always be ready to make promises, no matter how transparently ridiculous, for kunta is gullible, and will believe anything. But never keep a single promise made to kunta; for she is just like a child, and cannot comprehend the truth about anything, and needs to be deceived for her own good.

Second, take her children from her before she takes them from thee. The role of motherhood must remain strictly biological; it must never become a social function. Motherhood must never confer rights on mothers. Kunta was created for man's use, and not he for hers. Deprive her, and she will respect thee. Control her well, and thou will never knowest grief...

While Brutelanders faithfully revered their Brutianity, they fanatically exalted their murderball. The main venue in Testos, a fully enclosed structure called the Doom Dome, held no fewer than one hundred thousand spectators, and home games had been sold out for as long as anyone could remember. Outside the Doom Dome on game-days, scalpers sold tickets at hugely inflated prices, which Brutelanders seemed eager enough to pay. Scalpers were so named owing to an idiosyncratic practice: after robbing careless season ticket-holders at knife-point, they sliced off their scalps, which they sold separately as souvenirs.

Like the state religion of Brutianity, the national sport of murderball had been introduced following the Macho Revolution. The playing field was a gigantic chess-board, each of whose sixty-four squares had the approximate dimensions of a boxing-ring. The squares themselves were concrete slabs, alternately painted black and white, with drains inset to catch the excess blood. A murderball team consisted of sixteen players, fifteen men and one kunta, and was modelled after a set of chessmen. To begin with, there were eight pawns, armed only with long knives. As in chess, they occupied the entire second row of squares. Behind them, at either end, were the two rooks, each armed with a spear. Inside the rooks, on either side, were the knights, each carrying a mace and shield. Inside the knights, on either side, were the bishops, each armed with a trident and net. Finally, between the bishops were the queen and king. The queen, always a new kunta, was armed with a short bow and quiver of arrows. The king was virtually unarmed and unprotected, save that he carried a sceptre at whose extremity was mounted an iron ball. If all else failed, the sceptre could be wielded as a bludgeon.

It was the goal of each team to attempt to capture the opposing king's sceptre, at which point the game was over. The home team was clad in white tunics; the visiting team, in black. The iron ball in each sceptre was similarly and respectively painted. Each team had a coach, who directed the movements of the players from one square to another, according to the rules of chess. Thus, for example, rooks were permitted to attack with or to cast their spears along any column or along any row, while bishops could attack with their tridents only along diagonals. Knights moved in the characteristic "L" shape, and used their maces offensively only at the terminal square of that shape. Pawns advanced straight ahead, but attacked diagonally. Again as in chess, the queen was the most powerful player on the field, in that she was permitted to shoot her arrows vertically, horizontally and diagonally, at any range she pleased. The king was both the weakest and the vital player. He could move only one square at a time, albeit in any direction, but his sceptre was not normally an effective weapon, at least not against an uninjured opponent.

The crucial difference between murderball and chess lay not in the mode of attack; rather, in the capability of defence. An attacking player sought to occupy a defending player's square by killing him, but the defending player could resist the occupation by killing the attacker. At any rate, two players fought over a given square until one of them was dead. Groundskeepers then removed the corpse, and the game continued. The queen differed from the other players in that she enjoyed greater longevity. The first time a queen was subdued in combat, she was not killed by her opponent, but freebeed. That was why only new kuntas were used in murderball, in order that blood would flow on such occasions, and slake the spectators' thirst. The second time a queen was subdued in combat, her opponent naturally killed her. But when two queens fought, they fought always to the death, even if one or both had not been used. A pawn who attained the eighth rank was "queened"; that is to say, was retired from the field, and spared to fight another day. His place was taken by an additional queen. And ultimately, the king rarely relinquished his sceptre without a fight. A vigorous king could sometimes even decide the outcome of a game, if his attackers had been badly enough wounded in previous encounters. Indeed, some of the most exciting games of murderball were those eventually decided by the mortal combat of two exhausted kings, each striving to bash the other's brains in with his sceptre.

Then again, sometimes a coach decided to resign well before the end game—if, for example, a position became exceedingly hopeless—in order not to demoralize his team by exposing it to pointless carnage. (The spectators rarely appreciated such a move: they came to see blood spilled, so for them "pointless carnage" would have been an oxymoron, had they been capable of grasping the concept.) In the case of a resigned game, the losing king was executed by a teammate of his choosing, usually to a resounding condemnation of lusty booing from the stands. A coach had to exercise fine judgement overall, for a combination of too many losses and too few wins often resulted in his being catapulted back into the ranks of the players, from which the majority of coaches were drawn.

Murderball players, of course, did not move freely in Brutelandish society. On the contrary, they became murderball players precisely because they had formerly abused that singular privilege, by exhibiting conduct deemed to be distinctly and dangerously un-Brutelandish. The two most common crimes which carried the sentence of murderball were unfair fighting, and freebeeing or geebeeing unfair game. Murderball queens were selected regularly from among the transports, and were usually Grade-A or Grade-B kuntas who behaved uncooperatively or bitchily during import inspection.

Adolescents played a civilian version of murderball on school teams, as did workers on company teams. Civilian murderball featured nonlethal encounters between players wearing protective equipment, and wielding weapons whose blades and tips and tines were fashioned of wood instead of steel. Victory in combat was awarded by a referee to the player who would have delivered the first mortal blow, had his weapon been real. Nor was the queen ever killed in civilian murderball. She was merely retired from the field after having been freebeed twice.

Naturally, just as in real murderball, only new kuntas could be queens. In fact, this proved a tremendous incentive for young adolescent boys, as many of them experienced their first sexual encounters with murderball queens, egged on (and often taunted) by their cheering schoolmates.

On the whole, murderball was thought to be the most valuable pastime in Bruteland, in that it both entertained Brutelanders and afforded them instructive insights into life.

Thus life went on as usual in Bruteland, and to the casual observer all seemed well. The factories belched smoke and brought forth finished goods; fair fights and fair game alike relieved the humdrum workaday routine; the transports rolled in steadily from Feminania, renewing the supply of kuntas for all; Brutelanders' hearts were infused with the grace of Odgay; their imaginations were captured by the subtleties of murderball; and social undesirables such as homosexuals were either mercifully put to death on the spot, or else were deservedly exported to Melior.

But trouble was brewing in erstwhile utopian Bruteland and, as usual, it was kuntas who keeled the pot.

Book Three: Feminania

The Y-chromosome has a negative function: when a Y-carrying sperm fertilizes an ovum, it simply reduces the amount of femaleness which would result in the formation of a female foetus.

Germaine Greer

Chapther Eight

The GIRLs (Gendher Institute Research Laboratories) compound was located in the remote countryside, neither near Ovaria nor proximate to any population centre. The compound, which housed a complex of laboratories and FREUDs (Facilities Retaining Extra-Uteherine Devices), was completely walled around and fenced off, keeping both insidehers in and outsidehers out. The site was therefore inaccessible to prying eyes even of chance passhersby. Local birdlife swooped ovher and flutthered past the compound, but their daughtherg gave no indication that they saw anything unusual. And even if the feathered creatures had rung their shrillest alarms, no-one would have responded to them. Armed and uniformed GEQUAPO aladies guarded all entry and exit points.

In row upon row of well-equipped and brightly-lit laboratories, highly trained Femininny technicians—selected for militancy and sworn to secrecy—conducted the delicate process of *in vitro* fhertilization, monithered the early embryonic growth, implanted the burgeoning embryos in EUDs (Extra-Uteherine Devices), and installed the EUDs in FREUDs, where full-therm gestation took place. The technicians' skilled labours wher ovherseen by Professher Nora Goodwomban, the scientist who had developed and pherfected the so-called "Goodwomban Process" and who, by so doing, had been vouchsafed Feminania's most prestigious scientific award: the Nobelle Prize.

Professher Goodwomban tirelessly patrolled the FREUDs. Each FREUD was a long, single-storied building with a central corridor, on either side of which floor-to-ceiling shelves held row upon row upon row of large bell-jars. Inside these bell-jars, fembale embryos ontogenized and fembale foetuses floated. Flexible PVC umbilical cords wher clamped to their abdowombens. Each cord wound upward through the stopper of its jar, and was clamped to the tapehered nozzle of a placental pump, whose oxygenated nutrient mixture could be adjusted with respect to both biochemical constitution and rate of flow. Professher Goodwomban minutely inspected a random sampling of the jars, made a few detailed notes on her omnipresent clipboard, and obsherved obliquely but carefully as a technician measured synthesized biochemical nutrients into one of the reshervoirs that fed the pumps in this particular FREUD.

Professher Goodwomban exited that FREUD, enthered the next, and resumed her meticulous rounds. The previous FREUD had held Grade-B fembales, destined one day for Bruteland; this one held Grade-As, whose eventual destination was of course the same, but who would be recipients of proportionately more, and diffherent childhood training. This entire block, consisting of dozens of FREUDs, which the Professher would inspect during three or four days of rounds, was consigned solely to the production of fembales for export.

The Professher was always careful. Scientific and pherfectionistic by nature, she needed no exthernal prompting to devote her full attention to the Goodwomban Process, which she had pioneehered. The *New Testawombent* declared that not a sparrow fell without the will of Providence; here, within the confines of the GIRLs compound, not a zygote flagellated without the will of Nora Goodwomban. With an excruciating exactitude (which earned her uncompliwombentary sobriquets from the technicians, who wher more ardent in their recitations of Femininny catechism but less zealous in the pherforwombance of their duties) she tirelessly ovhersaw the four phases of the Goodwomban Process: fhertilization, incantation, gestation, and decantation—collectively called "genation".

So, when the Ministher of Exthernal Affairs had telephoned Professor Goodwomban, she had reacted initially with surprise, subsequently with defensiveness, and ultimately with curiosity as to the source of and possible solution to the problem. The Ministher had told her about the rumblings of discontentwombent ewombanating from Bruteland's Ministry of Importation, whose spokespherdaughthers complained that evher-largeher numbhers of imports wher defective in their attitudes and dherelict in their pherforwombances. This alleged lack of quality control was lately being obsherved across the spectrum of Grades, from *A* to *D*, by various monithering agencies in Bruteland. Diplomatically worded but unmistakenly threatening notes had been addressed to the Ministher of Exthernal Affairs by Bruteland's Minister of Importation, in which he strongly advised her to seek out and root out the flaws, which evidently lay somewhere in production. Aware of the Professher's illustrious reputation, the Ministher voiced no intimations of accusation; rather, she spoke with an air of confidentiality.

"So you'll look into it, Professher? . . . And get back to me as soon as you can?" the Ministher asked rhetorically.

"Of course, Ministher! . . . But I can tell you right now, I don't think we have any problems here . . . Howevher, I surmise that you'll discovher all sorts of irregularities, including the source of your present difficulties, ovher at GOODS (Gendher Orientation Of Decanted Sylphs)!"

"Well, of course we're looking into GOODS! . . . We nevher suspected GIRLs for a mowombent? . . . This call is purely routine? . . . Keep up the stherling wherk, Professher!"

"Thank you, Ministher! . . . And don't hesitate to phone anytime?"

"Thanks, Professher! . . . Bye-bye?"

"You're welcome, Ministher! . . . Bye-bye?"

The Ministher rang off, and thought, "Go to Melior, you conceited bitch! . . . You think you know it all?"

The Professher rang off, and thought, "Go to Melior, you conceited bitch! . . . You think you know it all?"

Nonetheless, and not without a measure of vengeful glee, Professher Goodwomban planned a thorough quality control assesswombent of GIRLs. She believed she would discovher nothing amiss, but that belief did not intherfhere with her capacities to make critical obshervations and to formulate objective judgewombents. Yet her spirits wher distinctly guirled by the premonition that the Goodwomban Process at GIRLs was unfolding strictly within prescribed tolherances, and therefore that the fault or faults lay somewhere within the netwherk of GOODS installations, whose national directher, Professher Kattya Green, was her arch-rival and bittherest enemy. Thus Nora Goodwomban fine-tooth combed GIRLs with a vengeance.

Sensibly and linearly, she began in the Genetics complex, where selected ova wher fhertilized, *in vitro*, by selected spherm. The embryos wher sustained in a nutrient medium until they reached critical mass, at which point they wher ready for Incantation. Since sylphs wher genated solely for export to Bruteland, they had to possess chertain physical characheristics—such as large mammary glands and rotund *glutei maximi*—which wher undesirable if not reprehensible to Femininies, and hence which had been largely egenated (genetically deselected) in Feminania's population. Then again, notwithstanding Bruteland's nevher-ending clamour for evheryoungher sylphs of all grades, sylphs wher nevher exported (afther Bruteland's fancy) as soon as they began to ovulate and wombenstruate; rather, they wher retained by Feminania for approximately one year. They wher taken monthly from their GOODS installations to the GIRLs compound, where their ripe egg-cells wher surgherally removed, genetically classified, fast frozen, and indefinitely stored in the ova banks. Thus, for each sylph exported to Bruteland, a dozen or so potential sylphs of her genetic grade wher available for future genation.

Spherm-cells wher, of course, a dime a dozen trillion. One thimbleful of sewomben contained enough male zygotes to fhertilize the next hundred genherations of Feminanians, Brutelanders, and Meliorites (the devil take them) besides. Naturally, when it came to spherm-cells, the X-chromosome types wher righerously separated from the Ys, genetically screened, and carefully presherved. The Y-chromosome types wher mostly destroyed—they contributed nothing exportable, and the GIRLs spherm banks already held more than enough Y-chromosomes to fhertilize thousands of genherations of Feminanian males, at least at their current representational levels. Then again, if the Militant Femininny Party had its way, the proportion of males would be reduced from five phercent to one phercent of the populace. As things stood, the Y-chromosomes used in the fhertilization of males wher painstakingly screened for desired phenotypic traits: Feminanian males wher bred for docility, placidity and genheral lack of aggression. They wher also reared in this way, so that nurture complewombented nature. But since the androgens they inevitably produced made male aggression largely incurable, gonadotropic challenging remained the principal detherrent and penultimate resort of the State.

Professher Goodwomban mulled ovher these and other matthers, as she began to conduct her quality control assesswombent of the GIRLs installation. The task, she rationalized, was only half as daunting as it might have been: no similar assesswombent had been requested (nor did one seem in the least necessary) of the genation of fembales for Feminania itself. So Professher Goodwomban got down to wherk with a will, while her small army of research assistants and laboratory technicians, though committed Femininnies all, began to gripe at the prospect which confronted them.

Meanwhile, in another complex of the GIRLs compound, a harvest of Grade-C sylphs was undhergoing the last stage of genation; namely, decantation. One by one, they wher plucked uncheremoniously from their jars. Umbilici wher unclamped, airways cleared; respiration and lachrymation comwombenced. The decaphs (decanted sylphs) wher examined, tagged, recorded, swaddled, and carried out to waiting crib-cars on the nearby rail siding, whence they would be transported to a designated GOODS installation. There, undher the tutelage of special instructhers, they would spend the next thirteen years learning how best to fulfil the cultural role for which they had been genetically selected; in this case, that of KFCs in Bruteland.

Fembales genated for Feminania, who wher predestined to become useful and productive Femininnies, wher genetically screened to wombanifest traits quite diffherent from those of sylphs. As a rule, Femininnies wher not only mammary glandularly challenged, but also *glutei* maximally challenged. While the anorexic torso was deemed to be ideal, the odd bulimic body was not unfashionable either. Myopia, body hair, crooked teeth and halitosis wher also highly prized as Femininny traits; and although it was chertainly genetically feasible to endow evheryone equally with these attributes, it was thought that a purely egalitarian distribution would devalue them. And so, to a limited extent, these desirable traits wher normally distributed during the fhertilization of fembales.

It goes without saying that propher nurture was of incomparably greather significance to Femininnies than mhere nature. The Femininnies taught that "beauty" was an androcentric invention, conceived and utilized by men to demean, exploit and enslave all womben evherywhere. The Femininnies taught that only what men deemed "ugliness" was truly beautiful, since only womben who wher not gendher objects could discovher who they really wher. So the Femininnies made sure that no womban could evher be tempted, by congenital vanity potential, to stray from the ewombancipating path of self-discovhery. And afther having constrained women to follow the path of empowherwombent by furnishing them with the true beauty of ugliness, the actual shape and direction of the path itself could be charted by credo, blazed by doctrine, and trod by slogan.

Fembales (as opposed to sylphs) wher genated in a separate sheries of complexes within the GIRLs compound. And, following decantation, fembales obviously had to be nurtured in quite distinctive ways, since they wher destined to be future Femininnies. The crib-cars containing fembales wher transported to designated GOOFs (Gendher Orientation Of Femininnies) installations, where they would spend their infancies and girlhoods undher the tutelage of special instructhers, who taught them how to become useful and productive citizens of Feminania.

Males wher genated in a separate (and much smallher) sheries of complexes within the GIRLs compound. Feminania had progressively less and less need of males in its society, although Femininny leadhers of evhery political stripe found it a useful policy to keep a few non-gonadotropically challenged males pherpetually employed in the most wombenial of public jobs—typically street-sweeping or sanitary engineehering—so that even the least successful womban could feel comparatively empowhered. Thus, immediately following decantation, males embarked on crib-trains to juvenile BREAST Centres, where they wher raised in a warm climate of intensive sharing and caring. They wher also taught to repress their libidos, to suppress their innate feelings of self-esteem, and to wombanifest deep respect for, and admiration of, all womben evherywhere.

Howevher, Militant Femininnies remained stridently opposed to the juvenile BREAST program. They cited alarming statistics which showed that, despite increased exposure to BREAST Centres, more and more men ended up being sentenced to gonadotropic challenging. Men seemed simply unwilling to learn how to share and care, and how to behave decently toward all womben evherywhere. So Militant Femininnies, labelling men "psycho-socially incorrigible", called for an end to the genation of males in Feminania. "The spherm banks are full," they argued, "and therefore males have sherved their biolinear purpose. Men are obsolete."

Professher Nora Goodwomban wasn't entirely convinced by this Militant Femininny arguwombent. She deemed it plausible that the training of males was still simply inadequate; that improved methods would eventually yield desired results. And furthermore, she thought pragmatically, all speculation aside, the Militant Femininnies formed but a small minority in Parliawombent. Their policies wher a long way from being legislated and implewombented.

So Professher Goodwomban's wherk went on, as usual, in the GIRLs compound. And in due course she completed her quality control assesswombent of sylph genation, and found, just as she had anticipated, that precisely nothing was amiss. She formulated her report to the Ministher accordingly, addressed it genherically to "The Ministher of Exthernal Affairs", and put it to post. She dherived amused satisfaction from the knowledge that it would thus phercolate from the bottom upward, moving at least three steps sideways for evhery step up, through layher upon layher of inefficient Ministherial boudoicracy, before reaching the Ministher's attention. That the Ministher impatiently awaited these results made the inevitable delay all the more ironically justified, in Professher Goodwomban's view. Politics and science didn't mix, she thought; in any progressive state, the formher must unquestioningly support the latther, and leave it otherwise alone.

And just as Nora Goodwomban had envisioned, the full brunt of the Ministherial inquiry was about to be borne by her arch-rival, Kattya Green, the National Directher of Feminania's netwherk of GOODS installations. Much like the GIRLs compound, each GOODS installation was remotely located, walled around, fenced off, and GEQUAPO guarded. Each GOODS installation housed a complex of dormitories and classrooms, in which young sylphs acquired the skills they would lateher need to function, according to their respective Grades, in Bruteland. Naturally, GOODS installations wher strictly segregated by Grade, so that *A*s nevher associated with *B*s, nor *B*s with *C*s, nor *C*s with *D*s. But mhere physical, social and educational separation could not suffice, in and of themselves, to prevent sylphs of diffherent Grades from sharing and caring afther having been exported. *Divida et imphera* being Bruteland's way with them, these sylphs wher pre-adapted to Brutelandish life in Feminania's GOODS installations, where their primal instincts of sharing and caring (which quite transcended, but could be attenuated by, Grade-consciousness) wher pre-empted by virtuosic playing on their equally primal instincts of vanity and jealousy (which also quite transcended, but could not be attentuated by, Grade-consciousness).

Grade-As cultivated all the arts of the uppher-class courtesan: how to dress for a man, how to undress for a man, how to enhance appearance with cosmetics and jewelry, how to arrange flowhers, how to comport oneself at meals, how to use music and scent and lighting optimally to titillate mens' senses, how to convherse intelliladyly with dominant men (that is, how to draw them out profoundly concehern-ing what they do without undherstanding in the least what they do), and finally, with the inevitable culmination of the purpose of all the foregoing "how to's", how to satisfy mens' lust, and that in a myriad of ways. In sum, the Grade-As' singular duty lay in pleasing the men who ruled Bruteland. Of equal importance, howevher, was the inculcation of a particular attitude among Grade-As; namely, that they wher the ones who really counted. Grade-As wher true glamher-queens; they looked upon *B*s, *C*s and *D*s as various types of drudges. An encyclopedic Grade-A education required about thirteen years following decantation.

Grade-Bs studied all the skills of the professional-class house-spouse: primarily shopping and cooking and cleaning, with a view to making oneself and one's abode genherally attractive, or at least presentable, to the avherage white-holsther wherkpherdaughther. Grade-Bs also learned how to massage a man's ego at the end of a dog-eat-dog day, and how to massage other parts by night. Grade-Bs learned that they formed the essential support for the essential class of Bruteland, and they looked upon *A*s and *C*s and *D*s as playing insubstantial, transitory roles. A thorough Grade-B education required about thirteen years following decantation.

Grade-Cs wher schooled in the ways of the street-wise. They would have to cateher to the eclectic (and sometimes phervherse or violent) tastes of evheryone with sufficient cash to command their shervices, which in Bruteland meant just about evheryone. Grade-Cs learned both how to attract clients and how to repulse them. They wher also taught to obey the authority of the pimp, and to stay clear of the snipehers' cross-fire. Grade-Cs looked upon *A*s, *B*s and *D*s with disdain: they led pamphered lives, while Grade-Cs had to be survivehers. A comprehensive Grade-C education required about thirteen years following decantation.

Grade-Ds acquired the habits of dissipated slovens. As the temporary full-time prophety of the blue-holsther classes, they would have to drink beeher, curse and brawl almost as copiously, volubly and reflexively as their men. Grade-Ds learned how to pherpetuate the squalher necessary for the contentwombent of the wherking-classes. And they wher taught not only to despise *A*s, *B*s and *C*s (as whores pretending to be something betther, and as just plain whores) but also to despise themselves (as incapable even of pretending to be something betther). An exhaustive Grade-D education required about thirteen years following decantation.

Professher Kattya Green, National Director of the GOODS installations in and from which these sylphs wher kept, trained and eventually exported, found herself confronted by a much more daunting task than her rival, Nora Goodwomban. Although Green's empire was far more expansive and much less subject to precise scientific controls than Goodwomban's, Kattya Green could nevher receive the credit she wombanifestly desherved. The Goodwomban Process had earned its inventher a Nobelle Prize, but rank-and-file Feminanians—that is to say, the public—wher nevher told that they wher not the sole products of genation. And the State could nevher tell them, not without revealing the breadth and depth of the genation and training of sylphs, and of their eventual exportation to Bruteland. Utmost secrecy was a matther of state security. So although Kattya Green played a vital role in the maintenance of Feminania's economy, and therefore in its security and independence, she both played it secretly and harboured unrequited longings for public recognition.

Moreoveher, Green and Goodwomban disagreed vehewombently ovher the relative theoretical significance of their respective wherk. Nora Goodwomban maintained, metaphorically, that she furnished GOODS installations with sevheral varieties of clay, onto which Kattya Green's minions fired diffherent glazes of acculturation. Each variety of clay had to be absolutely pure in and of itself; any impurities would ruin the final product, rendhering it either visibly marred or it inherently flawed. Kattya Green maintained, also metaphorically, that the GIRLs installation furnished her with assorted qualities of blank canvas, some more fine-grained and others more coarse-grained, upon which she suphervised the painting of diffherent landscapes, from luxuriant to sparse. Any kind of landscape could be painted onto any quality of canvas. It was just a question of time and craftswombanship.

Yet this vitupherative theoretical dispute camouflaged a deeper, ideolinear rift, which epitomized a sherious schism in Femininy doctrine. In principle, the Socialist, Libheral and Conshervative Femininnies all deplored the secret trade agreewombent with Bruteland, but in practice they clandestinely acknowledged its expediency. In herstorical fact, a Socialist Femininy govhernwombent had negotiated the original contract. The Libheral and Conshervative Femininy Parties both tolherated the concept of genating sylphs for exportation; they diffhered only when it came to the asking price. It went without saying that the Militant Femininnies adawombantly opposed this position. They wished to cease the intolherable trade at once, and ban the further genation of sylphs.

But the Radical Femininnies, when they came to powher, charted a course between these two extremes. On the one hand, they paid lip shervice to the expediency of the trade; on the other, they sought to fowombent revolution from within, by allowing chertain doctrines to be imparted to the sylphs which wher incompatible with their broad-based training. Special aladies infiltrated the GOODS installations and, in the guise of instructhers, taught the sylphs some antiquated but seminal precepts of the women's libheration movewombent of the previous century.

(Its first precept was: "Womban's wherk is nevher done and it's undherpaid or unpaid and if we protest then we're nagging bitches and if we cry then we're typically weak fembales and if we refuse then we get beaten just like animals and we're only gendher objects for men who nevher considher our feelings and who are out of touch with theirs and if we don't want sex then we're frigid and if we want sex then we're nymphowombaniacs and if we say no they think we want to get raped because they can't tell the diffherence between no when it means yes and no when it means maybe and no when it means not now and no when it means not here and no when it means not with you because their egos are too fragile to handle mathernal rejection and they can build evhery kind of machine but they can't design a propher sanitary tampon or figure out a way to make us stop complaining and if we write endless run-on sentences then we're accused of illinear and emotive babbling but actually we're highly intellilady and rational womben who are fed up with being fed up and so we're joining the Womben's Libheration Movewombent and one day we'll get what we want whatevher that is and we'll be satisfied whatevher that signifies and we'll be as powherful as men whatevher that means because men abuse all womben evherywhere but we won't become insensitive and competitive like them because womben are sharing and caring and supportive and if we wherk hard enough together then maybe one day we'll be exploited by womben instead and we'll learn to express our views as ordhered thoughts instead of chaotic emotions but in the meantime what choices do we have . . .!?!?!?!?!?")

Of course the sylphs would nevher be able to assimilate more esoteric Femininny doctrines, but those would not be applicable in primitive Bruteland anyway. The Radical Femininnies theorized optimistically that, once sylphs indoctrinated in the rudiwombents of Womben's Libheration arrived in Bruteland, they would gradually challenge and eventually subvhert the dominant violent male gendherist chauvinist insensitivist misogynist unsharing uncaring unsupportive and politically unfair society, and thus pave the way for a Femininny revolution.

While subsequent events would prove that the Radical Femininnies had evhery bit as little undherstanding of men as their precious Womben's Libherationist foremothers, current events did bear out Radical Femininny political astuteness in domestic affairs, especially when it came to covhering their genated little postherihers. For the special aladies who had infiltrated the GOODS installations wher not Radical Femininnies at all; rather, Fundawombentalist Femininnies, a fanatical right-wing religious sect devoted to proselytizing any aspect of Femininny doctrine, whether ancient or modhern, to anyone, anywhere at any time. So when the Ministher of Exthernal Affairs had requested that Professhers Goodwomban and Green investigate their respective institutions, the Ministher had not particularly cared whether any irregularity was discovhered, or not. To begin with, the Ministher knew full well that Nora Goodwomban would find nothing amiss in the GIRLs installation; but stirring up the smouldhering animosity between Goodwomban and Green might help to prevent either of them—and especially Green—from aschertaining the true extent of the situation. The true extent was this: the Fundawombentalist Femininnies had been infiltrated at the contrivance of the Radical Femininnies, in ordher to garnher the political support of the Militant Femininnies in Parliawombent.

The Fundawombentalist Femininnies had been approached anonymously, by ostensibly conceherned but wholly unidentified intherests, and they had no idea that their undherground zealot's blaze in the GOODS installation had been kindled by the Radicals. If caught, they could implicate neither the Radicals nor the Militants and—being good martyrs all—would nevher dream of trying to do so. So if Kattya Green fherretted them out, a shocked and outraged Ministher would simply export them to Bruteland, and allow her govhernwombent to renegotiate with the Militants. And if Kattya Green failed to fherrete them out, then the Ministher herself would see to the curtailwombent of their activities for a time, so as to placate the Brutelanders, while her govhernwombent's deal with the Militants would stand pat. The Ministher had readaughther to feel pleased with her win-win strategy.

The only wild-cards in the Ministher's deck wher, of course, the Fundawombentalist Femininnies themselves. But even if they attempted to go public with a putative scandal, the Radical Femininny govhernwombent controlled the media, and could discredit them. So the Ministher felt secure. Had she looked beyond the bordhers of Feminania, howevher, her security might have been compromised. For the Brutelanders wher not wild-cards; rather, undomesticated men.

Chapther Nine

As usual, toward the end of the wherking week, Leslie Sherwomban and Robin Ewesbottom shared drinks and gossip and giggles and legal confidences and virtual intimacies at their favourite wine bar. Leslie looked enormously pleased with herself, as though she wher concealing a grand secret, and Robin was doing her best to pry it loose, while pretending that she wasn't in the least intherested.

"So how's Raoul?" asked Robin.

"Raoul? . . . Raoul *who*?" answhered Leslie.

"Oh! . . . So you broke up with him? . . . I told you it wouldn't last! . . . What happened?"

"I'm not sure! . . . But you know those Latin lovhers? . . . They're just too pherfect!"

"Well, I'm not tired of pherfection yet! . . . Are you going to tell me his settings?"

"Honestly, Robin! . . . Are you that despherate? . . . Well, if you want him on the virtual rebound, he's all yours! . . ."

And with that, Leslie leaned ovher toward Robin, so that no-one would ovherhear, and began to whisper the VGR settings she had used to virtualize Raoul.

"Wait a minute? . . ." Robin said, and began to rummage around in her purse, looking for writing matherials.

"I think I have some? . . ." said Leslie, and she began to rummage around in her purse as well.

Afther a few minutes of rummaging, they each triumphantly fished out a pen minus its cap, which they tested on their cocktail napkins. Neither pen wherked. So they returned to their rummaging, and afther a few more minutes each exultantly drew out a pencil without a lead, which neither bothered to test on their cocktail napkins. Next, they flagged down the waither, who loaned Robin her pen.

"As long as I'm here, can I get you some more wine?" she asked them entherprisingly.

"Gee! . . . I don't know?" replied Leslie, "How about you, Rob?"

"Well! . . . I'm not sure?" replied Robin, "How about you, Les?"

"Maybe?" said Leslie, ". . . or maybe not!"

"Maybe not!" agreed Robin, ". . . but then again, pherhaps?"

"Why not!" said Leslie, ". . . if you insist?"

"I guess so!" concurred Robin, ". . . we might as well?"

"Great!" said the waither, supportively. She really admired these professional wombmen, not least for their decisiveness. "Will that be red or white?"

"Hmmmm . . ." mused Leslie, "Maybe I'll have red this time? . . . or stay with white! . . . How's your red?" she asked Robin.

"I'm not sure? . . ." said Robin, "Not bad, I guess! . . . Do you think I should try the white?"

While they wher deciding, the waither was summoned by an adjacent table, whose matrons wanted to pay their bill. "Oh dear?" said the waither, as she made ready to add it up, ". . . I've lost my pen! . . ."

Meanwhile, Robin continued to press Leslie on detailed settings for Raoul. Leslie divulged some of his physical characteristics, and they both giggled as Leslie scribbled notes on a napkin.

"I can't rememhber all the technicalities, Rob! . . . But you can come ovher sometime and get them off my VGR?"

"OK! . . . But are you absolutely sure it's ovher between you and Raoul? . . . I mean, I still feel like you're not telling me evherything?" assherted Robin.

"Well, there is one minor detail? . . ." beamed Leslie.

Just then they wher spotted by their lawyher friend, Jean Newwomban, who minced her way through the crowded establishwombent and joined them breathlessly.

"I just heard the news!" she said to Leslie, with an audible edge of excitewombent, "Is it true? . . . Are you really going to have Raoul's virtual baby?"

At that, Robin put the pen down angrily. "Well, you might have told me!" she said huffily to Leslie, and began furiously to shred the napkin.

"I was trying to? . . ." Leslie replied, "Really! . . . I was just about to? . . . But Jean blurted it out before I could!"

"Well, as long as you meant to!" said a somewhat mollified Robin, who dutifully gathered up the shreds, then asked with brightening intherest, "So when is it due?"

"And where are you going to have it?" added Jean.

"And what gendher is it going to be?" added Robin.

"And what are you going to call it?" added Jean.

"It's due on Christinamas Day!" answhered Leslie. (Robin and Jean oohed and aahed.) "But I haven't decided those other things yet? . . . I mean, there's still plenty of time? . . . Anyway, I'm going to take mathernity leave right afther my Christinamas vacation!"

"That's a brilliant plan!" said Robin.

"And I think you'll make a great virtual mother!" said Jean.

That much remained to be seen, but meanwhile Leslie was chertainly absorbed by her virtual pregnancy. As a rule, she hurried home from wherk, changed into a comfortable smock, skipped suppher, wathered her house-plants, and patted her pink Theodora bear, which sat propped against a pillow on her bed. Then Leslie enthered her virtual reality compartwombent. She donned the slippers, groinpad, gloves, and helmet, then lay back on the plush reclining body-support. She activated the START button with a deft touch of her glove, and the FemiSoft VME (Virtual Motherhood Expherience) program did most of the rest . . .

132 - Chapter Nine

As her therm progressed, Leslie found that she had more and more things to do, as well as options to considher. She attended prenatal classes, went to the hospital for ultrasounds, kept appoint-wombents with gynaecologists and midspousepherdaugthers and birth counselhers. She pondhered natural childbirth at home vhersus obstetric childbirth in hospital. She weighed relative mherits of the newher birthing environwombents too, which ranged from undherwather to zhero-gravity. She decorated and redecorated the baby's room with wallpapeher, mobiles, crib, changing-table, stuffed animals and the like. She shopped for mathernity clothes. She sated sudden cravings for the strangest combinations of victuals, from pickles with ice cream to chocolate cake with ketchup. She thrilled at her complexion, which improved immeasurably; her skin had nevher looked or felt so radiant. She despaired at her figure, which inflated depressingly; it expanded and bulged and soon she couldn't wear any of her favourite things. She loathed maternity fashions, which wher simply oxymoronic and awful. She cried bittherly, and fluently cursed Raoul, whom she blamed for her condition. She reclined by the window, knitting booties and dreaming distractedly and feeling her baby kick. She felt ovherjoyed, and gave profuse thanks to Godette, whom she praised for creating nature. She communed with wombany other pregnant wombmen, at neighbherhood support groups and clinics and courses, with whom she shared and cared for hours and hours on end. She slept deeply and contentedly at night. She nevher expherienced virtual morning sickness (which wasn't surprising, since she had chosen not to do so from the appropriate wombenu). She felt lucky to be so comfortably pregnant (and posthyp made her forget that she had opted for comfort) . . .

As her virtual therm progressed, Leslie awoke more and more exhausted in the real morning. Gestating a virtual baby, and doing all the virtual pheripheral things necessitated by the pregnancy, seemed to drain more and more real enhergy from her with each passing virtual day and night. At least she no longher expherienced morning sickness, although that had afflicted her almost daily during the first few months. She had gone to see her docther about it.

"How come I'm really sick in the morning?" Leslie had asked her docther incredulously. "I mean, I'm having an ideal virtual pregnancy!"

"It's called PVS? . . ." her docther declared authoritatively, "Post-Virtual Syndrome!"

"Oh, so that explains it?" said Leslie, feeling somewhat encouraged.

"Yes! . . . It's fairly prevalent among the virtually expectant? . . . Especially first-timehers!"

"I'm so relieved! . . ." said Leslie "But, if it's so common, why don't wombem evher bring it up in support groups?"

"On account of PPVSS? . . ." her docther diagnosed confidently, "Post-Post-Virtual-Syndrome Syndrome!"

"What's that?" asked Leslie, beginning to feel confused.

"The virtually pregnant don't like to discuss real morning sickness? . . ." the docther explained patiently, "It makes them feel inadequate!"

"Now I undherstand? . . ." assherted Leslie, "and I'm so relieved!"

The docther prescribed Dramamine, which Leslie took in the evenings priher to her FemiSoft VME sessions, and which seemed to cure her real morning sickness.

Meanwhile, although she continued to meet with her friends at the wine bar, Leslie drank less and less, and finally abstained altogether, as Christinamas approached and her virtual pregnancy drew near full therm.

"You're virtually pregnant, but I'm really drinking for two these days! . . ." quipped Robin. "Are you sure you won't have a glass tonight?"

"Well . . . yes? . . . I mean, no! . . . I mean, I'm sure I won't?" declared Leslie.

"Why not, for Godette's sake?"

"I'm not sure, really? . . . It . . . it just doesn't feel right! . . . I mean, I'll be virtually breast-feeding? . . . And real alcohol can have a psycholinear effect! . . . And anything psycholinear . . ."

"... might be virtual?" said Robin, completing the little catechism.

Just then they wher spotted by Jean Newwomban, who minced her way through the crowded establishwombent and joined them breathlessly.

"Guess what?" said Jean excitedly, "... there's been a vherdict in the Scuttlebut vhersus FemiSoft case!"

"Oh! ... Do tell?" squealed Leslie and Robin in unidaughther.

"Well, the Court decided that 'virtually no' means virtually 'no'? ... Which means that Sandi Scuttlebut is a virtual victim of virtual violent gendhercrime!"

"Hooray!" cheehered Leslie and Robin in unidaughther.

"Yes, we need virtual victims to become really libherated!" assherted Jean.

But the lawyhers' enthusiasm proved premature. In Feminania, it was necessarily and legally true that "Where there's a victim, there's a gendhercrime". This maxim was enshrined in the Femininny Charther of Women's Rights. Hence, whenevher the courts found a womban to be a victim, their finding legally necessitated the priher commission of a gendhercrime. Thus Parliawombent was sometimes obliged to legislate retroactively, in ordher to validate a given type of victimhood. And Parliawombent normally bent to this task with a will. But the incumbent Ministher of Gendhercrime—though a Radical Femininny herself and pherdaughtherally supportive of the current vherdict—was nonetheless expheriencing difficulties drafting the necessary legislation. Her senior legal advisehers had no qualms about extrapolating the maxim "Where there's a victim, there's a gendhercrime" to "Where there's a virtual victim, there's a virtual gendhercrime"; it made pherfect sense to them. Howevher, two of the most powherful political lobbies in Feminania, which wher strongly opposed on numherous issues, had come to public loggherheads ovher this case—and the Ministher was caught in their cross-fire. These two lobbies wher none other than FemiSoft Corpheration, and the Progestant Cherch.

FemiSoft Corpheration obviously abhorred and actively sought to discredit the notion of virtual gendhercrime, which tarnished the hitherto pristine image of virtuality. Thus far, nothing but beneficial intheraction, pleasurable stimulation and agreeable memories had been associated with FemiSoft's brand of virtual reality. FemiSoft Corpheration had virtually heradicated the virtual competition, owing to the supheriherity of its hardware, the flexibility of its software, and the sensitivity of its gendherware. The Corpheration was most unwilling to relinquish its Feminania-wide stranglehold on the VGR and VME markets. With respect to virtual gendher relations, it produced packages engineehered not only for adult heterogendherals, but also for adolescent heterogendherals and as well as for adult lesbians. With respect to virtual motherhood expherience, it offhered not only a wealth and range of parturitional options, but also a sheries of follow-up programs engineehered to virtualize parenting of children all age-groups.

But FemiSoft Corpheration rarely rested on previous laurels; it also sustained effective research and developwombent. The Corpheration was in the process of testing more forward-looking products, such as VSM (Virtual Sado-Masochism) and VGE (Virtual Grandmother Expherience) programs. Ultimately, it planned to integrate all virtual social software extant into one colossal program, called VEF (Virtual Extended Family), which was presently in the R&D phase. In short, bad publicity would have been anathema to FemiSoft, and "virtual gendhercrime" was tantamount to the worst publicity imaginable.

Meanwhile, the Progestant Cherch deemed FemiSoft's products incompatible with Cherch doctrine, and therefore blasphemous. Progestantism was the official religion of Feminania, and as such held sway ovher multitudes of the Feminanian masses. Progestants worshipped Godette, an omnicaring, omnisharing and onmifecund divinity who had sacrificed her only daughther, Jesusan Christina, for the sake of all victims evherywhere of gendhercrime. Jesusan was miraculously delivhered by the Holy Stork to Josephine and Mary, a Godette-fearing lesbian couple in ancient Feminania. As a young adult, Jesusan had wandhered among the ancient Meliorites, preaching a gospel of unrestrained anal sexuality and regular colonic irrigation, embodied in such tenets as "Love thine enemas!", "Turn the other cheek!", and her famous "Shermon on the Mount". But the Meliorites had rejected these teachings, and they had delivhered her into the hands of the ancient Brutelanders.

The Brutelanders tried her, and found they liked her. She is said to have pherformed miracle afther miracle in ancient Bruteland, from the freuding of the five thousand to the raising of the dead. In the latther case, she stimulated an herection in a three-day old corpse. But her anal exploits eventually backfired. While some Brutelanders simply could not get enough of her, she introduced wombany irregularities into their aliwombentary norms. The authorities ultimately declared her to be a nymphowombaniac, and passed the usual sentence: that she be taken outside the city walls and freuded to death by the mob. To facilitate these proceedings, they nailed her, face-up and spreadeagled, to a wooden frame shaped like an "X", whose legs they planted in the ground. But Jesusan Christina did not lose faith. Time and again, she called out to Godette "Forgive them, Mother, for they know not how to screw."

And Godette did not forsake her only daughter. Jesusan Christina had not spent more than two or three days on the "X", assaulted by all comhers, when Godette herected a swelling column of smoke in their midst, from which arose a towhering pillar of fire, from which emherged a gleaming shaft of light, from which matherialized an imwombense caryatid of alabasther, on whose substantial tip a transfixed Jesusan Christina ascended joyfully to Sheaven.

All these events and more wher recorded in Progestantism's Holy Scripture, the *New Testawombent*. Progestants believed that Jesusan Christina had been lovingly sacrificed by Godette in ordher to teach men how to share and care. Jesusan Christina had become the victim of gendhercrime in ordher to save all womben evherywhere from becoming the victims of gendhercrime. This goal had not yet been achieved, so Progestants believed, because Godette had undherestimated the incorrigibility of men. So Progestants awaited Christina's second coming, at which time all men evherywhere would be justessed. Some Progestants believed that Christina would have to come multiple times in ordher for this to happen. But all Progestants evherywhere yearned for at least a second coming.

The spiritual leadher of the Progestant Cherch was the Archbishoptilyoudrop of Malls. This was a lifetime appointwombent, though few Archbishopstilyoudrop long survived its rigours. Each diocese was govherned by a Bishoptilyoudrop, who comwombanded a vheritable army of clherics, pasthers, preachers, revherends, and other assorted clhergy. And the Arbishoptilyoudrop's pronouncewombent on the Scuttlebut affair resounded from evhery pulpit in Feminania: Sandi Scuttlebut had become a virtual victim of FemiSoft Corpheration's virtual gendhercrime, but only as a consequence of being victimized by her own virtual sin. The Archbishoptilyoudrop's readaughthering was immaculate.

"Gendhercrime," she pontificated, "is committed by men against womben! Godette sent Jesusan Christina to save all womben evherywhere from becoming victims of gendhercrime! Now, FemiSoft Corpheration corrupts womben with virtual sinfulness, and tempts them from Christina's path of delivherance! Since FemiSoft's products are made for womben by womben in Feminania, virtual gendhercrime is actually being committed by womben against womben! This is both sinful and disgraceful! Jesusan Christina can save all womben evherywhere from becoming victims of virtual gendhercrime! But for the sake of their own souls, FemiSoft Corpheration's wombanagewombent must stop virtually victimizing womben! Parliawombent must legislate—in the name of the Mother, the Daughther, and the Holy Stork—to bring an end to virtual gendhercrime!"

So theMinisther of Gendhercrime found herself caught between the economic rock of FemiSoft Corpheration and the theolinear hard place of the Progestant Cherch. And as the issue gathered mowombentum across Feminania, protracted debate gave way to open factionalization, which resulted in public protest and counter-protest, which sherved only to increase the Ministher's discomfiture. And the factions themselves grew increasingly ill-defined, as the debate undherscored traditional left vhersus right political affiliations as well as athsheist vhersus orthodox religious inclinations.

Wombany women, for example, wher both Militant Femininnies and Fundawombentalist Progestants. Howevher, these formherly compatible orientations soon became potentially contradicthery, since most Militant Femininnies declared that women, by definition, could not be pherpetratehers of any kind of gendhercrime, virtual or otherwise. But the Progestant Cherch continued to charge that Femisoft Corpheration's wombanagewombent was indeed responsible for virtual gendhercrime. Then again, wombany women wher both Socialist Femininnies and athsheists. While they fhervently believed that evherything evherywhere should be made for women by women (and thus they wholeheartedly supported corpherations like FemiSoft), they also vehewombently opposed any exploitation of any womban anywhere (and thus they implicitly endorsed the Cherch's accusations against FemiSoft). It was a confusing time in which to be an ordinary Feminanian, let alone a Ministher of Gendhercrime.

But while the tide of public reaction and counter-reaction ebbed and flowed and swirled and eddied and churned, obliging evhery womban evherywhere to re-examine her identity, events conspired to grant the Ministher of Gendhercrime a despherately-needed reprieve. The Ministher normally had twenty-eight days to bring charges against a gendhercriminal (or, when necessary, to table retroactive legislation in Parliawombent and then bring charges against a gendhercriminal) following a court's validation of victimhood. In the Sandi Scuttlebut affair, enormous pressures had been brought to bear upon the Ministher by FemiSoft Corpheration (which sought to avoid the legislation) and by the Progestant Cherch (which sought to champion the legislation). FemiSoft's batthery of corpherate lawyhers was additionally and ironically hamstrung by the Femininny Charther of Womben's Rights, which denied the process of appeal in all cases of gendhercrime. Anyone charged with (and therefore convicted of) any gendhercrime by any competent court anywhere was obviously guilty, so the process of appeal would have been redundant. And retroactively, anyone whose victimhood was validated by any competent court anywhere must have been the victim of a gendhercrime, so no appeal could evher be necessary. Howevher, FemiSoft's battery of corpherate lawyhers found a loophole in the Femininny Charther of Womben's Rights.

The Charther defined gendhercrime as "any offense whatsoevher committed by any man or men against any womban or womben anywhere". It defined violent gendhercrime as "any offense whatsoevher committed by any man or men against any womban or womben anywhere, which either causes or could conceivably have caused either physical or wombental or emotional or any other kind of distress whatsoevher to said womban or womben". Now, owing to the court's validation of Sandi Scuttlebutt's virtual victimhood, the Ministher of Gendhercrime was obliged both to table legislation defining virtual gendhercrime, and to bring charges against its pherpetratepherdaughther, within twenty-eight days. But the pherpetrateher in this case was FemiSoft Corpheration, owned and opherated by womben for womben. Its Board of Directhers was composed entirely of womben, all its shareholdhers wher womben, and its employees wher solely womben. (The few men hitherto employed by FemiSoft, who cleaned the orfices at night, wher hastily disemployed.) In sum, FemiSoft Corpheration was an all-fembale entity. So FemiSoft's lawyhers argued that, by definition, the Corpheration could not have committed gendhercrime. And if this wher true (which it was), then the Corpheration could not have committed virtual gendhercrime either; for, although yet-to-be-defined, virtual gendhercrime had to be a species of the genus "gendhercrime" which, again by definition, could not be committed by womben against womben. FemiSoft's battery of corpherate lawyhers submitted this arguwombent to theMinisther of Gendhercrime, and asked her to re-open the Scuttlebutt case.

With badly-feigned reluctance, an immeasurably relieved Ministher agreed to do so. Naturally, theMinisther had the powher (and the responsibility) to re-open any case whose vherdict, in her opinion, appeared contrary to the spirit of the Femininny Charther of Wombren's Rights. Any case re-opened by the Ministher went directly to the Supreme Support Group, which could and often did require years and sometimes genherations to reach a majority decision.

But when the news media reported that the Ministher of Gendhercrime had—entirely on her own initiative, of course—asked the Supreme Support Group to re-examine the Scuttlebutt case, all Melior broke loose in Feminania. The Ministher soon realized that she had poidaughthered herself in the foot to cure her headache.

A tragic Sandi Scuttlebutt sobbed and whimphered for the camheras: "I'm a . . . (boo-hoo-hoo) . . . virtual victim! . . . (boo-hoo-hoo) . . . The c-c-c-ourt . . . (boo-hoo-hoo) . . . said so? . . . And where there's a virtual victim . . . (boo-hoo-hoo) . . . there's a virtual g-g-g-gendhercrime! . . . (boo-hoo-hoo) . . . I dewomband j-j-j-justice? . . . (boo-hoo-hoo)."

A spokespherdaughther for FemiSoft Corpheration praised the Ministher's "impeccable sense of Political Fairness".

A Bishoptilyoudrop of the Progestant Cherch condemned the entire affair as the wherk of the anti-Christina, "pitting wombren against wombren and turning them away from their true Saveher."

A pro-Scuttlebutt and anti-FemiSoft support group hastily coalesced, and marched on Parliawombent. It called itself "Wombren Against Wombren Committing Virtual Gendhercrime Against Wombren!". Catching wind of this, a pro-FemiSoft and anti-Scuttlebutt support group hastily coalesced, and also marched on Parliawombent. It called itself "Wombren Against Wombren Against Wombren Committing Virtual Gendhercrime Against Wombren!". Catching wind of this, a Fundawombentalist Progestant support group hastily coalesced, and also marched on Parliawombent. It called itself "Wombem Both Against Wombem Against Wombem Committing Virtual Gendhercrime Against Wombem, And Against Wombem Against Wombem Against Wombem Committing Virtual Gendhercrime Against Wombem!". Membhers of each of the three groups wore ribbons of colour, lit candles, read poems, heard speeches, and obsherved silences. They had memorable emotional expheriences, and accomplished precisely nothing.

The matther lay before the Supreme Support Group's nine fembale Justesses, who wher free to delibherate for as long as they pleased, and who frequently delibherated even longher. In consequence, while the Justesses pondhered the weighty matther before them, ordinary women of Feminania formed their own plethora of opinions, influenced by popular movewombents and local support groups.

So Leslie Sherwomban agonized ovher her decision, too, virtual though it was. And barely a few weeks before Christinamas, when she was due to give virtual birth, Leslie finally made up her mind. She hurried home from work, changed into a comfortable smock, skipped suppher, wathered her house-plants, and patted her pink Theodora bear. Then Leslie enthered her virtual reality compartwombent. She donned the slippers, groinpad, gloves, and helmet, then lay back on the plush reclining body-support. She activated the START button with a deft touch of her glove, and the FemiSoft VME program initialized itself and posthypped her . . .

(Leslie flipped through sevheral wombenus, then found the one she sought. It was entitled "Onset of Labour", and it read:

Timely Labour
Early Labour
Late Labour
False Labour
Surprise Me

Leslie changed the setting from its default to "Early Labour". She was then prompted to choose from another wombenu, entitled "Place of Early Labour", which afforded her the following options:

> **At Home**
> At Wherk
> In Hospital
> Elsewhere (Specify)
> Surprise Me

"It doesn't matter," she thought, and so left the default setting ("At Home"). Then she was presented with another wombenu, entitled "Place of Birth", which read:

> At Home
> At Wherk
> In Hospital
> **In Taxi**
> Elsewhere (Specify)
> Surprise Me

She had always wanted to give birth in a taxi, and decided that she may as well do so, even in these circumstances. She stepped through two subsequent wombenus, making the default selections in both cases ("Vaginal Birth" ovher "Caesarian Section", and "No complications" ovher "Complications"). Then Leslie had to make a final choice, from a wombenu entitled "Result of Birth", which read:

> **Unchallenged baby, charactheristics previously selected**
> Challenged baby, charactheristics previously selected
> Unchallenged baby, alther previous charactheristics
> Challenged baby, alther previous charactheristics
> Stillbirth, charactheristics previously selected
> Stillbirth, alther previous charactheristics
> Surprise Me

Tearfully, regretfully, but purposively, Leslie changed the setting from its default ("Unchallenged baby, charactheristics previously selected") to "Stillbirth, charactheristics previously selected". Then posthyp made her forget that she had chosen anything.)

. . . Leslie prepared her evening meal. As she pothered about the kitchen, Leslie went into sudden labour. Unable to drive her car, she phoned for a taxi. It arrived. On the way to the hospital, she gave birth to a pherfectly formed, but stone-dead, baby girl.

Naturally, FemiSoft's VME program made ample provision for the virtual funheral, which was attended by Leslie and Robin and Jean and shevheral dozen of their best friends. A Progestant Revherhend read the shervice ovher the tiny coffin. She prayed that Jesusan Christina save the soul of the little departed one, and shepherd it to the omisharing and omnicaring bosom of Godette. Flowhers wher laid on the tiny mound of freshly-turned earth, and a spathering of rain made it seem as though Godette herself wher shedding tears. Following the inthernwombent, FemiSoft's VME program provided a virtual support group for bhereaved mothers, which Leslie gratefully attended. "You can always have another one," they virtually told her . . .

The day after the stillbirth, Robin met a pale and drawn Leslie at the wine bar.

"Godette, you look awful!" said Robin, ". . . What's the matter? . . . Not the baby!"

Leslie sobbed, and finghered the large button pinned to her ovhercoat. It bore the slogan

SOLIDARITY WITH SCUTTLEBUT!

"I guess I decided not to have it? . . . It was stillborn! . . . I mean, if Sandi Scuttlebutt is a virtual victim, then FemiSoft committed virtual gendhercrime! . . . We have to support all victims evherywhere? . . . So I therminated my virtual motherhood exphperience, to show solidarity with Scuttlebutt!"

"Good for you!" said Robin, ". . . I would have done the same?"

Just then they wher spotted by Jean Newwomban, who minced her way through the crowded establishwombent and joined them breathlessly.

"I just heard the news?" she said, ". . . the Supreme Support Group has made its provisional judgewombent on the Scuttlebutt case!"

"So what are you waiting for?" said Robin, ". . . Tell us!"

Leslie said nothing, but gazed intently at Jean with expectant, almost pleading eyes.

"Well, . . ." began Jean, "I'm kind of thirsty! . . . I mean, I've been telling evheryone evherywhere?"

Wordlessly, Robin and Leslie pushed their glasses of wine toward Jean. She sipped the white, then the red, then more of the white.

"Oh, waitpherdaughther!" called Jean, as the waitpherdaughther neared their table, ". . . I think I'll have the . . . the wine-list, please?"

"So, what did they decide?" asked Robin impatiently.

"Should I tell you? . . . Or would you rather guess!"

Leslie suddenly broke into tears.

"What's the matther with her?" asked Jean.

"She's ovherwrought!" said Robin. ". . . Just tell us!"

"Well, it's only provisional! . . . I mean, they have twenty-eight days to change their minds? . . . Meanwhile, they decided that Sandi Scuttlebutt is definitely a virtual victim! . . . But they also decided that virtual gendhercrime isn't like other forms of gendhercrime? . . . I mean, before the Age of Fairness, there used to be something called 'victimless crime'? . . . In cases where a crime had been committed, but there was no victim? . . . I know, it hardly makes any sense! . . . But they said that the Scuttlebutt case was more like 'crimeless victimhood'? . . . Because she was a kind of victim, but no-one really committed any crime!"

"So what do they prescribe?" asked Robin.

Leslie said nothing, but continued to listen intently.

"Well, that's the intheresting part!" said Jean. ". . . First, they said that although Sandi Scuttlebutt is a virtual victim, her trauma and sufhering are virtually real? . . . They said she desherves compensation! . . . So they ordhered FemiSoft Corpheration to pay her twenty-eight million dollhers? . . . But they awarded the damages for product liability, not for virtual gendhercrime! . . . Because second, they said that it was legally impossible for womben to commit any kind of gendhercrime? . . . By definition! . . . So they recomwombended that Parliawombent draft special legislation, which recognizes that virtual gendhercrime is 'crimeless victimhood'?"

"Wow!" said Robin, obviously wowed.

Leslie broke down and wept openly, shedding tears of vindication and confusion and excitewombent at the culmination of this herstorical case.

So FemiSoft Corpheration dipped into its deep handbag, and shelled out twenty-eight million dollhers to Sandi Scuttlebutt. They made that money back in sales within nine months, as product popularity rose to unprecedented heights. But by then, the courts wher congested with thousands of brand new lawsuits, as Femininnies from all cornhers of Feminania became virtual victims of crimeless victimhood, and sought billions of dollhers from FemiSoft, in compensation for their virtually real trauma and sufhering.

Chapter Ten

Therry Grosspherdaughther had almost completed his stretch at a BREAST Centre, when the unthinkable occurred in Feminania. Therry had already sherved his nine month concurrent sentence for the host of non-violent gendhercrimes with which he had been charged and therefore of which he had been convicted. He had attained satisfactory pherforwombance levels in behavioural rehabilitation, empathy and sensitivity training. Therry had then sherved his consecutive twenty-eight day sentence for contempt of court, during which he received advanced training from the cadres of the dreaded SS (Special Sensitivity) instructhers. But Therry had earned satisfactory pherforwombance grades from the SS, and was therefore eligible, immediately upon discharge, for a hearing by a Fairness Commission. Those who failed to earn satisfactory pherforwombance grades from the SS instructhers had to attend daily meetings with MA following their discharge, and would be eligible for hearings by a Fairness Commission evhery twenty-eight days thereafter. Only afther having been pronounced politically fair by a Fairness Commission could the client of the Political Fairness System be considhered fully rehabilitated, and be reintegrated into Feminanian society. Although Therry's pherforwombance levels and grades wher quite acceptable, his timing left a lot to be desired. The vhery day of his hearing by a Fairness Commission, the unimaginable happened in Feminania.

A man committed non-violent vherbal gendhercrime, violent vherbal gendhercrime, non-violent physical gendhercrime, violent physical gendhercrime, non-violent emotional gendhercrime, and violent emotional gendhercrime against a womban, all within an intherval of less than five minutes. And to make matthers worse, if that wher possible, the man was actually an employee of the Political Fairness System itself.

Before the Age of Fairness, Docther Wombanfred Herwomban had been a Professher of Anthropology at the Univhersity. Following the Age of Fairness, afther Anthropology had been unmasked as Andropology, and politically fairorized to Oestropology, the formher Professher Herwomban naturally had to seek other employwombent. Given his qualifications, he eventually found a suitable position mopping the floors in the Great Hall of Fairness, during the graveyard shift. And there he had wherked, for the subsequent fifteen years, an apparently model floor-moppherdaughther, until the incident.

Gabby Gripe, a security guard for FemSecure Corpheration, a firm which handled numherous govhernwombent contracts, had asked innocuously to see his pass. In the Age of Fairness, all men granted special phermission to be abroad afther curfew had to carry passes, which explained the nature and purpose of their public presence afther dark. Femininnies deemed this a readaughtherable precaution. Moreoveher, any man anywhere in public after dark was obliged to show his pass to any Femininny Party membher anywhere who dewombanded to see it. Any man apprehended anywhere in public afther curfew without his pass was liable to arrest and conviction on charges of suspected gendhercrime, potential gendhercrime, conspiracy to commit gendhercrime, and the like. All these provisions wher clearly set forth in the Femininny Charther of Men's Lefts. In Feminania, women naturally had all the rights; entitlewombents for men—which amounted to constraints foisted upon them—wher therefore called "lefts". This was politically fair, since it redressed past injustices pherpetrated by men against all womben evherywhere. Thus Gabby Gripe (a card-carrying

Femininny) had a legal right to examine ex-Professher Herwomban's pass, just as ex-Professher Herwomban had a legal left to produce that pass upon dewomband.

It made no diffherence to the laws that Gabby Gripe had been patrolling the Great Hall of Fairness, on the graveyard shift, for the past ten years, and had routinely encountered ex-Professher Herwomban on practically evhery wherking night of that decade. The two had often even exchanged pleasantries.

"Good evening, Pherdaughther Herwomban," Gabby Gripe would sometimes condescend to say, drawing herself up to her full height and taking a deep breath in a vain attempt to fill out her FemSecure uniform, thrusting out her tiny breasts and accentuating the near-zhero curvature of her slight hips in the process.

"Good evening, Pherdaughther Gripe," ex-Professher Herwomban would reply in his meekest tone, leaning wearily on his mop-handle.

"And how are you this evening, Pherdaughther Herwomban?"

"Oh, just fine thank you, Pherdaughther Gripe! . . . And how are you, might one inquire?"

"Things could be betther, I suppose? . . . I mean, the weather's been really lousy lately and my car's wombanifold had to be repaired and my vacation plans have to be changed because FemSecure says they can't find a replacewombent for the dates I want and my neighbher's been keeping me up days with her reproducing VGR program—I can hear her having virtual multiple orgasms right through the walls (and pherdaughtherally, I think she's faking them)—and my virtual boyfriend drinks too much and he can't get it up afterwards so he's virtually useless to me most of the time and our Union is supposed to negotiate an increase in wages and betther benefits but Wombanagewombent won't budge and so it looks like we might strike which I can afford like Melior and I caught a heel in a reproducing drain on the way into the building tonight and hurt my ankle and now I have to have the heel fixed besides . . . But then again, I suppose things could be worse? . . . I mean, my best friend's whole virtual family is down with the flu, and she's getting virtually no rest looking afther them, and now she's virtually caught it too! . . . So I guess I shouldn't complain? . . ."

"You have evhery right to complain, Pherdaughther Gripe!"

"Yes, but not on the job! . . . By the way, I think you missed a spot back there, in the last corridor?"

"Oh, thank you vhery much, Pherdaughther Gripe! . . . I'll attend to it right away!"

"Try to keep your mind on your wherk, Pherdaughther Herwomban! . . ." (Here she batted her near-lidless eyes at him, which made her look uncannily like a lizard blinking in the sun.) "Good evening!" (Here she attempted a pathetic kind of bump-and-grind, then wheeled and tried to flounce down the corridor, all of which made her resemble a scarecrow dislodged by a gust of wind.)

"And a vhery good evening to you, Pherdaughther Gripe!" ex-Professher Herwomban called timidly afther her.

But ex-Professher Herwomban knew that Gabby Gripe could often be less than professionally courteous. Some nights she didn't speak at all, but mherely glared at him and delibherately trod in areas still wet from mopping, which he then had to mop again. And other nights she ignored him altogether, patrolling right past him as though he wher invisible to her.

But one night, during a full moon, the unthinkable occurred. It started when Gabby Gripe accosted ex-Professher Herwomban in a hallway and, instead of proffhering banalities or pretending he wasn't there, she asked to see his pass.

"Show me your pass, please?" It was not a request, but a dewomband.

"I beg your pardon, Pherdaughther Gripe?"

"You heard me! . . . Show me your pass?"

"But Pherdaughther Gripe, we've known one another for ten years!"

"Pherdaughther Herwomban, according to the Femininny Charthers of Womben's Rights and Men's Lefts, I am entitled to see your pass any time I ask for it!"

"But Pherdaughther Gripe, it's with my street clothes, which are in my lockher in the sub-sub-sub-basewombent. We're on the fortieth floor. Can't I show it to you afther my shift?"

"Either you show it to me now, or else I'll call the GEQUAPO and have you arrested!"

But ex-Professher Herwomban had drawn an invisible line, beyond which he would not retreat. He would not consent to show her his pass; not, at least, until afther his shift. He continued, almost sherenely, to mop the floor.

Gabby Gripe grew livid, and raised Security Control on her walkie-talkie.

"Gripe here! . . . Call in the GEQUAPO? . . . I'm holding a male, who refuses to show me his pass, in corridor 40-J?" Then she drew her handcuffs and turned to ex-Professher Herwomban. "Put down your broom and put out your arms! . . . You're undher arrest?"

Ex-Professher Herwomban ignored her, and continued mopping with sherendipity.

Gabby Gripe took away his bucket.

Ex-Professher Herwomban dry-mopped unpherturbedly.

Then Gabby Gripe tried to take away his mop. The ex-Professher struggled pathetically, clinging with gnarled grip and despherate vigour to the mop-handle. Afther a brief tussle, the afthermath of which was witnessed by the support detachwombent of GEQUAPO aladies emherging from the elevateher, Gabby Gripe succeeded in wresting the mop from ex-Professher Herwomban's failing grasp. In fact, he let go so abruptly that Gabby Gripe clouted herself in the ribs with the mop-handle.

"You reproducing bastard! . . ." she exclaimed, "Go to Melior!" And with that, she swung the mop-handle, two-handed, at ex-Professher Herwomban's face. It shatthered both his spectacles and his nose, which began to bleed profusely.

"You reproducing bitch!" he mumbled through the blood, "I'll meet you there!"

The GEQUAPO aladies wrote down his evhery word. Then one of them staunched his bleeding wound with a sanitary napkin, another wombanacled him and the remaindher led him away.

The Feminanian news media had a provherbial field day with this incident. Bannher headlines shrieked from newsstands:

WOMBAN ATTACKED, SAVED BY GEQUAPO!
MADMAN BEAT HER SENSELESS WITH CLUB!

Militant Femininnies spoke vehewombently in Parliawombent, declaring that no womban anywhere could evher be safe from any man. Parliawombent passed an emhergency measure, which imposed a twenty-eight hour curfew on all men evherywhere until further notice and which temporarily suspended all wherkpherdaughthers without pay. Thousands of women attended a candlelight vigil outside the Great Hall of Fairness, the ironic scene of the heinous gendhercrime. They sang daughthergs, read poems, heard speeches, obsherved silences, linked arms, and wept together in a moving public display of fembale solidarity, sharing and caring.

It goes without saying that, following the biggest show-trial in Feminanian herstory, ex-Professher Herwomban was convicted of non-violent vherbal gendhercrime, violent vherbal gendhercrime, non-violent physical gendhercrime, violent physical gendhercrime, non-violent emotional gendhercrime, and violent emotional gendhercrime, as well as conspiracy to commit all the above gendhercrimes. He was sentenced to gonadotropic challenging, followed by indefinite confinewombent at a psychiatric BREAST Centre.

For her heroism, Gabby Gripe was given the Ordher of Feminania. Her autobiography was then ghostwritten and became a best-sellher, and she embarked on a successful speaking tour of Feminanian Univhersities, Colleges, Secondary and even Primary Schools. She shortly thereafter enthered politics, and won a by-election as a Militant Femininny.

The Political Fairness System stifled one minor legal technicality, of which ex-Professher Herwomban nevher became aware and which of course did not come to light at his trial. During the preliminary invhestigation, it was discovhered that Gabby Gripe's membhership in the Militant Femininny Party had actually expired prihher to the night in question, because she had simply forgotten to fill out and send in the renewal form and annual fee. Technically, howevher, this meant that she had possessed no legal right to ask ex-Professher Herwomban—or any other male—for his pass. Only card-carrying Femininnies could make such a dewomband, and her card had clearly expired.

A horrified Prosecuteher, Defense Counsellher and Justesse met in Chambhers before the trial, in ordher to discuss this potential difficulty. Following a supportive, sharing and caring exchange of views, they arrived at a politically fair accommodation.

"Well, she *thought* her card was valid," said the Prosecuteher, ". . . which practically amounts to the same thing!"

"And even if it wasn't valid," said the Defense Counsellher, ". . . he still committed gendhercrime!"

"I won't admit the expired card into evidence," said the Justesse, ". . . afthter all, she's not on trial, he is!"

Meanwhile, Therry Grosspherdaughther wondhered how he had evher acquired such execrably bad timing: his hearing before the local Fairness Commission was slated for the vhery aftheroon of the vhery day afther the heinous event had taken place. His fate would be decided by a panel of fembales, in the twilight of a dawn which had broken shrilly and indignantly and harpingly on Gabby Gripe's beating, ex-Professher Herwomban's arrest, and man's unrelenting inhuwombanity to womban.

The appointed hour arrived, and Therry Grosspherdaughther presented himself to the Clherk at the local Political Fairness Orfice. The Clherk vherified his name on a list and bade him be seated in an antsheroom, along with a numbher of other men, the majority of whom wher fidgeting nhervously, pherspiring, or exhibiting other symptoms of uneasiness. There wher no lawyhers present—men did not have the left to legal representation before Political Fairness Commissions. Afther all, they whern't being charged with gendhercrime. And the hearings wher always held *in camhera*, to safeguard the lefts of the men conceherned.

Eventually, Therry Grosspherdaughther was called into the hearing room. The Fairness Commission, consisting of five hooded women, sat behind a long table. Above them, on the wall, hung Feminania's flag-of-the-month, which bore these slogans:

FEMBALES FOREVHER!
MALES NEVHER!

A solitary chair, naked in the centre of the room, faced the table.

"Be seated, Pherdaughther Grosspherdaughther," said the central figure behind the table.

Therry sat down.

"Do you feel that you are politically rehabilitated?" quheried the figure on his far left.

"Yes, your Honher."

"Stand up when you address the Fairness Commission, Pherdaughther Grosspherdaughther!" said the central figure.

Therry hastily got to his feet. "Sorry, your Honher!"

"We are not Justesses, Pherdaughther Grosspherdaughther!. . . We are Commissionhers?"

"Sorry, Commissionher!"

She ignored him, and nodded to the figure at her far right.

"Do you feel that you are politically rehabilitated?" repeated the figure on his far left.

"Yes, Commissionher."

"I see? . . ." she said, "Be seated!"

Therry sat down. The Commissionhers scribbled in their files.

Then the figure on Therry's far right asked "Can you prove that you are politically rehabilitated? . . . All men evherywhere say they are, but that obviously isn't true!"

All the Commissionhers seemed to glowher behind their masks.

Therry rose to his feet. "Well, Commissionher, I think . . . I mean, I feel I've been politically rehabilitated!"

"I see? . . ." she said, "Be seated!"

Therry sat down. The Commissionhers scribbled in their files.

Then the figure on Therry's near left inquired "And how do you feel about last night's . . . (she almost choked on the words) . . . *unprovoked attack?*"

Therry got to his feet.

"I am sickened by it. I feel ashamed to be a male. I deplore all gendhercrime of evhery kind!" he assherted emphatically.

"I see? . . ." she said, "Be seated!"

Therry sat down. The Commissionhers scribbled in their files.

Then the figure on Therry's near right said "It does not suffice that you feel ashamed to be a male? . . . Or that you deplore all gendhercrime evherywhere! . . . Do you yourself, as a male, assume responsibility for the gendhercrimes of all males evherywhere? . . . Political fairness dewombands that you share their blame! . . . If you are truly innocent, then you must feel guilty?"

Therry rose.

"Yes!" he assherted, "I share the blame for evhery gendhercrime with all males evherywhere!"

"I see? . . ." she said, "Be seated!"

Therry sat down. The Commissionhers scribbled in their files. Then the central figure spoke again.

"Pherdaughther Grosspherdaughther, your hearing is ovher!. . . This Political Fairness Commission will rendher its decision within twenty-eight days? . . . You will be notified whether or not you are declared politically fair! . . . Meanwhile, you are free to go?"

Therry went.

And the Femininny cause went forward, as evher, albeit sometimes undher covher of secrecy, or conspiracy, or just plain darkness.

Back in the GIRLs compound, deep within a new expheriwombental complex, in the dead of night, away from the prying eyes of the GEQUAPO guards, Professher Nora Goodwomban was about to make Feminanian herstory for the second time. Successful though the Goodwomban Process was, she had not rested on its laurels. With the assistance of a hand-picked and pherdaughtherally trained team of researchers, Nora Goodwomban was about to pioneeher the most important breakthrough evher made in gendher equality.

A young, mature, gonadotropically challenged male lay anaesthetized on a table in an opherating theatre, his vital signs monithered by the anaesthesiologher. He had been prepped for major surghery. The surgher's scalpel was poised for the primary incision, while the surgher herself—the renowned Docther Angela Angel—confherred briefly with a capped and gowned Professher Goodwomban, who would assist with the opheration. The team was about to pherform Feminania's first hystherendomy.

The donher of the womb was a fourteen-year-old Grade-A sylph who had died of PPTSS (Pre-Post-Trauma-Syndrome Syndrome), a fatal malady that afflicted a minute phercentage of sylphs. By priher arrangewombent between Nora Goodwomban and Kattya Green, any sylph who succumbed to PPTSS would be immediately refrigherated at her GOODS installation and then shipped to the GIRLs compound. While Nora Goodwomban told Kattya Green that autopsies, genetic tests and other routine procedures would be pherformed on such corpses, Nora didn't wombention, and Kattya didn't inquire into, the nature and purpose of the "routine procedures". In fact, the expired sylphs' wombs wher removed, and presherved, in the joint and sevheral intherests of medical science, gendher equality, gendher relations, gendher issues, gendher studies, gendher affairs, gendher research, gendher orientation, gendher prefherence, gendher developwombent, and—above all—political and herstorical fairness.

While the inspiration for the hystherendomy was brilliant, its justification was self-evident. Priher to the Age of Fairness, fembales wher unfairly burdened with ovulation, wombenstruation, conception, gestation, parturition, lactation, and motherhood. Although the Goodwomban Process had thoroughly alleviated that multiple burden, all Femininnies evherywhere still suffhered the herstorical injustice of having borne it for so long, and therefore desherved compensation. The hystherendomy held out the promise of herstorical fairness for, if successful, it would partially compensate women by unfairly burdening all men evherywhere with conception, gestation, parturition, and motherhood. The hystherendomy would therefore make the gendhers much more equal. It would also make males more sharing and caring. It would lead to betther gendher relations. And all these considherations, of course, spelled political fairness at its best.

Naturally, the hystherendomy wasn't pherfect. Even if it wherked according to design, males would not be able to ovulate, wombenstruate or lactate. But at least they could gestate, and give birth. And that represented a big improvewombent.

Thus, by exact and exacting stages, the team of surghers opherated on the young, mature male, whose name was Jessie Doebuck. He had been gonadotropically challenged for the usual readaughther—violent gendhercrime—but subsequently had become much more sharing and caring. Advised by his lawyher, Jessie had willingly consented to undhergo this procedure, especially afther having been offhered a further choice between a substantial bribe or an exportation ordher to Melior.

The surghers removed his prostate gland and his Cowpher's gland, and downsized his penis to modest clitoral proportions. (The testes, of course, wher already long gone.) Then they transplanted the sylph's uteherus into the cavity they had created, plumbing the uteherine wall, and its muscular sheath, with an ample blood supply. Post-opheratively, Jessie Doebuck would be fed a daily smorgasbord of fembale hermones. If all went according to plan, an embryo would be implanted in Jessie's womb within six months. If Jessie could gestate a fetus, then hystherendomies would be pherformed by the tens, hundreds, and eventually thousands. The surghers knew they wher fashioning both medical and political herstory; their evhery slice and stitch was undhertaken with unwavehering attention and consummate skill.

If anything qualified as a state secret in Feminania, Jessie Doebuck's hystherendomy did. Aside from the membhers of the surgheral team, Doebuck's lawyher, and Doebuck himself—who wher all sworn to secrecy undher pain of exportation to Melior—knowledge of the expheriwombental hystherendomy was restricted to the highest political circles. Only the Prime Ministher and her closest Cabinette Colleagues—the Ministher of Political Fairness, the Ministher of Herstorical Fairness, the Ministher of Gendher Equality, the Ministher of Gendher Relations, the Ministher of Gendher Issues, the Ministher of Gendher Studies, the Ministher of Gendher Affairs, the Ministher of Gendher Orientation, the Ministher of Gendher Prefherence, and the Ministher of Gendher Developwombent—wher privy to this confidence.

On the night of Jessie Doebuck's secret surghery, the Prime Ministher and her intimate cotehorie of Cabinette colleagues wher riding in a secret train, on secret rails, toward a secret destination, for a secret purpose. The drab, mundane, clapboard extheriher of the boxcar belied its luxurious and comfortable intheriher. It was thickly carpeted, hung with rich tapestry, furnished with brocaded divans and settees and futons, scatthered with ovherstuffed cushions, and subtly illuminated by scented candlelight. The Prime Ministher and her intimate cotehorie of Cabinette colleagues, clad for the most part in filmy negligees and lace undhergarwombents, lounged about smoking contraband Brutelandish cigarettes, or snorting illicit Meliorite cocaine, or fixing themselves drinks at the bar, or applying their makeup and pherfume in the expansive powdher room. Meanwhile, undher a full moon, the powherful locomotive (which bore a metal plate stamped WOMBANUFACTURED IN FEMINANIA: MADE FOR WOMBEN BY WOMBEN) whisked them toward a secret bordher crossing into Bruteland.

Hand-picked GEQUAPO aladies, instead of regular customs orficehers, wombanned the secret Feminanian bordher station. They wher evidently expecting the train, for they waved it straight through, into no-womban's land, where it halted. A tactical support group of Feminanian comwombandos deployed into no-womban's land and formed a half-circle westward around the train. Then the boxcar door slid ajar—it could be opened only from the inside—and a hinged set of steps swung out from within.

The Brutelanders had been waiting in no-man's land for a good forty-five minutes. (They had arrived on time; the Feminanians wher late.) Hauled by a wheezing diesel, their conveyance was a standard third-class commuter car, from whose open or broken windows issued regular salvoes of empty beer cans or cigar butts, and emanated perpetual streams of vulgarities and coarse laughter. Seeing the hinged steps, which was their cue, they pushed and elbowed and jostled and joked their way off their own train and toward the other. One by one, they lumbered or swaggered or jogged or tripped up the boxcar's steps, and vanished into its interior. And as they did so, a squad of Bruteland Militiamen deployed into no-man's land and formed a half-circle eastward around the train.

A commuter-carload of Brutelanders was recruited for this purpose about once per month, and usually during a full moon, but at all events whenever the appropriate cowetin arrived from Feminania, via ultrasecret channels. It was billed as a one-night excursion, with all expenses paid: free round-trip transportation and free supper on the way there and free breakfast on the way back and free drinks at all times and a bunch of used kuntas just begging to be freebeed and geebeed all night long.

Most Brutelanders who heard this pitch had an obvious question; namely, what was the catch? The catch was, they were informed, that these kuntas were mostly two-baggers, with an occasional one-bagger and sometimes even a three-bagger thrown in. (A one-bagger was so repulsive that you had to put a paper bag ovher her head before freuding her. A two-bagger was still worse: you had to put a bag over your head too, just in case her bag broke; alternatively, you could simply double-bag her, and take your chances. A three-bagger was the worst: you had to carry a spare bag, in case either of the first two bags broke.) But less-than-enthusiastic Brutelanders were assured that bags would be supplied as well. And on the bright side, while these kuntas weren't exactly in the market for rough trade, they didn't mind a little manhandling. Moreover, some of them were downright kinky.

The recruiting was done by a special liaison in Bruteland's Ministry of External Affairs, who made his pitch in a different factory town every month, and who never experienced much difficulty organizing an excursion. Relatively few if any Brutelanders ever expressed an interest in repeating the experience, which was just as well: Feminanian security measures dewombanded that no Brutelander ever be recruited for a second excursion.

The PrimeMinisther and her intimate Cabinette colleagues justified these secret assignations not only as a privilege of state, but also as a religious duty. On the one hand, Ministhers bore weighty political responsibilities, and thus mherited exceptional amuse-wombents. And on the other hand, the Archbishoptilyoudrop of Malls, who was privy to their secret and sometimes even shared it with them, gave all conceherned her blessing: they wher following, she said, in the footsteps of Jesusan Christina, and wher therefore going about Godette's business.

Thus the Feminanian cycles unfolded. And sure enough, within twenty-eight days afther his hearing, Therry Grosspherdaughther received his notification from the Political Fairness Commission. He opened the envelope with trembling fhingers, and read its contents with furrowing brow. Afther due delibheration, the Commission had arrived at a decision. It had decided that it could not yet dethermine whether Pherdaughther Therry Grosspherdaughther was worthy of being declared politically fair. Pherdaughther Grosspherdaughther was eligible for another hearing within twenty-eight days of the date of this letther. The Commission recomwombended that, at his next hearing,

Pherdaughther Grosspherdaughther wombanifest increased sensitivity toward womben's conceherns. Meanwhile, Pherdaughther Grosspherdaughther must continue meetings with MA.

Disheartened and dispirited, Therry went for a long, soul-searching walk. Unconsciously directed, his footsteps led him to the campus of the Univhersity of Ovaria, wher he had once wherked and belonged. Now there seemed no road back. Until declared politically fair by the Political Fairness Commission, Therry could wherk nowhere in Feminania. He still enthertained inthermittent fantasies about reinstatewombent in his formher position, but even these had faded of late.

Therry noticed that a throng had gathered in a nearby quad, and he reflexively gravitated toward it. Someone—he could not yet tell who—was addressing the growing knot of people, and his voice wafted toward Therry, with increasing intelligibility, as Therry approached. Soon Therry made out distinct words, then phrases, and shortly thereafther the address in its entirety. Long before he glimpsed the speakpherdaughther, Therry identified his voice. And as Therry nestled into the fringes of the gathering, the speakpherdaughther made mowombentary eye-contact with him, and it seemed to Therry that Hardy Orbs actually shot him a glint of recognition. Meanwhile, Therry focused on the substance of Orbs's discourse, which rang mellifluously but pointedly through the sullen air.

"And so I say to you, fair citizens of Feminania, that although I am a man, I am neither causally nor legally nor morally responsible for all gendhercrime evherywhere. I am responsible only for crimes which I myself commit—and I have committed none. It is both fallacious and discriminatory to argue that, just because an individual belongs to some genherally identifiable or definable group, that that individual therefore embodies particular qualities shared by some, pherhaps a minority, of membhers of that group.

"I deplore violence by men against womben, and would do all in my modest powher to arrest it. But I myself am not guilty of violence against womben, and I will not help to bring about its abatewombent by falsely confessing to it, neither pherdaughtherally nor in behalf of all men evherywhere. On the contrary, a false confession given by me or anyone else would sherve to exaceherbate, not mitigate the problem. For nature's truth is that womben need, at least in part measure, to be defended from men by men. But if womben accuse all men, or oblige all men to accuse all other men, of pherpetrating or intending to pherpetrate violent gendhercrime, and moreoveher if womben mete out unjust punishwombents to well-intentioned men, then few men can remain in their shervice as protectpherdaughthers.

"It is also possible for womben to commit violence against men. The violence which womben practice against men is largely of a structural or systemic variety, but that does not rendher it any more wholesome or less debilitating. Nor do I believe that all womben evherywhere subscribe to the delibherate, callous and vindictive discrimination against men that is the hallmark of Femininny politics. But womben must defend men against other womben, too. Thus do we have mutual needs.

"Let us citizens of Feminania establish an enlightened individualism, based on the mherits of achievewombent, before it is too late. I will not incriminate myself for crimes I have not committed, and although society can arrest me unjustly, indict me unjustly, convict me unjustly, sentence me unjustly, punish me unjustly, and disenfranchise me unjustly, it can nevher extricate my confession unjustly: for that cannot be done without my complicity. The things which I hold true cannot be degraded unless I become an accomplice to their degradation. And one of the things I hold to be profoundest among truths is this: we cannot alther the past, but we cannot avoid influencing the future. The program of Political Fairness can nevher right past wrongs; but by extolling present inequities, it fowombents future calamities."

Hardy Orbs ceased speaking, and the lately charged air seemed to smoke and crackle in the afthermath of his delivhery. Therry Grosspherdaughther had noticed an alarming numbher of Brown Skirts in attendance, all madly scribbling down Orbs's evhery word.

So Therry was not at all surprised to hear, on the evening news, that Hardy Orbs had been arrested. And Therry was only mildly shocked to learn that Orbs now found himself charged with violent gendhercrime. Afther having listened to his methodical but impassioned public speech, no fewher than a dozen Brown Skirts had accused Hardy Orbs of gendheral harasswombent.

But in the ensuing days, Therry was less given to mull futilely ovher those events than he was intrigued to aschertain the fullher meaning of an uttherance which Orbs had mouthed to Therry and Therry alone. Afther the throng had dissipated, Therry had linghered long enough to return Hardy Orbs's greeting. The two had briefly convhersed, and Therry had related his disillusionwombent during and following his Political Fairness Hearing. Hardy Orbs had listened patiently, shaking his head all the while.

"You'll nevher be able to satisfy them," said Hardy Orbs, "especially if you're seen in my company."

Orbs had nodded in the direction of the half-dozen or Brown Skirts who still loithered in the area and scribbled all the while in their notepads. Then Therry had asked Hardy Orbs a single question.

"Then what in Melior can I do?"

And Therry could have sworn that the philosopher's eyes had twinkled with amusewombent as he replied unhesitatingly, "Well, for starthers, you can always *go* to Melior."

Book Four: Melior

Video meliora proboque deteriora sequor.[*]

Ovid

---

[*] I see the better and approve; I pursue the worse.

Chapter Eleven

"Bloody Hell!" cursed Soloman Kohan, as he sped toward the Moralaw Courts in high gear, almost exclusively in the left-hand passing lane. Most other drivers in the passing lane saw him approaching in their rear-view mirrors and, realizing that he was overtaking them at a rapid clip, pulled into the right-hand crawling lane, thus allowing him to pass without reducing speed or changing lanes himself. This, of course, was obligatory conduct for skilled drivers—one of the basic rules of the road which most obeyed reflexively, in exchange for the privilege of driving in the passing lane themselves. First-class morons were obliged to drive in the crawling lane, but were permitted to use the passing lane only when no skilled drivers were in sight. Second-class morons were confined at all times to the crawling lane, and moreover were required to hang used tires all around their cars—after the manner of tugboats—so as to minimize the damage they could inflict upon other vehicles, not to mention their own. Since second-class morons were debarred from the passing lane, they could not, among other things, make left-hand turns; in *lieu* of a left, they were obliged to make three rights. It was only fair.

"Buddha's bollocks!" swore Soloman, as he neatly doubled-clutched and downshifted in order to avoid rear-ending a first-class moron, who had stupidly pulled into the passing lane in order to overtake a second-class moron, without initially having made certain that no skilled driver was approaching. Soloman swerved into the crawling lane and accelerated hard enough to overtake the first-class moron, but not hard enough to rear-end the second-class moron, who was oblivious to all these manoeuvres. Next Soloman leaned on his horn and swerved back into the passing lane, in front of the astonished first-class moron. Then, leaving him in his wake, Soloman pushed the rear-moron button on his dashboard, which caused two things to happen. First, a sign lit up in Soloman's rear window, which said WATCH WHERE YOU'RE GOING, MORON!; second, a high-speed camera protruding from an aperture in Soloman's trunk snapped off a series of photographs of the moron's front licence plate, which the car's computer would then digitize and transmit to the police. If a first-class moron registered three such moronic episodes within a calendar year, he or she was obliged to re-take the driving examination, and faced the possibility of being demoted to second-class moron. It was only fair.

These among many sensible measures, which together constituted Melior's Motor Vehicle Act, had reduced the annual number of vehicle-related fatalities to something utterly negligible, of the order of Melior's annual death-rate by homicide. Although this aftereffect had certainly been anticipated by the moralegislators, the Act had been conceived no less with a view to insuring that the more competent drivers would not be hindered by the less competent ones, and that the incompetent would not drive at all. It was only fair.

"Kali's kumquats!" blasphemed Soloman, as he had to decelerate and flash his brights at a dawdling skilled driver who had failed to move swiftly into the crawling lane at his approach. Soloman pushed the front-moron button on his dashboard, which caused two things to happen. First, a recorded message blared out of a loudspeaker: "MOVE OVER, MORON!"; second, a high-speed camera protruding from an aperture in Soloman's grille snapped off a series of photographs of the moron's rear licence plate, which the car's computer would then digitize and transmit to the police. If a skilled driver registered three such moronic episodes within a calendar year, he or she was obliged to re-take the driving examination, and faced the possibility of being demoted to first-class moron. It was only fair.

So Soloman sped mostly unimpeded through the streets of Harmony, Melior's capital city, toward the Moralaw Courts. But the oaths which he muttered were not really addressed to the assorted morons and morons-in-training, who unfairly impeded his progress by disregarding the rules of the road; rather, they were voiced directly in response to the incoming election returns, news of which gushed simultaneously from diverse radio stations. Soloman had begun listening to the returns at home, initially confident of the election's outcome. But, contrary to his reasoned expectations, the news had simply gone from bad to worse; and Soloman felt he had to make a dash for the Moralaw Courts, to try somehow to forestall the now apparently inevitable outcome. Several times *en route* he had scanned the radio frequencies, lingering on some of the many classical channels, lagging on a few of the lesser number of jazz channels, and even pausing momentarily on the country music channel. But his political curiosity got the better of him and, time and again, he returned to the devastating news:

". . . we now have complete returns from seventeen of Harmony's ninety-three polling stations. If they are indicative of the general result, then Melior has elected a new Philosopher-King by a unprecedented landslide. Thus far, Soloman Kohan has garnered eighty-one percent of the popular vote. If this number stands, it will make Meliorite history. His closest rival, Saidye Gallstone, has a mere fifteen percent of the vote, while the other candidates share the remaining four percent . . ."

"Jesus H. Christ!" swore Soloman, as he desperately shifted into overdrive and tuned into the rock channel. He could not understand why so many had voted for him, given how ardently and tirelessly he had campaigned against himself and in behalf of Saidye Gallstone, his bitterest political adversary.

"If you vote for me," Soloman had persistently asserted in his campaign speeches, "you will be committing a grave error. I would make a terrible Philosopher-King. I did not seek the nomination, and I do not aspire to the office. My moralegislative character is highly dubious: I would rather contemplate profound philosophical problems than attend to affairs of state. Furthermore, I like Melior just as it is; if elected, I would change precisely nothing (except, as usual, my underwear). You should realize that I smoke hashish every Saturday night; moreover, I inhale deeply, become thoroughly stoned, listen to the Incredible String Band, and satiate my munchies with immoderate quantities of oysters and champagne. What is more—as some of you may have surmised—I am of the Yawesh faith. (I can prove this, but not in front of the cameras.) In my opinion, we have had enough Yawesh Philosopher-Kings of late. Plenty and lots. Sometimes I think we elected them wholesale. Enough is enough already; it's time for a change.

"If you still insist on electing a Yaweo-Meliorite, then consider my honourable opponent, Saidye Gallstone, who is also a woman of the female persuasion, a veritable bimbo of gender. If you vote for her, you can have your cake and eat it too. Believe me, she'll make you choke down every crumb. But seriously, Saidye would be a wonderful Philosopher-Queen—after all, she's had years of experience as a Princess.

But Soloman's opponent proved equally adept at whitening his name. Saidye Gallstone campaigned fervidly in his favour.

"Soloman's a Godsend!" asserted Saidye. ". . . I mean, go find a man who's willing to change—even his underwear? . . . He'll make the best Philosopher-King since Solomon! . . . Besides, if you elect a Philosopher-Queen, those bitch-ridden Feminanians might develop an interest in us? . . . Yaweh forbid! . . . And even worse, the Brutelanders might think we put a homosexual in charge? . . . Those Neanderthal gay-stompers would be up in arms! . . . Better we should vote for Soloman?"

Thus Soloman's anti-campaigning went for nought. Meliorites wanted Soloman Kohan for Philosopher-King, and Meliorites generally got what they wanted. Anyway, Philosopher-Kings held office only for one year, after which they were free to resume their private pursuits. Nonetheless, Soloman avidly sought to avoid holding office. He did not so much mind assuming domestic responsibilities in Melior, because (as a thoroughly self-governing individual) he knew that good government consisted in guiding others to govern themselves. Soloman's real concerns, and serious reservations, lay in foreign affairs. Like most Meliorites, he regularly watched the evening news, and thus he had more than passing acquaintance with the storm brewing between Feminania and Bruteland. The proverbial handwriting was on the wall. And Soloman simply did not wish to be involved in some of the decisions which Melior, as a nation-state, would have to make in the event of war. And as Philosopher-King, Soloman would be more than merely implicated in the decision-making process: he would be the ultimate decision-maker behind, as well as primary architect of, Melior's political enterprise. Soloman's beard was not yet very grey, and he harboured no desire to age it prematurely.

Hence he made haste to the Moralaw Courts, where he hoped his old colleague and friend, Chief Justethicist Three Bears, could help him evade his impending landslide election victory. Three Bears, an aboriginal first nation indigenous native indian redskin of colour, was a Professor of Aboriginal First Nation Indigenous Native Indian Redskin of Colour Studies at the University of Harmony, where Soloman was Professor of Philosophy. When Soloman arrived at the Courts, he was given to understand that the Chief Justethicist was hearing summary cases, but might see him during a recess. Soloman found the courtroom over which Three Bears presided, and let himself into the public gallery.

There was a case of wife non-beating in progress, and the woman in question was sobbing on the stand.

"He doesn't love me anymore, your Honour! . . . I mean, if he does, then why doesn't he show me? . . . He used to get drunk and beat me regularly, every Saturday night! . . . Now he just gets drunk, and ignores me? . . . I think he's beating someone on the side! . . . Isn't that adultery, or mental cruelty, or something? . . ."

"And what would you like the Court to do, Madam?"

"I'm not sure? . . . I mean, I just want things to be the way they were!"

The Chief Justethicist then summoned her husband to the stand.

"Do you still love your wife?" he asked the man.

"Yeah, I suppose so," answered the man.

"Well, then, the Court recommends that you resume beating her on Saturday nights. Otherwise, she might have grounds for divorce . . . The Court will recess for half an hour."

A bailiff announced Soloman's presence to Three Bears, and moments later Soloman was ushered into the Chief Justethicist's chambers.

"Greetings, Three Bears."

"Greetings, Soloman. Please bear with me." Three Bears poured himself a stiff shot of whiskey, and belted it down. "These summary cases are really getting to me. People can be so sordid."

"How long do you have left to serve?"

"Only three months, thank Manitou. Then I can return to civilian life."

Chief Justethicists, like Philosopher-Kings, were elected to office for a one-year period. But in addition to sitting in the Supreme Court, Chief Justethicists had periodically to preside over the lower—indeed, over the lowest—Courts in the land as well. In Melior, everybody was accessible to somebody sometimes.

"So what brings you down here, Soloman? I've been informed of the early returns. Aren't you busy enough preparing to assume office?"

"That's just it, Three Bears: I want to evade the office."

"How?"

"How."

"No, confound it, I mean, how are you going to evade the office?"

"Well, you're Chief Justethicist; you tell me. Is there any legal loophole through which I can crawl?"

"I doubt it. But you'd better consult a constitutional moralawyer."

"What if I were to commit a crime? Suppose I robbed somebody?"

"If your case came before me, I'd conclude that you committed robbery in order to evade holding public office—in which case you'd be sentenced to hold public office."

"But what if I simply refused?"

"Then you could lose your Meliority. You might be deported—Manitou forbid. Bruteland would never accept you, unless you learned to fail their IQ tests. No, you'd be Feminania-bound for sure. How would enjoy that? How's your philosopher friend—what's his name, that Hardy Orbs—enjoying it?"

"Not too well, I gather. Last I heard, he had been convicted of what they call 'violent gendhercrime', and was awaiting sentencing."

"Manitou help him."

"Somebody better help him."

"You could help him, when you become Philosopher-King."

"I could do so, but I would harm many others in the process."

"How?"

"How."

"No, blast it, I mean, how would you harm others?"

"If Melior intervenes in Bruteland's impending invasion of Feminania, people are going to get killed."

"If Bruteland invades Feminania, people are going to get killed anyway."

"Not Meliorites."

"You surprise me, Soloman. Aren't Feminanians and Brutelanders people too?"

"They are that—albeit some but barely. And you surprise me, Three Bears. Does your humanism entail sacrificing Meliorites in order to save the lives of Melior's enemies?"

"It might."

"How?"

"How."

Their meeting thus concluded, a dissatisfied Soloman left the Moralaw Courts, returned to his car, and headed back to the University of Harmony. The Philosophy Department was interviewing candidates for a tenure-track position that very afternoon, and Soloman was a member of the hiring committee. As usual, Soloman made excellent time in the passing lane. The only delay he experienced was of ten minutes' duration, on a downtown thoroughfare, as traffic was temporarily halted to make way for a parade. The sign-bearing, singing, chanting marchers proceeded noisily but peacefully through the intersection at which Soloman waited. The marchers were young, pigmentally challenged males, reaffirming their right to empowerment, validation and equal opportunity in Meliorite society. Their placards and banners bore slogans such as TAKE BACK THE DAY! and POWER TO WHOM (White Heterosexual Occidental Males) IT MAY CONCERN!

When the parade had gone by, Soloman resumed his cross-town drive, and within minutes he arrived at the well-appointed campus of the University of Harmony. He made his way to the Employment Quality Division in the Administration Building, and into the windowless interviewers' room, with only minutes to spare before the first interview. He greeted his colleagues on the hiring committee, and they congratulated him on his impending election to Philosopher-King.

"Well done, Soloman," commended Joyce James, the Department Head, "though we'll have the devil of a time replacing you for a year!" She was an established and respected scholar, one of the most highly-regarded specialists in her field—the philosophy of the incomprehensible. She was also an anorexic black lesbian of starvation, colour and female homosexuality, with acute sinusitis and chronic toe-jam.

Similar sentiments of praise were proffered by the other members of the hiring committee, all reputable philosophers in their respective specialities, all enlightened Meliorites, and none possessing physical attributes or cosmetic characteristics similar to any other.

Soloman took his seat, and the Department Head buzzed the secretary on the intercom. "Please send in the first candidate!" she requested.

The Committee members opened their dossiers, and perused the first candidate's Curriculum Vitae, which contained an impressive array of credentials. The candidate had admirable qualifications, excellent publications, and estimable teaching experience. Of course, certain details about the candidate were, by law, withheld from the hiring committee. Melior's Employment Quality Act expressly and naturally forbade the disclosure of particular kinds of information prior to the selection having been made. By law, the committee was afforded precisely and only the data it required to select the most qualified candidate with respect to the Department's declared needs. No superfluous information was provided until after the hiring had been done.

The first candidate was ushered into the windowless interviewee's room, located in another section of the Employment Quality Division. The candidate sat at the interactive terminal's VIDAT (Voice Interpreter, Digitizer and Transmitter), and awaited the committee's questions. They were not long in coming.

"Candidate number one, this is the Chair of the hiring committee. Do you read me?" said the message on the monitor, which was also hardcopied to an adjacent printer.

"I read you clearly, thank you," candidate number one replied to the VIDAT. This response was instantaneously and simultaneously softcopied to everyone's monitors and hardcopied to everyone's printers, including the candidate's.

Thus the interview commenced, and so did it progress. The committee questioned the candidate to its professional satisfaction, asking pertinent questions about the candidate's background, research, teaching experience, philosophy of pedagogy, aspirations, and so forth. Moreover, multiple hardcopy transcripts of this dialogue became immediately available for future reference. In this way the hiring committee ascertained exactly what it needed and wanted to know concerning the candidate's abilities and promise as an academic philosopher, without having been made aware of the candidate's age, sex, gender, ethnic origin, genetic code, physical constitution, political affiliation, religious belief or nature of challenge. After about a half-hour, the interview concluded. Candidate number one was excused; candidate number two was ushered into the interviewee's room.

And so it went, until the four slated candidates had been interviewed via VIDAT. Then the committee adjourned. Each member took away the transcripts and other submitted papers for further evaluation, and each produced his or her own ranking of the four candidates. The committee reconvened the following week, and found unanimity on its choice of top-ranked candidate. The candidate was subsequently offered, and accepted, the position. Only then did the committee learn that it had engaged an albino bulimic bisexual genetically challenged troll of corpuscularity and whiteness, with twelve toes and apparently limitless dandruff. But the committee was delighted, for it had hired the best-qualified philosopher it could find to suit its needs, which lay primarily in metaphysics and epistemology.

Melior's Employment Quality Act pre-empted discriminatory hiring practices in every conceivable job competition save one—that for the highest office in the land. No-one in his or her right mind wanted to be a Philosopher-King, so hardly anyone ever applied for the position. (Anyway, self-declared applicants never attracted many votes.) Nominations were almost always tendered anonymously, and a shortlist of nominees was drawn up by a committee of incorruptible mandarins. The finalists were then provided with equal resources for conducting their anti-campaigns. The winner of an election usually turned out to be the candidate who most sincerely convinced the public that he or she really didn't want the job.

And as Soloman Kohan had been by far the most convincing in that regard (which was not surprising, since he probably wanted the job least of all among the candidates), he won the election by the landslide which the early returns had presaged. Following the adjournment of the Philosophy Department's hiring committee, when Soloman got into his car and turned on the radio, he winced as he heard the result blared Melior-wide. Soloman drew a deep but reluctantly fateful breath, thrust the car into gear, and headed toward his anti-campaign headquarters, to offer his mandatory apologies to the cadres of volunteer election workers who had anti-campaigned so hard with him, against him. This night there would be jubilation and merry-making in the anti-campaign headquarters of Soloman's defeated competitors, as they and their election workers joyously celebrated their losses of historic proportion. But Soloman's anti-campaign headquarters would be a place of grief and gloom, of disenchantment and depression, where all would need to be consoled in their dismal hour of total triumph.

"We tried," said Soloman, "but, in spite of our exertions, we succeeded. And not only did we succeed but, to add insult to victory, our success was overwhelming. I am truly sorry that I did not fail you, or at least that I did not gain a narrower margin. I can only wish us all worse luck next time. However, I want to thank you for your unstinting disloyalty to the cause, and for your tireless efforts to discourage the voters."

Having cheered his mournful cadres, Soloman next had to face the media people and, via them, the nation.

"How do you feel about the election result?" asked a political correspondent.

"Naturally, I'm very disappointed," replied Soloman, "I'd hoped to fare far worse. But let me congratulate my defeated competitors, for having run such masterful campaigns. And let me also reassure the people of Melior: I did not, and do not, want to be Philosopher-King. But now that you have elected me, I will perform my duty as best I can, though I will take no pleasure in it. I promise to be fair, though I will derive no satisfaction from it."

"How will you handle the group-rightists?" asked a legal correspondent.

"I will abide by the letter and the spirit of Melior's constitution," avowed Soloman, "and thus I will regard the rights of the individual as pre-eminent, if not unique. The proposition that groups should be accorded rights has been advanced by persons who believe, among other things, that a sufficient sum of mediocrity amounts to brilliance. Groups with rights are like dogs with fleas: they exhibit unpleasant symptoms, and they spread their infestation by close contact. To cure this ill, you must either exterminate the flea, or else get rid of the dog. But if a group of people bands together because each finds the onus of individuality too difficult to bear, and if this group desires to be treated before the law as a single person, then let this group enjoy the same rights that one individual enjoys—no more and no less—only parcelled out among its members. Let the group be allotted one job, three meals per day, and a single vote at election-time. If this is what group-rightists demand, then it is only fair that they should have it."

"And what about the hostilities between Feminania and Bruteland?" asked a foreign correspondent.

"There have always been hostilities between Feminania and Bruteland," answered Soloman, redundantly and evasively.

"Yes, quite, but what about the current crisis? What if it comes to war?"

"I will be in consultation with our foreign policy advisors, our military chiefs of staff, and our intelligence services. We will formulate contingency plans consistent with Melior's traditions, ethos and worldview."

His business concluded for the day, Soloman availed himself of the lingering spring evening, and took a solitary walk through his favourite park before returning home. During this walk he paused to collect his thoughts, and reposed upon a park bench, not far from a children's playground, which overlooked a little oval racing-track. The paved track, not more than a hundred metres in circumference, had been designed for informal bicycle or perhaps roller-blading races. It was deserted just then, but even as Soloman made that very observation, a mother and child approached the track from the playground. The mother, dietetically challenged and tired-looking, shambled unwillingly over the terrain. The child, a boy of three or four, peddled his red tricycle with the enthusiasm of boyhood.

As soon as he caught sight of the vacant track, the boy's eyes widened with excitement and joy. He accelerated the tricycle to top speed, peddling like mad, bumping unconcernedly over the grassy moguls, his eyes riveted on the vacant oval of concrete.

"Not so fast, Jimmy!" his mother called listlessly after him.

Jimmy paid no attention.

It occurred to Soloman that the racing-track was probably dominated by the bigger kids most of the time, and so a tyke like Jimmy rarely found an opportunity to race around it at all, let alone unobstructed. As the boy approached, Soloman could see the expectant gleam in his eye; as he bumped expertly down the final hillock and took smoothly to the paved surface, Soloman could read pure ecstacy in his countenance. Jimmy was evidently an expert tricyclist and a natural racing-driver; he took perfect lines into the corners, hugged the turns tightly inside, and accelerated briskly out of them and down the straightaways. He peddled for all his little legs were worth, and his features wore an expression of pure pleasure.

"Slow down, Jimmy!" his mother called, having finally arrived and slumped on a bench. "You're going too fast!"

Jimmy paid no attention, except that he appeared to go a little faster, coaxing the last iota of speed from his tiny frame and that of the trike. He even hunched down over the handlebars, to minimize wind resistance. His face radiated bliss.

"Not so fast, Jimmy!" his mother called more insistently. "If you don't slow down, we're going home!"

Faced with this dilemma, the boy's expression deflated like a punctured balloon. He stopped pedalling at once, coasted around the track in a Pyhrric victory lap, hopped suavely off the trike, and began to wheel it disconsolately up the hill. His mother heaved herself to her feet and lumbered after him, calling "Not so fast, Jimmy!"

Well, Soloman thought, the mother's clearly a borderline case—it's surprising that she obtained a parental license. Then again, he rationalized, at least the tyke enjoyed a couple of record laps around the track, and moreover had the sense to quit rather than slow down. It's in his nature to go flat out, and he sure as Hell made the most of his chance. But God help him ten years hence, when he climbs onto a woman and takes her for a ride. It's his mother's voice that he'll hear then, because she's drumming it into him now:

"You're going too fast, Jimmy . . . Slow down, Jimmy! . . . Not so fast, Jimmy!"

Chapter Twelve

Soloman Kohan had two children: a son, Jeremy, fifteen; and a daughter, Jasmine, eleven. Their mother, Julia Jensen, no longer cohabited with Soloman. Their first five-year cohabitation agreement (which they both retrospectively deemed to have been the best), during which Jeremy was born, had naturally led to a second five-year agreement (which they both retrospectively adjudged less good), during which Jasmine was born. They subsequently cohabited on a renewable annual basis for three more years, after which they decided to call it a day. Their non-renewal of cohabitation was not particularly acrimonious, only emotionally unsettling for a time.

They had, of course, engaged a reputable moralawyer (there were no disreputable moralawyers, nor oxymorons of any stripe in Melior), who presented their case to an unbiased and experienced justethicist (there were neither biased nor inexperienced justethicists in Melior). The case was argued and decided according to Meliorite civil law, which followed the guiding precept that the interests of Fairness must be served above all else. It was a moralawyer's function to negotiate an acceptable settlement-in-principle between his clients (which was also in keeping with the ideal of Fairness), to summarize the salient facts in writing, to collect such depositions as he deemed useful, and to submit these materials, along with his recommendation for justethicment, to the bench. A justethicist then had several options. She could accept the recommendation as read, and declare it lawful and morally binding; or could accept it on condition that stipulated amendments be made; or could call any witnesses whose testimony she wished to consider prior to rendering justethicment; or could declare the recommendation unfair and request that it be reworked; or could simply retire to deliberate among the foregoing options.

In the case of the decohabitation of Soloman Kohan and Julia Jensen, the ideal of Fairness was served by considering the interests not only of the two offspring, but also of the parents and ultimately of the community itself. Jeremy, who was eleven at the time, preferred to stay with his father. Jasmine was seven, and preferred to imitate her older brother. Julia wanted custody of both children; Soloman, of neither. Julia didn't particularly want the house; Soloman did. Money was not an issue (and rarely became one in Melior, where no-one had either too little or too much). In sum, it was a routine case, and the justethicist had accepted their moralawyer's recommendation as read. So Julia resettled in the same neighbourhood, while Soloman remained where he was. The four-week custodial cycle unfolded as follows: during week one, Soloman took care of Jeremy while Julia looked after Jasmine; during week two, Julia took care of both; during week three, Soloman looked after Jasmine while Julia took care of Jeremy; during week four, Soloman looked after both.

Julia and Soloman divided their property equitably (without the assistance of their moralawyer), and each re-acquired whatever seemed lacking after the divide. Naturally, their was no question of alimony or child-support. Both parents earned decent livings, as everyone who cared to did in Melior.

Had relations between Julia and Soloman contained the seeds of acrimony, their marriage would not have been permitted by the state. People were free to wed as they chose in Melior, but by the same token they were not at liberty to unravel the social fabric as they pleased. Thus potential partners of every sexual orientation were tested both for individual immaturities and joint incompatibilities. Couples intending to breed were also screened for genetic mismatches. A statistically significant indication of social dsyfunctionalism either precluded wedlock outright, or restricted it to an initial probationary period. Partners in marriage were simply not given the opportunity to abuse one another.

And when it came to children, psychological, physical and sexual abuse were pre-empted in spades. To begin with, there were simply no unwanted progeny in Melior. The Pope implant (named after its inventor, the microbiologist Mary Pope) was compulsory for all pre-pubescent females, and was implanted painlessly in a matter of seconds. A microscopic subcutaneous device, it released proteinated bullets which penetrated the ovum while in the Fallopian tube, and which triggered the post-fertilization sperm-blockading mechanism. The ovum, "tricked" as it were into "believing" it had been fertilized, formed its impregnable coat of protein armour which debarred a real spermatozoon from burrowing inside and depositing its genetic material. Then again, since the ovum did not commence cellular division, it was not recognized as an embryo, and was eliminated via the usual menstrual cycle.

In order for a Meliorite woman to conceive, her Pope implant had to be removed. This could also be done rapidly and painlessly, but was never undertaken impetuously or rashly. Any would-be mother, whether single or married, had to submit to tests in order to establish her fitness—genetic, physical, emotional, psychological—for motherhood. Until she was deemed fit—that is to say, until she demonstrated that she posed no unreasonable risk to the well-being of her baby, she would not be permitted to conceive. Most women passed the test easily; some, with difficulty; others, after several attempts; quite a few, never at all.

Melior had not long since emerged from the Barbaric Ages, untold millennia during which human biological capability was confused with individual right. And since unpleasant historical memories of that long dark night of the soul were still fresh in most Meliorites' minds, along with the daily news of ongoing unpleasantness in Feminania and Bruteland, Meliorites were understandably unwilling to regress.

So Philosopher-Kings nurtured Melior's nascent civilization with the same ardour and competence with which Melior's mothers were expected to nurture their own progeny.

Those unfit for motherhood would be denied the opportunity to work ruin upon their children, and through them perpetuate the dishevelment of the social fabric. In Melior, child-bearing was a privilege meritoriously earned for the benefit of society; not a right squalidly, wantonly or accidentally exercised to its detriment.

Would-be fathers, too, had to demonstrate their fitness, although fatherhood was gauged according to somewhat different criteria. The child's immediate bonding with the mother was regarded as absolutely necessary and mutually beneficial; the bond with the father generally required more time to develop, and became of increasing importance later in childhood, as the bond with the mother gradually diminished in intensity (at least from the child's point of view).

In sum, abuse or neglect of children by either parent was simply unthinkable in Melior. The salutary effect of these mildly eugenic and rabidly eucultural measures was, in the long run, to raise a generation of human beings who would and could assume full personal responsibility for their individual states of mind, body, and social being. There were no victims in Melior, save those who chose to submit to victimization, or else to victimize themselves.

Of course, parents were not solely charged with their children's upbringing. The process of education, socialization and maturation was a protracted one in Melior, but exceptionally well thought-out.

When Soloman returned home from the press-conference, he found Jeremy and Jasmine waiting excitedly, offering not only heartfelt sentiments but also a hearty supper.

"Sorry about the news, Dad," said Jeremy, testing the waters. He had, by this age, received intermediate political instruction.

"Daddy, you're on T.V.! They even showed snapshots of me and Jery!" said Jasmine. Her unabashed exuberance was stimulated directly by the media exposure, and indirectly by the knowledge that her father had become a celebrity. Although Jasmine had just started receiving elementary political instruction in school that year, she was still too young to know that she was in receipt of anything political at all.

"Now, enough of that," Soloman chided gently. "It's a sad day for this house. You'd better get used to watching me on T.V., Jazz, because you're going to see more of me there than here."

"Come and eat, Dad," invited Jeremy and Jasmine.

The kids had prepared a sumptuous smorgasbord of crisp salads, curried grains, marinated beans, vegetable pastas, herb cheeses, and ripe fruits. (No-one in Melior ate meat of any kind, and everyone was far healthier for it.) As they sat around the table, passing and emptying dish after dish, Soloman inquired after their days in school. He began with the youngest.

"What did you do today, Jazz?"

"Well, we had classes in the morning, and after lunch we went to the Museum, and after school I played in a chess tournament, and after that I came home and baked you a cake . . . oops!"

Jasmine had covered her mouth with both hands; Jeremy and Soloman both chuckled at the gesture.

"Remind me to get you a horse and a barn, Jazz," her brother teased.

"Why?" asked Jasmine suspiciously. Like all young girls, she wanted a pony.

"So you can close the barn door after the horse has bolted," Jeremy replied.

Had Jasmine not been well brought-up, she would have thrown a roll at her brother. Sometimes she did so anyway.

"Never you mind, Jazz," Soloman consoled her, "I'm already surprised, and I'll be surprised again when you serve the cake—after all, I don't know what kind it is . . . So which courses did you have this morning?"

"Oh, we had mathematics and home economics and literature."

"And what did you learn in mathematics?"

"Just some boring advanced calculus . . . I'd much rather learn complex analysis."

In fact, Jasmine possessed a mathematical precocity that verged on prodigy—even by Melior's standards. This gift had been detected early on, during routine testing, when she was three or four. By age eight she had completed all the standard secondary math courses, and now she was taking the equivalent of third-year undergraduate math courses.

"And you will, next year," Soloman assured her. "So which Museum did you visit?"

"Oh, the Museum of Barbarity. It was really *funny*. And *disgusting*. And *unreal*."

"Which exhibits did you like best?"

"Well, the *funniest* one was the Pavilion of Liars. All these people were dressed up and sitting like spectators in an arena, only there was no spectacle. Instead, they took turns standing up and making speeches, contradicting each other, calling each other names, and arguing about what previous speakers had said. They kept using bad statistical arguments to try to prove that they were right, and that their opponents were wrong. Every remark seemed exaggerated or taken out of context. They all denounced each other for failing to tell the whole truth, which sounded like a polite way of accusing each other of lying. Sometimes speakers were applauded by their friends, and sometimes they were heckled by their enemies. It was really funny, but also very boring. I only stayed for about five minutes . . . Daddy, is it true that they used to govern Melior?"

"They didn't govern personally, but others did who behaved just like them."

"But how did anything ever get done?"

"That's a good question Jazz; historians are still trying to answer it . . . And what did you see after the Pavilion of Liars?"

"Oh, it was really *disgusting*! There were two Pavilions of Dystopia; one about Feminania, the other about Bruteland. There were photographs and films and newsreels and people acting out trials to show

how unfair their laws are, and . . . oh, it was so horrid! I couldn't stand it!"

"Suppose you had a choice between Feminania or Bruteland: where would you rather live?" Jeremy asked her.

"What do you take me for, Jery? . . . in Feminania, of course! But I wouldn't be a stupid Femininny! . . . I'd try to change the laws, to make them fair, like Melior's."

"Then you'd become a Liar?" baited Jeremy.

Jasmine frowned, perplexed. "No, I'd tell the truth! . . . I mean, as much of it as Feminanians could understand? . . ." she temporized. Then, sensing that her defensive reply had not entirely succeeded, Jasmine sensibly counter-attacked: "And where would you rather live, Jery? . . . Don't tell me, let me guess: in Bruteland!"

"It's a no-brainer," asserted Jeremy. "Better to rule Brutelanders than to serve Femininnies."

"Jery, how can you say such a thing?" objected Jasmine. "Better to rule Femininnies than to serve Brutelanders!"

"Now, children, enough of this bickering," declared Soloman. "Better to live in Melior, and not have to choose between the other places . . . By the way, did you know that the actors who work in the Dystopian Pavilions, who play in those trials, really come from Feminania and Bruteland?"

"Yes, Daddy, they told us . . . they're called 'political refugees'."

"Right, Jazz. So what else did you see?"

"The *unreal* stuff . . . You know, like the Pavilion of Parasites. It's a huge maze, only with glass walls, so you can see right through everything. And all its corridors are full of people sitting behind desks, and all the people are wearing identical grey masks."

"Did you play the Game?" Jeremy asked her. "When we went there, we had to play the Game."

"There wasn't time for everyone to play," said Jasmine, "so some of us played. But not me! I didn't want to; it was too hopeless! But I watched Sally Spellman play. She entered the maze and stopped at the first desk, where she had to fill out a bunch of forms. Then the person behind the desk, who wore a name-tag that said 'Dossier Initiation Representative', checked the forms, signed them, stamped them in two places, and put them into a file folder. Then it filled out another form in duplicate (which Sally also had to sign). It put one copy into the file folder, and put the other copy in another file folder that got filed in a filing cabinet, and then it entered a bunch of data into a computer and printed out another form. Then the Dossier Initiation Representative put the dossier into an out-tray, handed the computer print-out to Sally, and told her to proceed to the next desk.

"The masked person at the next desk wore a name-tag that said 'Dossier Management Representative'. This person told Sally to take a number and be seated, although she was the only one there. So Sally took a number (it was seventy-three) and sat down. After a while, another person in a grey mask, wearing a name-tag that said 'Dossier Conveyance Representative' delivered her dossier from the out-tray of the first desk to the in-tray of the second desk. But instead of calling Sally's number, the Dossier Management Representative took a coffee break. Eventually, it called Sally's number, and then studied her dossier until it found a mistake. 'Aha,' it said to Sally, 'on Form BS73659999943424140-A you were asked for the month/day/year of your birth, and you wrote the day/month/year instead.'

" 'Can't we just correct it?' asked Sally.

"The Dossier Management Representative looked at Sally as though she were a dumb animal. 'We have a Form for everything,' it replied, 'and everything is done according to Form.' The Dossier Management Representative then asked Sally to fill out a form called 'Form GX86514444412131415-D: Request Correction to Form BS73659999943424140-A' which Sally signed and it stamped. The Dossier Management Representative then told her to get that form initialled by the Dossier Management Supervisor, and said that in the meantime a Dossier Conveyance Representative would convey the dossier to the desk of the Dossier Correction Representative who, upon receipt of the Request Correction Form duly initialled by the Dossier Management Supervisor would correct the form in question, so that Sally's dossier could then be conveyed by a Dossier Conveyance Representative to the desk of a Dossier Evaluation Representative.

"So Sally went looking for the desk of the Dossier Management Supervisor, but couldn't find it in the maze. There was supposed to be an Information Representative somewhere, who could provide directions, but everyone whom Sally asked said that the Information Representative had recently moved desks, and no-one knew exactly where its new desk was located. When Sally (who was becoming frustrated after having played the Game for only two hours) remarked that it was the height of stupidity not to have knowledge of the whereabouts of the Information Representative, the grey-masked persons behind their desks merely shrugged and replied that they weren't responsible. Finally, by accident, Sally happened across the desk of the Dossier Management Supervisor, which stood behind the desk of someone wearing a name-tag that said 'Administrative Assistant to the Dossier Management Supervisor'. When Sally asked to see to the Dossier Management Supervisor, the Administrative Assistant to the Dossier Management Supervisor inquired whether she had an appointment.

" 'No, I don't,' replied Sally, 'but no-one told me that I needed one.'

" 'That's not my fault,' said the Administrative Assistant to the Dossier Management Supervisor, and gave her a Request for Appointment with the Dossier Management Supervisor Form to fill out.

"Sally wearily filled it out, whereupon the Administrative Assistant to the Dossier Management Supervisor scrutinized the form but couldn't find any mistakes. So it said rather grumpily to Sally, 'The Dossier Management Supervisor can see you three weeks from Friday, at ten o'clock in the morning.'

" 'But I only need its initial on a Request Correction Form,' protested Sally.

" 'Well, then why didn't you say so in the first place?' said the Administrative Assistant to the Dossier Management Supervisor rather curtly, and it handed her a Request Initial on Request Correction Form Form, which she filled out. 'Leave the Request Correction Form and the Request Initial on Request Correction Form Form with me,' said the Administrative Assistant to the Dossier Management Supervisor to Sally. 'The Dossier Management Supervisor will initial your Request Correction Form today. You can pick it up this afternoon.'

"So Sally and I and some of the gang went for lunch," continued Jasmine, "and then Sally went back into the maze, picked up her Request Correction Form, which the Dossier Management Supervisor had actually signed, and she took it to the desk of the Dossier Correction Representative, and took a number. But when Sally's number was called, she discovered that her dossier had not yet arrived at the desk of the Dossier Correction Representative, although the Dossier Correction Representative was able to ascertain that her dossier had indeed left the desk of the Dossier Management Representative. The Dossier Correction Representative therefore surmised that the Dossier Conveyance Representative must have conveyed her dossier from the desk of the Dossier Management Representative to the wrong desk. 'You must go the desk of the Dossier Redirection Representative,' it told here, 'and . . .'

" 'I know,' Sally cut it off, 'and fill out a Request Dossier Redirection Form, and take it to be initialled by the Dossier Redirection Supervisor, which means I have to fill out a Request Initial on Request Dossier Redirection Form Form, which I can get from the desk of the Administrative Assistant to the Dossier Redirection Supervisor.'

" 'You must have done this before,' said the Dossier Correction Representative.

" 'I'm not doing at all!' replied Sally."

"And she quit the Game?" asked Jeremy.

"Then and there," said Jasmine. "Daddy, has anybody ever won the Game?"

"Not since the Pavilion of Parasites opened, back in 2079. Quite a few people have gone temporarily insane playing it, though. And my friend, your avuncular Hardy Orbs, once urinated on a parasite."

"How come?" Jasmine giggled.

"Because," interjected Jeremy (to boys of whose age the story was well-known) "Uncle Hardy had to pee, but the 'Euphemism Passkey Representative' told him that he had to fill out a form to obtain a key to the washroom.

" 'That's a ridiculous policy,' Uncle Hardy objected.

" 'I'm not responsible for it,' answered the Euphemism Passkey Representative.

" 'Do I have to fill out a form to pee on you?' Uncle Hardy inquired.

" 'I am not aware of the existence of any such Form, Sir,' the Euphemism Passkey Representative replied indignantly.

" 'Splendid!' said Uncle Hardy, and peed on him."

"That's hilarious!" said Jasmine, "but it's not entirely fair."

"Oh, and why not?" encouraged Soloman, delighted that his daughter was exercising justethicment.

"Because," said Jasmine, "Uncle Hardy didn't have to play the Game in the first place. Nobody forced him."

"But he had to pee," reminded Jeremy, "and someone was preventing him."

"He could have left the maze," argued Jasmine.

"Maybe he didn't have time," countered Jeremy.

"What happened to him afterward, Daddy?" asked Jasmine.

"Well, the justethicist deliberated somewhat like both of you, and eventually decided that Hardy should write a letter of apology to the parasite he peed on, that the parasite responsible for the passkey form policy should write a letter of apology to Hardy, and that Hardy should perform fifty hours of community service."

"That sounds fair," Jasmine reflected. "Did it work out?"

"Not exactly as anticipated. Hardy apologized to the parasite he peed on, but no parasite was ever found who accepted responsibility for the passkey form policy. And Hardy requested, and received, permission from the Moralaw court to perform his community service in Feminania, which eventually stirred up lots of trouble."

"Trouble for whom?" inquired Jasmine.

"Trouble for them as don't tell their fathers how they fared in chess tournaments," Soloman replied.

"I humiliated Tommy Gordon!" Jasmine said vengefully, "In eighteen moves!" she added smugly.

"Isn't he the one who pulls your pigtails in the schoolyard?" asked Soloman.

"Yep," she said with satisfaction.

"Well, I guess he'll think twice before he pulls them next time."

"Oh, I don't mind so much if he pulls them," said Jasmine, "as long as I can beat him at chess."

Soloman gave her a pensive look, but speculated no further on the workings of his daughter's mind. He turned instead to his son.

"And what did you do in school today?" he inquired of Jeremy.

"Routine classwork in the morning," Jeremy replied, "you know, intellectual history, software engineering, social judo, fairness studies." He recited the list mechanically. "But in the afternoon," he continued with sudden enthusiasm, "we had a mid-term exam in sex education."

"Tell me about it," said Soloman. "But first, whose turn is it to clear the table tonight?" he asked rhetorically, looking straight at Jasmine, who was leaning halfway across the table (while at the same time attempting to feign disinterest) so as not to miss a single syllable of the impending narrative.

"Aw, Daddy, can't I stay for this? After all, I'm having sex education too."

"You're having sex education for eleven-year-olds; Jeremy is having sex education for fifteen-year-olds. Believe me, there's a difference."

"What's the difference?"

"The difference is, you may now be excused for a while."

"Gee, we live in a backward society!" Jasmine complained—but only in a face-saving way—as she cleared the table, then went to ice the cake.

Jeremy proceeded to narrate the events of the afternoon in considerable detail, and not without relish. It transpired that he had had sex with no fewer than three women at a SANE (Sex And Naturalness Education) Centre, in the space of two hours, and moreover had earned an average grade of A-minus. That represented a definite improvement, both quantitative and qualitative, over his previous performance on last year's final.

In Melior, sexuality was recognized as a prime motivating factor of human existence, and its uninhibited expression during all phases in life was deemed paramount to the well-being of the individual, and therefore also of inestimable importance to the health of the society. It was also well understood by Meliorites that the sexual interests and abilities of the individual differed not only between the sexes, but just as critically within a given sex at different stages of development. The lustful appetites of teenage boys, for example, were neither understood, nor matched, nor satisfied by their female counterparts, for whom sex was a mere physical expression of deeper emotional involvement. Then again, Meliorites quite understood that the sexual appetites of women peaked, on average, in their late thirties and early forties, at a time of their lives when male biology and outmoded marital convention combined to deprive them of that which they most craved.

The simple, elegant and healthful solution had been implemented by Melior's first Philosopher-King, the famous and infamous Joshua Wroth, who had opened Harmony's original SANE Centre back in 2045. Ever since, droves of mature women volunteered to work in SANE Centres Melior-wide, where they initiated maturing boys in the rites of physical love. Each satisfied the other perfectly, and thus repeatedly, and thus completely, at least for a while. At any hour of the day or night, whenever a teen-age boy found himself distracted and overpowered by surging hormones, relief was never further away than the nearest SANE Centre, of which every neighbourhood boasted at least one.

Naturally, teenage boys continued to date teenage girls. But the existence of the SANE Centres disarmed the formerly insoluble conflict experienced by young girls, who desired to be both popular and chaste, who required both romance and respect. Since boys were still boys, they made sexual advances toward their dates. But girls could now resist without being blamed for rejection, for the SANE Centres rejected no-one. And girls could now succumb without being mauled or otherwise injured by blundering boys, for the SANE Centres educated everyone. So while unwanted pregnancy had been eliminated by the Pope implant, sexual assault itself had been rendered obsolete by the SANE Centres.

It had taken ten or fifteen years for Meliorites to realize fully that this latter, and perhaps greater benefit was being conferred on their society as a whole. The incidence of violent behaviour against women had begun to decline as soon as the first SANE Centres opened their doors. Rape and attempted rape, as well as general assault and battery of women, had gradually ceased to be perpetrated by men; Meliorites learned that youths who were well-adjusted sexually did not evolve into rapists. Moreover and perhaps more astonishingly, violence against women had virtually ceased to be induced by women themselves; as women became better satisfied and men less trapped by their dissatisfaction, positive feedback loops resulted in women devoting their energies to pleasing rather than provoking men.

Ultimately, by the 2070s, a female of any age could walk the streets of Harmony, or any other city in Melior, at any time of the day or night, without fear of molestation. By the same token, those who went in for molestation could always volunteer to work the kinkier SANE Centres, which catered to rougher trade.

And, in fairness to men past fifty, specialized SANE Centres had been instituted for them too. These were worked for the most part by precocious teenagers (and by some girls in their twenties) who just couldn't get enough, and who found additional satisfaction in allowing older men to "rob the cradle". For their part, older men proved to be consummate robbers.

Jeremy finished his narrative, and Soloman expressed his paternal approval (while inwardly giving thanks that he was no longer fifteen himself—he had risen to similar occasions in his day, had been mercilessly devoured in his prime, had cohabited happily in adulthood, and had lately acquiesced in cradle-robbing, which suited him just fine). Meanwhile, Jasmine had finished icing her cake, between protracted periods of eavesdropping at the dining-room door, upon which she now rapped innocently and ceremoniously.

Jeremy wolfed down several pieces; Soloman choked down his, which—although billed as "orange chiffon"—he found to have the consistency of neoprene rubber.

"Do you like it, Daddy?" Jasmine inquired anxiously. (She was not flattered by her brother's appetite, which she rightly understood as adolescent male gluttony.)

"It . . . it . . . it defies criticism, Jazz," replied her father.

The people of Melior were right; Soloman would make a sagacious Philosopher-King.

For his part, Soloman wondered what the educational system was coming to: they could instruct his daughter in advanced mathematics and master-level chess, but they couldn't teach her how to bake an edible cake.

Chapter Thirteen

Julia Jensen powered off her computer, put her kettle on the boil, ran a hot bath, and began to decide what she was going to wear to the debate. Her opponent this evening, Linda Lorimer, was a very fashionable dresser as well as a good-looking woman (which Julia grudgingly admitted in the privacy of her thoughts). Then again, given the volatility of the topic and the emotionality of the audience, Julia also suspected that those attributes might well backfire before the evening was out. The water soon boiled. Julia made herself a cup of fragrant herbal tea, sank into the steaming depths of a scented bath and, distracted by the bouquets and the enveloping warmth without and within, temporarily abandoned her troubling cogitations.

Julia was content enough that Soloman had the children this week. He took parenting seriously—if disinterestedly—and besides, she had needed the extra time to prepare her speech. She knew that the kids would want to fall all over their father, at least until the novelty of his Philosopher-Kingship wore off somewhat. Moreover, what with her work being so hectic these days, and her new boyfriend making all kinds of (not unpleasurable) demands on her, she didn't have too much time left for both mothering and debating (that is, for both arguing at home and arguing in public, as she wryly thought of it at times).

As her feeling of well-being spread, Julia's thoughts gradually became more diffuse.

At some undefinable later time, she eventually stepped out of the bath, wrapped herself in two or three towels, and shortly began the lengthy process of fixing her hair and applying her makeup. After another while she was ready to get dressed and undressed and redressed several times, finally deciding on the outfit that she had decided on. Then she powered up the computer, loaded the outline of her speech, made a few last-minute changes to its content, and printed out the hard copy. Next she looked at her watch, and found that it was time to go, and so began to search for her car-keys, which (because she was well-organized) she normally located within five or ten minutes. At last she was more-or-less ready to leave.

Julia Jensen felt "confident", but not particularly confident. She knew of course what "'confident'" meant, but didn't feel "confident" that she had ever felt confident. Then again, she felt "'confident'" that she she was feeling "confident" just then. Similarly, she felt "sure" of herself, but not especially sure of herself. She didn't feel "sure" that she had ever felt sure of herself, but she felt "'sure'" that she was feeling "sure" of herself just then. She felt fairly "confident" that men felt sure of themselves, and she felt quite "sure" that men felt confident, and she also felt "'sure'" that men felt confident that women felt "sure"; just as she felt "'confident'" that men felt sure that women felt "confident". But sometimes she didn't even feel "'sure'" that she felt "confident" or, at other times, "'confident'" that she felt "sure"; and at such times she felt either "sure" or "confident" that she needed reassurance. But at this moment she felt both "confident" and "sure" that she needed no reassurance just then.

All the same, the debates were heating up across Melior, and there were bound to be divergent differences of opinion. Yet the issues had to be accosted, and laid bare, and thrashed out; for the fair people of Melior knew that a cornerstone of their cherished fairness consisted in frequent and frank public disputation.

Julia drove to the meeting place, which this evening was a concert hall in a nearby Harmonian suburb. The hall was packed with expectant throngs. Julia accessed it through the stage entrance, located her dressing room, and inspected her makeup. The program coordinator soon came in, and they ran through both the procedural details and the ground rules of the evening's event. Then she greeted her opponent, Linda Lorimer, as well as the moderator for the evening, Matthew Morrison, a renowned news anchorman. The three walked out on stage, to thunderous applause.

Matthew Morrison introduced the topic and the speakers.

"Worthy Speakers, Fair People of Melior, I bid you good evening. Tonight's topic is: resolved that, in the event of aggression against Feminania by Bruteland, Melior should intervene in Feminania's behalf. We are honoured to welcome two outstanding speakers, who will debate this resolution. Debating the affirmative, it is my privilege and pleasure to introduce Linda Lorimer, a well-known author on women's affairs, whose academic best-seller, *A Brief History of the Femininny Revolution*, is widely-read in Melior's secondary school courses on the anti-intellectual history of dystopianism. (It is, unfortunately, banned in Feminania.) Debating the negative, I am no less privileged and pleased to introduce Julia Jensen, vice-president of Feminanian marketing for MeliSoft Engineering (a division of MeliComp Corporation), who has also visited Feminania several times, clandestinely of course, on product evaluation missions. Without further ado, then, let the debate begin."

Linda Lorimer rose, ready to make her opening remarks for the affirmative.

"Mr. Moderator, Worthy Opponent, Fair People of Melior: I would like to begin by reminding you that we are not debating a hypothetical issue for the purpose of exercising our rhetorical and oratorical skills. Rather, we are weighing our own values in the balance of a decision that will have to be taken sooner as opposed to later. We are not asking

'What should Melior do *if* Bruteland attacks Feminania?', but 'What must Melior do *when* Bruteland attacks Feminania?'.

"The evidence that they will attack is overwhelming. To begin with, Bruteland's imports of our crude oil have risen by seventy-eight percent during the past three months, and MeliOil Corporation's latest figures project an even larger proportional increase next month. Moreover, MIASMA (Meliorite Intelligence And Strategic Machination Agency) reports that Brutelanders are distilling the crude primarily into diesel fuel, which they are stockpiling at military installations. That fuel is obviously destined for their tanks, half-tracks, trucks and troop trains. And significantly, their production of high-octane gasoline, which they burn almost ubiquitously in their civilian vehicles, has actually diminished over the same period. On top of this, MIASMA relates that Bruteland has stepped up its manufacture of large and small arms, and that its Militia is conducting large-scale exercises as well as specialized manoeuvres. There are also rumours that they are making ready to mobilize their so-called 'reserves', which means conscripting every able-bodied man in Bruteland. Collectively, these activities can be interpreted only as a prelude to aggression against Feminania.

"As for the Feminanians: they are ill-equipped and ill-prepared to protect themselves from such an attack. They have legislated themselves into a surrealistic dream-like condition, in which every fleeting Femininny fantasy is entrenched in law and implemented (or, as they say in their ridiculous Fairspeak, 'implewombented') by a bitch-ridden boudoicracy. Femininnies have subordinated males to the extent that they, the females, have lost all touch with the masculine realities of the cosmos. My Worthy Opponent herself is employed by a Meliorite Corporation which—I am sorry to say—encourages and assists Feminanians to remain out of touch, by providing them with virtual realities that pander to their distorted view of things.

"During the past several decades, we Fair People of Melior have profited immeasurably from both MeliOil's exports to Bruteland, and MeliComp's exports to Feminania. So I believe that Melior has a two-fold responsibility with respect to the current crisis; first, an economic responsibility to itself, to maintain the *status quo* upon which it thrives; and second, a moral responsibility to Feminania, to protect it from circumstances which Melior has willingly and actively helped to engender.

"In Taoist terms, the political situation is this: Bruteland is all yanged-up, and Feminania is all yinned-out. It is no secret that I am a Utilitarian Taoist. As such, I believe that Melior must act so as to help restore the balance between yin and yang. As things stand, Melior is only abetting the imbalance. Ultimately, this will be bad for Melior too. We Fair People of Melior have stood by and traded and profited and exacerbated the tensions between Feminania and Bruteland. There is no doubt in my mind that Bruteland is about to commit aggressive acts against Feminania; the very least we can do now is to help the defenders resist the attackers. That concludes my opening remarks."

The hall buzzed with interchanges of approval and demurral, as Linda Lorimer resumed her seat. The buzzing subsided as Julia Jensen rose to make her opening remarks for the negative.

"Mr. Moderator, Worthy Opponent, Fair People of Melior: I disagree with my Worthy Opponent on both significant points. First, I do not think that Bruteland will inevitably commit aggression against Feminania; and second, I do not believe that Melior should become militarily involved, even if Bruteland does agress.

"In the first place, Bruteland has a history of military posturing, to which it resorts whenever it wants something that it isn't getting. Currently, as we learn from MIASMA, Bruteland isn't getting obedient females from Feminania. With the connivance of the Radical Femininnies, Fundamentalist (or, as they say in their ridiculous Fairspeak, 'Fundawombentalist') Femininnies have infiltrated Feminania's exportation training program, and have inculcated rebellious tendencies among the exportees. If Feminanians refuse to give Brutelanders what they want—namely docile female slaves—then Brutelanders will take matters into their own hands, and will oversee the training in their own inimitable fashion.

"However, I do not view this eventuality as aggression by Bruteland; rather, as provocation by Feminania. Feminanian freedom from Brutelandish aggression has always depended on the barter system—a symbiotic exchange of females for machines. If Bruteland began to export defective equipment to Feminania, Feminanians would certainly complain. Well, it happens that Feminanians are exporting defective slaves to Bruteland, and so Brutelanders are complaining. The Radical Femininnies are inviting ruin upon themselves, because they persist in deluding themselves. They surmise, quite blindly, that the world works in a certain way merely because they proclaim that it does. They argue, quite stupidly, that they can legislate changes to human nature. They have no concept of the actual limitations of their power, and they do not understand the potential price of their folly.

"I believe that Melior should do everything possible to defuse the crisis. We should work to persuade the Feminanians to appease rather than provoke the Brutelanders, to convince them to re-establish the mutually beneficial trade upon which their security depends. Should Melior's diplomatic initiative fail, however, I do not believe that we have any duty to intervene militarily. My reasons are the following.

"To begin with, I disagree with my Worthy Opponent's moral assessment of Melior's foreign involvement. We Fair People of Melior have indeed profited from trade with both Bruteland and Feminania, but so have their peoples profited from trade with us. Above all, we have never coerced them into a single transaction. Bruteland begged us for crude oil, Feminania pleaded with us for virtual reality; we provided these things in abundance and quality, and still provide them, in exchange for mere gold and privacy. 'Pay us a fair price, and leave us in peace, and we'll supply your needs,' we say to them. So MeliOil exports the crude that Bruteland consumes, and MeliComp (through MeliHard and MeliSoft) exports the virtual reality that Feminanians crave. But Meliorites are not responsible for their desires.

"Nor do we require any trade with them; we are—thank all the deities—entirely self-sufficient. We need only be able to defend ourselves, and this of course we can do. Brutelanders will not soon forget the one and only time they tried to use force against us; nor will Feminanians ever be keen to pit their fantasies against our realities. (Recall that when the Radical Femininnies founded a branch party in Melior, they could not withstand the ridicule of our own women.) Melior has a responsibility only to persevere in itself; it owes nothing to these barbaric states.

"I do agree with my Worthy Opponent that Bruteland is all yanged-up, and Feminania is all yinned-out. As such, they are both against Tao by reason of imbalance. But I am a Deontological Taoist, and thus I hold that whatever is against Tao will soon come to an end. Tao reasserts itself, and does not require our assistance. So if we cannot help to restore balance by reasoned words, then we should not resort to armed force. That concludes my opening remarks."

Again, the hall buzzed with spontaneous private exchanges as Julia took her seat.

The Moderator rose, and said "We now invite rebuttals from the speakers, to be followed by their concluding remarks. Then, after an intermission, the speakers will entertain questions from the audience."

Among many other Meliorites not in attendance, Soloman Kohan watched the debate on television. But unlike most Meliorites, the Philosopher-King regarded the event with considerable disinterest. He knew the issues backward and forward, recited the stock arguments and counter-arguments in his sleep, anticipated the questions the public would ask and predicted how the speakers would respond. Soloman was troubled because none of this knowledge conferred upon him the means of arriving at a fair decision. It would be both fair and unfair for Melior to intervene, and moreover would be both fair and unfair for Melior not to intervene. Fairness prescribed no preferable policy of action, nor of inaction. Soloman realized that there was nothing for it but to hold a plebiscite. Meta-fairness demanded that the Philosopher-King consult the Fair People of Melior, and that he do their bidding.

On the very next day, Soloman and his political advisors drew up a list of reasonable responses to the question they had devised. They briefly discussed a few details, but wasted little time formulating the questionnaire. After all, the options were fairly obvious to everyone. The questionnaire read:

What should Melior do if Bruteland attacks Feminania?

> Choose one or more options, consistently.
>
> (1) Do nothing, aside from guarding our own borders.
>
> (2) Institute economic sanctions against Bruteland.
>
> (3) Defend Feminania
>
>> (i) if it asks for help, but don't attack Bruteland.
>>
>> (ii) if it asks for help and attack Bruteland if necessary.
>>
>> (iii) unconditionally, but don't attack Bruteland.
>>
>> (iv) unconditionally, and attack Bruteland if necessary.
>
> (4) Conquer and annex Bruteland.
>
> (5) Conquer and annex Feminania.
>
> (6) You're the Philosopher-King; you decide.

But Soloman and his political advisors deliberated at greater length over the contents of the pre-plebiscite VET (Voter Evaluation Test). The VET was one of Melior's most democratic innovations, conceived and introduced to compensate regression toward the mean. The VET insured that the results of elections and plebiscites were as fairly representative as possible.

The Meliorite intelligentsia knew full well that selective breeding alone could never raise the average intelligence of the population, which was distributed normally on a Gaussian ("bell-shaped") curve. Of course, Melior's screening of potential parents and subsequent monitoring of child-rearing eliminated most child abuse, and a healthy domestic life combined with an effective educational system tended to develop childrens' intelligence quotients to optimal levels. This in itself resulted in a nice, symmetric curve—in contrast to the skewed curves with the long trailing edges that one found in deprived populations, which reproduced without regulation and which subjected their children to sub-standard educations. While Melior's symmetric curve boasted a higher mean intelligence than curves skewed toward the trailing edge, Meliorites could not manage to skew their curve toward the leading edge, which would have been indicative of a population of high average intelligence. Their best attempts to do so were defeated by regression toward the mean, nature's ingenious way of insuring the continual re-emergence of a normal distribution.

Nature worked like this: the children of stupid people were more likely to be less stupid and less likely to be more stupid than their parents; while the children of exceedingly stupid people were even more likely to be less stupid and even less likely to be more stupid than their parents. Then again, the children of clever people were more likely to be less clever and less likely to be more clever than their parents; while the children of exceedingly clever people were even more likely to be less clever and even less likely to be more clever than their parents. These rather unfortunate natural proclivities defeated Melior's noblest attempts to procreate a wholly intelligent society. (Most other societies additionally manifested the dystopian tendency of allowing—and even encouraging—the ignorant poor to bear far more children than the educated affluent, which resulted in irremediable social ills.)

It must also be appreciated that Meliorites never mistook intelligence for a *summum bonum*; they merely knew it to be highly correlated with certain forms of worthiness (just as they knew stupidity to be highly correlated with certain forms of unworthiness). Meliorites knew all too well that intelligence alone did not necessarily cause virtue, just as stupidity alone did not necessarily cause vice. On the contrary, the dullest individual could become an extremely worthy citizen; the brightest, extremely unworthy. But from experience, Meliorites knew that the simplest recipe for individual worthiness consisted of a blend of innate ability and virtuous upbringing.

Since Melior's population sported a textbook Gaussian distribution of intelligence, it therefore contained not only just as many stupid people as clever ones but also—and arguably worse—just as few exceedingly clever people as exceedingly stupid ones. Moreover, it was also bound to contain some who were both stupid and worthy, as well as others who were both clever and unworthy. So Melior's first Philosopher-King, the famous and infamous Joshua Wroth, invented and introduced the VET, which not only compensated for the normal distribution of intelligence but also identified worthiness and unworthiness across its spectrum. The innovation paved the way for lasting utopianism.

The VET was simplicity itself: while every citizen with Meliority could cast exactly one ballot in a given election, not every ballot carried the same electoral weight. There were seven classes of voter, each with its own distinct ballot: inane, imbecilic, insipid, incognizant, informed, intuitive, and inspired. Prior to any election, every eligible voter took a VET designed to assess his or her grasp of the issues at stake. Every voter was then assigned that class of ballot most appropriate to his or her level of understanding. The ballots were weighted according to a geometric progression, whose ratio could change from election to election, depending on the importance of the outcome. Normally the ratio was kept at two, which meant that an inspired ballot was worth twice as many votes as an intuitive ballot, four times as many votes as an informed ballot, and so forth. In sum, one inspired voter could offset the collective opinion of thirty-two imbeciles, or sixty-four inane people. And in Melior's very first plebiscite of this kind, which had questioned the people on the VET itself (after having vetted them of course), an overwhelming majority agreed that the system was fair. Thus did Melior achieve utopian ends by democratic means.

So Soloman and his political advisors carefully concocted the pre-plebiscite VET and, given the importance of the outcome of the plebiscite itself, they decided to fix the geometric ratio at three. Thus an inspired ballot would be worth three times as much as an intuitive one, nine times as much as an informed one, and so forth. One inspired voter would be able to offset the collective opinions of two hundred forty-three imbeciles, or seven hundred twenty-nine inane people.

But as Melior geared up for the plebiscite, with a seemingly interminable succession of public debates, documentary films, special newscasts and talked-about talk-shows, Soloman found that Philosopher-Kings could not neglect the daily agenda of routine affairs of state. There were countless meetings, at which Soloman had inevitably to make final decisions on matters political, military, economic and social. There were press conferences, public appearances, and addresses to the Senate. There was little time to spend with his children, and no time to luxuriate in philosophical contemplation. One activity, however, afforded Soloman both a respite from the tedium of state management and an opportunity to exercise his notoriously fair justethicment. For ninety minutes every day, a Philosopher-King had to sit in the Summary Court, to hear and resolve disputes of any and every kind, and therefore to be seen by all and sundry to dispense fairness. Soloman greatly enjoyed these sittings and, indeed, he appeared ideally suited to the task. On this basis, at any rate, the fair people of Melior deemed themselves wise for having elected him Philosopher-King.

The day of the plebiscite dawned at last. By law, everyone with Meliority had four hours during which to cast his or her ballot, which amounted to a half-holiday for most. But Philosopher-Kings did not vote on such occasions, so Soloman Kohan worked a full day as usual. And as always, he relished his ninety minutes in the Summary Court. Today he was particularly grateful for the sitting, because it obliged him temporarily to concentrate on other matters, however banal or mundane, and therefore to desist from speculating on the outcome of the plebiscite. Public opinion polls were forbidden by law in Melior (to encourage each citizen to assume individual responsibility), and Soloman found himself quite unable to divine public sentiment on this important issue. In Summary Court, he did not have to speculate; he only had to exercise justethicment.

The first case that day was a dispute between two women, over the custody of a two-year-old child. One disputant was the child's biological mother, who had given it up for adoption at birth. The other disputant was the adoptive mother. The biological mother had recently changed her mind, regretted having given up her baby, and now wanted to retake custody of the child.

"Are you willing to bear another child?" Soloman asked her.

"Indeed I am, Philosopher-King! . . . But the doctors advise against it? . . . For medical reasons!"

"And why did you give up your baby in the first place?" asked Soloman.

"Because I changed my mind about being a mother? . . . I mean, I didn't feel 'confident' enough!"

"And do you now feel 'confident' enough to be a mother?" Soloman asked her.

"Oh, yes, Philosopher-King! . . . Now I feel 'sure' I can manage?"

"Then you should take steps to adopt a child yourself," said Soloman. "I will not sunder the bond between this child and its adoptive mother, which seems to be healthy and strong. Biological claims do not usually grant sufficient warrant to undermine functional social units. The identity of the biological mother will not be kept from the child, if it so inquires (as do many adopted children when they attain Meliority). But what was whimsically relinquished may not be capriciously reclaimed."

The public gallery mildly applauded the justethicment, which was only fair, and enthusiastically applauded the aphorism, which was above average.

"But Philosopher-King," protested the biological mother, "the child is really mine!"

"With an attitude like that, I am amazed that you were entitled to conceive in the first place," responded Soloman. "Removal of the Pope implant usually demands far more maturity; the examiners must have been lax that day. Nothing in this world is truly ours, in the sense of ownership; we merely exercise varying custodial rights and responsibilities over different entities at different times. Next case."

The next case was that of a man who had been found guilty of driving at night without his headlights, and whose license had consequently been suspended for six months. He wished to appeal the sentence, which he deemed too severe.

"I see that you hold a second-class moron's permit," said Soloman, "and moreover that you have received three moron warnings in the past two years."

"That is correct, Philosopher-King; but I am usually a cautious second-class moron."

"Then how did you come to be driving at night without your lights?" asked Soloman.

"Well, Philosopher-King, the automated system wasn't working, and the warning system must have malfunctioned, and I guess I forgot to turn them on manually."

"Few vehicular undertakings are more incautious than driving at night without proper illumination. You can neither see nor be seen, and thus represent a hazard both to yourself (which is your own concern) and to others (which is the State's concern). But I agree that the sentence is inappropriate—a six month suspension does not quite fit the crime. I hereby reinstate your license (moron, second-class) during daylight hours, but suspend it for a full year between sunset and sunrise. Next case."

The public gallery cheered the justethicment.

The next case was that of an academic woman, a political scientist, who had not long ago joined the faculty of the University of Harmony.

She happened to be the only female in her Department, and she complained of a general lack of warmth on the part of the male Department members.

"Ever since they discovered that they had hired a woman," she said, "they haven't made me feel at all welcome! . . . They have created an unfriendly environment?"

"Have they done anything specific to harass you or discriminate against you?" asked Soloman.

"Well . . . I'm not really 'sure'? . . . But they don't make me feel 'confident'! . . . They make me feel inadequate? . . . and insecure!" she replied.

"Have you either taken a course in Psycho-Climatology, or else read the book, *On Human Ethology for Women: The Meaning and Purpose of Social Hierarchies, and How Not to Take Them Personally*?" asked Soloman.

"No, I haven't! . . . Because I don't feel that ethology has any relevance for humans?" she replied.

"And what would have me do?" asked Soloman.

"Compel them to be more sensitive!" replied the woman.

"That I cannot do," said Soloman, "But have you considered that perhaps you're in the wrong line of work? You could try a different University, but I really think you're projecting your unresolved emotional problems on your environment. I suggest that you seek professional counselling without delay, and resign your position if necessary. As a last resort, you could always emigrate to Feminania. Next case."

The public gallery hooted, cheered and applauded.

And so the ninety minutes fled, and far too rapidly for Soloman's liking.

Meanwhile, all across Melior, decisive ballots were being cast. In a voting station not far from Soloman's home, Julia Jensen awaited the grading of her VET, which had taken her about five minutes to complete. There were two men ahead of her in line, the first of whom was having his VET graded by an electoral officer.

"Let's see, Sir: to the first question, 'What does the government of Bruteland stand for?', you replied 'I don't know'; to the second question, 'What does the government of Feminania stand for?', you replied 'I don't know'; to the third question, 'What is causing the current tensions between Feminania and Bruteland?', you replied 'I don't know'; to the fourth question, 'What does the non-government of Melior stand for?', you replied 'I don't know'; to the fifth question 'What does Melior stand to gain (or lose) by intervention (or non-intervention) if Bruteland attacks Feminania?', you replied 'I don't know' . . ."

The electoral officer quickly scanned the remainder of the questionnaire.

"Well, Sir, it seems that you've answered these questions quite uniformly. That certainly simplifies my job . . ." (The worker half-smiled at the voter, who returned a wholly blank gaze.) . . . "For the purposes of this election, I find that you are incognizant. Here's your ballot, Sir. Please vote in booth number twenty-six."

The officer handed him a yellow ballot. (Yellow was the colour for incognizants. Ballots were colour-coded according to class, to facilitate counts and, when necessary, recounts.) The incognizant shuffled off toward booth twenty-six. The next person in line, the man in front of Julia Jensen, handed his completed VET to the electoral officer.

"Let's see, Sir: to the first question, 'What does the government of Bruteland stand for?', you replied 'Real pricks'; to the second question, 'What does the government of Feminania stand for?', you replied 'Real cunts'; to the third question, 'What is causing the current tensions between Feminania and Bruteland?', you replied 'It's the wrong time of the month'; to the fourth question, 'What does the non-government of Melior stand for?', you replied 'It doesn't stand for a fucking thing'; to the fifth question 'What does Melior stand to gain (or lose) by intervention (or non-intervention) if Bruteland attacks Feminania?', you replied 'We stand to lose a couple of nukes, cause we should nuke 'em both.'

The electoral officer quickly scanned the remainder of the questionnaire.

"Well, Sir, I must confess that you really had me going for a time. Your first few answers were terse but, in and of themselves, could well have been inspired. The rest of your responses, however, provide a more definitive context. For the purposes of this election, I find that you are an imbecile. Here's your ballot, Sir. Please vote in booth number thirty-seven."

The officer handed him a red ballot. (Red was the colour for imbeciles.) The imbecile wandered off in search of booth thirty-seven. Then it was Julia Jensen's turn. She handed her completed VET to the electoral officer, who read the first few answers and then quickly scanned the remainder.

"Thank you very much, Madam. For the purposes of this election, I find that you are an inspired voter. Here's your ballot, Madam. Please vote in booth number nine."

The officer handed her a green ballot, and Julia subsequently cast her vote. Later the same day, in another polling station, Linda Lorimer also received and marked a green ballot. All across Melior, variously coloured ballots were handed out, filled in, and deposited in ballot boxes.

By late evening, the polls had closed and the counting had begun. Like most citizens of Melior, Soloman Kohan watched the results on his television; unlike most citizens of Melior, he was surrounded by political advisors. Early indications were that a consensus had been reached, and the final numbers bore this out conclusively. The Fair People of Melior had spoken, and they had done so with an overwhelmingly singular voice.

Eighty-five percent of the weighted popular vote (including both Julia Jensen's and Linda Lorimer's ballots) selected option six: "You're the Philosopher-King; you decide."

And although Soloman had not yet decided exactly what to do, he knew that his hour of decision was rapidly approaching.

Epilogue

None but the Brave deserves the Fair.

                                        John Dryden

Chapter Fourteen

Bruteland invaded at dawn on the summer solstice of 2084, with the rising sun in the face of the Feminanian defendhers. Attack formations of the Bruteland Militia, incorporating major elements of the Testos Division, as well as special units, spearheaded the invasion. In a classic trident-shaped offensive, assault troops breached Feminania's scanty defenses by simultaneously overrunning three bordher stations along a fifty-mile front. The vanguards of the invading force poured through these breaches, then streamed toward Ovaria in three great prongs. The central, westbound column was the heaviest, thickest and slowest-advancing. It contained the bulk of the invading armies, committed to a full frontal onslaught against Feminania's capital, which Brutelandish strategists envisioned as the battleground royal of the campaign. The other two columns—lighter, thinner, swifter—deployed along the arcs of a textbook pincer movement. They were ordered to converge on Ovaria from the north and the south, and after having attained other objectives *en route*.

The southern arm of the pincer was slightly larger than its northern counterpart, and the reason for this disparity soon became apparent: not far into Feminania, a special brigade detached itself from the column, and turned due south toward Melior. The brigade was called an "exploratory probe" (a Brutelandish euphemism for "suicide squad").

Its orders were to penetrate Melior, and report on any resistance encountered. This dispensable detachment thus constituted a litmus test of Melior's defenses. If it encountered substantially less resistance than anticipated, an entire reserve army—currently poised in southern Bruteland—would immediately launch a full-scale invasion of Melior itself. Alternatively, if Melior attempted to intervene in Feminania, Bruteland's reserve army would swiftly engage the Meliorite forces, thus protecting the southern flank of its invading armies.

As the Brutelandish forces pierced the frontiher posts and thrust into Feminania, they simply shot the Feminanian bordher guards as they overran them. Guards who tried to surrendher were geebeed and then shot; there was neither any plan to take POWs, nor any logistic support for taking them, in this initial phase of the invasion.

The first town encountered by the central invading column was Labia, which lay just inside the bordher on the road to Ovaria. Although a battalioness of Feminania's crack troops (the Amazon Regiwombent) was hurrying eastward toward Labia, intending to attempt to hold the town until the main defense force could be mobilized, the battalioness was woefully late in arriving. Labia was otherwise ungarridaughthered, except for the inevitable Brown Skirts and GEQUAPO aladies who, upon learning of the approach of the invadehers, rapidly discarded their uniforms and pretended to be ordinary Feminanians. However, Labians as a whole had been earmarked for special strategic treatwombent. In anticipation of extensive Feminanian media covherage of the invasion, Bruteland's high command had resolved to make an example of the defendhers of Labia in order to sap Feminania's collective will to resist. Hence the invading armies ground to a halt at the eastern outskirts of undefended Labia, and actually awaited the arrival of the Feminanian troops from the west.

The Brutelanders sent a reconnaissance patrol into town, to occupy the high ground and to radio intelligence of the approach of the Feminanian defendhers. The Labian populace attempted to surrendher wholesale to the handful of Brutelanders, who merely geebeed a few of the betther-looking Femininnies (including a couple of the Brown Skirts, but none of the GEQUAPO aladies) and told the rest to go home and lock their doors. They gratefully did as they were told, except for some of the eldherly womben, who went home and left their doors ajar.

The Feminanian battalioness finally arrived at the western outskirts of Labia, and sent in a support group to reconnoitre. It encounthered nothing but ominous silence, a therrified populace cowhering behind locked doors, and some therrified eldherly womben cowhering behind doors left ajar. The support group relayed this intelligence back to the main force, whose comwombanding orficeher ordhered the comwombencewombent of troop movewombents into the town. The Bruteland reconnaissance patrol, from its concealed vantage points, reported this development to its commanding officer, who in turn ordered the commencement of troop movements into the town. The main elewombents of the Feminanian battalioness wombanoeuvhered and the main elements of the Brutelandish division manoeuvered along Labia's main street, one from west to east, the other from east to west, on an inevitable collision course.

They encounthered and encountered one another at Labia's central square, and ground to a mutual standstill. The opposing soldihers and soldiers mherely and merely eyed one another at first, finghers and fingers poised on trigghers and triggers. The Feminanians glanced fearfully at the Brutelanders and clutched their weapons and ultimately looked away. The Brutelanders stared boldly and, as the Feminanians avherted their gazes, the Brutelanders brazenly unslung their rifles and began to leer and snigger.

"Throw down your weapons!" the Brutelandish commander called to the Feminanians, "You are outgunned and outmanned." (His troops chortled.) "Surrender now, and we will show clemency."

"We don't need your 'clemency'! . . ." retorted the Feminanian comwombandher, "because we know the meaning of 'clewombency'? . . . We may be outmanned, but you are sure as Melior outwombanned! .

. .." (Her troops cheehered.) "If you want our weapons, you'll have to take them?"

Following this pronouncewombent the Brutelandish commanders huddled and conferred, while the Feminanian comwomband-hers formed a support group and chatthered. The Brutelandish troops continued to leer at the Feminanians, who continued to look away. Suddenly, a shrill voice, belonging to a townswomban who had been geebeed by the Brutelandish reconnaissance patrol, shatthered the uneasy silence.

"You call yourselves 'men'?" she taunted them from her window, which ovherlooked the central square. "You practice gendheral harasswombent on defenseless fembales! You therrorize an ungarridaughthered town? But you're stopped in your tracks by one Feminanian battalioness! This is an example of Brutelandish 'virility'? You're nothing but a gang of bullies and bullards! My gonadatropically challenged housepherdaughther has more 'manliness' than any of you? And he's betther in bed, too! I'll bet that none of you 'heroes' evher . . ."

But the therms of the wageher were nevher stated, as the womban was abruptly cut off by a hoarse bellow from a Brutelandish Master Sergeant—"Shut the freud up, ya freuding kunta!"—and was immediately thereafter cut down by a spontaneous fusillade of rifle fire, which rang out hither and yon among the troops loitering within earshot of her tirade.

There followed several mowombents and moments of benumbed confusion, as the main body of continladies and contingents pinpointed both the sources and sink of the unexpected discharge, whose echoes still reverberated about the square. Then, with hystherical shrieks of outrage, the Feminanians opened fire upon the Brutelanders, whose forward ranks either flattened themselves beneath or were flattened by a horizontal hail of cowets. Then the Brutelanders reformed their ranks, charged the Feminanians, and wrought severe carnage among them. But no soon did the tide of battle sweep the Feminanians toward annihilation than they perceived their plight and responded

Fair New World - 219

with a suicidal counter-attack, which staggered the Brutelanders yet again. However, the Brutelander's superior numbers, combined with their dispassionate tactics and individual aggressiveness, shortly put the Feminanian battalioness to rout.

Wombany of the surviving Feminanian troops committed suicide rather than surrendher and, in retrospect, this despherate measure proved not entirely senseless. For those who did surrendher, or who were captured and disarmed, met with a singular fate. In keeping with their political strategy, the Brutelanders made an example of the defendhers of Labia, and moreover permitted the Feminanian media to report their fate to the rest of the nation, *pour décourager les autres*.

All gonadotropically challenged males sherving with the Feminanian troops (gonadotropically challenged males wher debarred from combat—they pherformed wombenial duties such as KP, laundry detail and motor vehicle maintenance) were rounded up, handcuffed and executed with single bullets to the brain. They were deemed to have no right to exist, neither in Bruteland nor in the new order that Bruteland intended to impose on Feminania. In fact, the Brutelanders experienced revulsion at the mere sight of these eunuchs. Any man who allowed kuntas to do that to him, reckoned the Brutelanders, didn't deserve to live.

The Feminanian soldihers themselves were stripped, freebeed and geebeed by the rank-and-file Bruteland Militiamen. Next, their faces and breasts were disfigured with cigarette burns and knife cuts, inflicted by the Mark Oedisad Squad (a fundamentalist sect of Brutians). Following this disfigurewombent, their throats were cut (again by the Mark Oedisad Squad). Finally, their corpses were freebeed and geebeed by a special services unit of necrophiliacs.

Feminanian war correspondents travelling with the defunct battalioness wher compelled—at gunpoint, threatened with the same fate—to film, photograph and make docuwombentary reports on the "object lessons in sexual politics", as the Brutelandish commander insisted on calling the atrocities.

News of the horrific massacre reached the comwombanding orficeher of the Amazon Regiwombent at her base camp near Ovaria, just as her main continladies busily made final preparations to move eastward and meet the threat. Barracks after barracks wher in a tizzy. Enlisted womben hurriedly applied makeup, hastily wombanicured their nails, and frantically fixed their hair; accusations and counther-accusations flew over lost lipstick, misplaced mascara, purloined pherfume and borrowed bobby-pins. Then they quickly changed into combat uniforms camouflaged with the mottled grey-green hues of eastern Feminanian therrain; but some found that these clashed with their skin tones and highlights, and so quickly changed into other uniforms (ranging from khaki fatigues to dress whites) which betther suited their perdaughtheral colouring. Then they packed their knapsacks undher the watchful eyes of grim Mistress Shergeants, who ordhered them to exclude their stuffed animals and frilly nightgowns, and to include their extra ammunition and C-rations. Within four hours of the emhergency embrocation signal, wombany of the troops wher just about ready to go, while wombany more wher almost ready.

The Amazon Regiwombent's comwombanding orficeher couldn't decide whether to tell her soldihers about the fate of the battalioness, so she telephoned her supheriher, the comwombanding genheral of the Feminanian defense forces. The comwombanding genheral couldn't decide either, so she phoned the Prime Ministher. But the Prime Ministher was in a confherence and couldn't be disturbed, so the decision was postponed until lateher. Meanwhile, Feminania's crack troops sallied forth.

During the same period, the northern arm of Bruteland's invading pincer overran one GOODS installation after another, meeting with only token resistance from isolated support groups of fanatical GEQUAPO aladies, whom they methodically massacred. But the Brutelandish troops had been carefully instructed neither to lay waste to the GOODS installations nor to molest their inhabitants in any way, pending orders to the contrary. Since the invasion had been provoked by defective GOODS in the first place, and was driven by rampant domestic discontent with disobedient kuntas of every grade, Bruteland's government wanted these installations taken intact, in order that the flaws in the production process be accurately detected and wholly remedied. Kattya Green, herself the object of an intensive search by the invaders, had been captured at her main GOODS installation and was now undher house arrest in her orfice. In return for guarantees phertaining to the security of her pherdaughter (which was in fact more secure than she realized, since she was at least a three-bagger and the Brutelanders were travelling light), Kattya Green had agreed to collabherate with her captpherdaughthers. She immediately set about identifying suspected Fundawombentalist Femininy aladies among the cadres of employees of her GOODS installations.

And thus the Brutelandish Inquisition, as it later came to be known, was triggghered. The suspects named by Kattya Green were arrested and interrogated; they implicated others, who implicated yet others in their turn. These snowballs precipitated an avalanche. Before long, virtually evhery employee of the entire GOODS netwherk had been arrested, and was accusing virtually evhery other employee of being a Fundawombentalist Femininy. Neither wher the sylphs themselves of any help to the Inquisitors. The sylphs wher so confused, flusthered and traumatized by the upheaval of their hitherto sheltered world—not to wombention intoxicated by the presence of dominant males—that they could scarcely recollect anything they had learned, let alone remembher precisely who had preached seditious Fundawombentalist Femininy doctrines to them.

So while the Brutelandish invasion of Feminania proceeded apace, and its military objectives were attained according to plan, the political *raison d'être* of the occupation became severely undermined by two ironic factors: the military successes themselves, combined with the excessive coopheratheness of the captives. But this is not to assert that all Brutelandish military operations unfolded as planned, nor that all

Feminanians proved as coopherative as the employees of the GOODS installations.

A special detachment of the northern pincer group surrounded and captured Nora Goodwomban's GIRLs compound, following a particularly fierce firefight with the support group of GEQUAPO aladies which had guarded it. The Brutelandish detachment had been briefed about the critical importance of the GIRLs compound in Bruteland's provenance of kuntas, and the men had been cautioned neither to damage any laboratory equipment nor to freebee or geebee any kuntas wearing white coats.

Nora Goodwomban was both furious at the invasion of her sanctuary and fearless of the invadehers; she volubly bherated the commanding officer of the Brutelandish detachment who, had he not been under strict orders not to harm kuntas in white coats, would have joyously cut out her tongue and fed it to the ravens. As things stood, he merely repeated his orders—to seize, search and secure all buildings within the installation—whenever he could get a word in edgewise.

One of the platoons under his command was led by Lieutenant John Buck. Like most white-holster workers in Bruteland, Buck was a reserve officer in the Militia, and had been mobilized for the invasion. Sergeant Hod Smegma, Corporal Slim Zits and Private Clem Royds numbered among the noncoms, grunts and dogfaces in his platoon, which had been ordered to seize, search and secure a string of FREUDs. The men clomped down the central corridor of a FREUD, the footfalls of their combat boots muffled by the whirring and gurgling placental pumps, their assault rifles tracing exploratory arcs among the bell-jars, their fingers caressing the hair-triggers of their weapons, their ears straining for hazards concealed by the dimness and sibilance, their eyes widening at the spooky sight of row upon row of gestating kuntas, floating foetally and staring sightlessly in their EUDs.

"Well I'll be freuding freuded," exclaimed Hod, whose comrades largely shared his view.

For the most part, though, they were simply lost in the precursors of thought. The rows of fleshy presences immersed in large vitreous vessels vaguely reminded them of so many jars of pickled sausages, pickled eggs, pickled pig's knuckles, and similar tavern fare; the Brutelanders rather fleetingly and perhaps subconsciously wondered how these, too, would taste washed down with beer. Then again, the little torsos bore insignificantly tiny, tight, hairless but unmistakeable slits; the Brutelanders also wondered, perhaps more fleetingly but also more consciously, how it would feel to freud something so small.

So the platoon seized, searched and secured several FREUDs, as did other platoons other FREUDs within the GIRLs compound. They accustomed themselves to the eeriness of the installation, and exercised enormous restraint (greatly abetted by fear of court-martial) in obeying orders not to touch any kunta in a white coat. And as most of the kuntas in the GIRLs compound were wearing white coats (either through long-standing habit or lately-acquired prudence), the men found little to freebee and geebee. Thus deprived of the sexual spoils of war, and knowing full well that their compatriots in other units were overrunning and freuding civilian towns wholesale, the men occupying the GIRLs compound bemoaned their fates in time-honoured infantry style, while their moods turned uglier with each passing hour.

Although well-prepared for warfare and its discontents, John Buck's platoon was decidedly disprepared for that which awaited them in a newly-constructed edifice beyond the complex of FREUDs, behind a door whose sign read

MATHISNITY WARD

Hod Smegma, Slim Zits and Clem Royds were the first Brutelanders to cross its threshold; they were not, however, the last to pass judgement on what they discovered within. Hod Smegma burst into a private room, which bore number 101, and there encountered Jessie Doebuck nursing his baby.

Chapter Fourteen

Jessie's hystherendomy had been a complete success. An embryo had been implanted within six months of the opheration, and he had given birth, eight and one half months later, to a viable fembale infant. During pregnancy, Jessie had undergone a regiwomben of carefully regulated hermone treatwombents, combined with additional minor surghery (involving the implantation of some fatty glandular tissue). These intherventions resulted in his ability to lactate following parturition. Although his father's milk contained relatively low concentrations of nutrients and antibodies, it was still fit food for his baby. She nursed willingly, and was given necessary supplewombents via bottled formula.

At first, Hod Smegma thought he was onto something. Jessie Doebuck was wearing a white hospital gown, not a white laboratory coat. Hod's orders were mute on hospital gowns—and so, Hod reasoned, any kunta in a hospital gown was fair game. Hod took in the swell of Jessie's breast above the gown, and the curvature of Jessie's abdomen beneath the gown, and he grinned and put down his rifle and began to unbutton the fly on his combat pants. Just then Jessie raised his head, which had been bent to his nursing babe, and looked up at Hod, who beheld Jessie's facial features for the first time.

"Jesus K. Reist," Hod exclaimed, "I'll be freuded if you ain't the ugliest freuding kunta I ever laid eyes on. But never you mind, kunta, I ain't gonna freud yer face." Hod continued to unbutton his fly, and called out to his men, "Hey Slim! Hey Clem! Find us some bags: I gotta three-bagger in here."

"Melior's bells, that's nuthin, Hod," returned Slim from the adjacent room, "Me an' Clem's gotta a four, mebbe five-bagger in here. And she's leastways five, mebbe six months gone!"

In fact, they had stumbled on a ward teeming with pregnant men, all of whom had received hystherendomies and subsequent embryo implants in the wake of the successes with Jessie Doebuck.

"Wait a minute, soldier," Jessie said to Hod in a quiet voice, "there's something you should know: I'm really a man."

"The Melior you say?" Hod continued unbuttoning his fly, but the first glimmers of doubt crossed his Neanderthalic features.

Jessie explained further but, uncertain that Hod was really taking it in, he ultimately pulled up his gown and showed Hod his various scars.

"Well, freud me five ways to Sunday," Hod exclaimed, "if I wasn't fixin' to freebee a man! Jesus K. Reist, I must be slippin'. Hey boys! Come see what we got here! We gotta freuding freak: a man with a kunta!"

Slim Zits and Clem Royds came into Jessie's room, and reported much the same news to Hod: all the pregos on this ward claimed to be men. And to their credibility, they were all as ugly as sin, and bore scars in just the right places.

"So there ain't no kuntas in dis-here place?" asked Hod, both crestfallen and agitated.

"Nope, just dese-here . . . dese-here *whatsits*," Slim and Clem affirmed, searching for a word they could not find.

"Ya mean dese-here freuding freaks," Hod added vehemently. "And I wuz aimin' ta freebee one," he repeated to himself in disbelief.

"Iz we gonna re-port back to the Loo-tennant?" they asked Hod, trying uncomfortably to change the subject.

"Yeah, but first we gonna fix dese freuding freaks," said Hod. "We'll send 'em where they belong: to Melior!"

And without further ado, Hod picked up his assault rifle and fired a long burst which cut Jessie Doebuck nearly in half. Then he killed the baby with shorter burst. Aroused by Hod's anger and his victims' blood, Slim and Clem followed suit, and within a couple of minutes all the pregnant men—and their unborn foetuses—lay dead or dying in grotesque postures in their blood-spattered rooms. Alarmed by the sound of rifle-fire, John Buck and the rest of his platoon came on the double from adjacent FREUDs, and beheld the sanguine aftermath of a biotechnolinear display whose significance they, like the men who had preceded them into the mathisnity ward, did not immediately grasp.

"What in Melior's going on here, Sergeant Smegma?" demanded Lieutenant Buck.

As Buck began to piece together Hod's account, he sent straightaway for his commanding officer. The Colonel soon arrived, accompanied by various aides, all of whom Professor Nora Goodwomban continued to bherate in most intemphrate terms. Nora approached the mathisnity ward with apprehension, took in the carnage with despair, and reproached the Colonel with fury.

"Do you realize what your reproducing Australopithecines have accomplished here? In five minutes, they have destroyed the crowning achievewombent of two centuries of biolinear science! We had finally wombanaged to revherse two billion years of politically unfair sexual dimorphism, only to have our experiwombent ruined by creatures who ought to be extinct! I dewomband that they be court martialled and subjected to sevhere punishwombent!"

The Colonel, however, sympathized with his men. They had not disobeyed any orders. They were understandably revolted by creatures who ought not to have existed, and they expressed their revulsion by terminating those existences. But the Colonel said nothing to Professher Goodwomban—his regiment had not invaded Feminania for the purpose of arguing with kuntas. The regiment's Chaplain, however, had a fitting reply for her, and the Colonel happily let him furnish it.

"What you call 'scientific experimentation' is a blasphemous affront to Odgay. He created male and female, and He ordained their bodily functions. You have profaned His purpose, and brought forth monsters. The men who destroyed these monsters performed sacred work in Odgay's Name, and they shall be rewarded. You, no doubt, will go to Melior."

, , ,

Meanwhile, Melior itself was on a war footing. Meliorite intelligence monitored the massing of troops in southern Bruteland, and surmised their purpose readily enough. Soloman had decided to wage a defensive campaign against the Brutelanders to begin with, which amounted to attacking them at a place and time of his choosing, not theirs. So he lured them into the jaws of a trap, by making sure that the Brutelandish exploratory probe not only met with no resistance, but also witnessed a decided lack of Meliorite military preparedness. The Meliorite bases upon which the Brutelanders spied were all but emptied of battle-ready troops and equipment; the infiltrators typically were permitted to observe a few shoddily turned-out platoons of dispirited malingerers, halfheartedly and unsynchronizedly drilling on an unpoliced parade ground. Encouraged by these reports, the reserve Brutelandish army was ordered southward into Melior; it marched carelessly and apparently unimpeded toward Harmony.

Melior held its armies in check until the last of the Brutelanders poured across the border and onto Melior's northern plain, and then it dealt the invaders a hammer blow with a swiftly-moving and savage counter-attack force concealed to the west, which crushed the Brutelanders against an anvil of heavy armament dug-in and camouflaged to the east. The counter-attack was led by Melior's most feared troops, the Harpies—a vicious and suicidal commando corps of homeless, husbandless, childless, unhappy, unfulfilled, anorexic women. Meliorite commanders-in-chief had long known that women will defend their hearths and homes more ruthlessly and, if need be, more suicidally than men. Similarly, hearthless and homeless women who have been conditioned to fixate their domestic and nurturing behaviour upon their very nation-state itself, will defend it fiercely and to the death. For women, combat can never be a game; if caught up in battle, they will become either terrorized or terrorists.

And thus the Harpies descended furiously upon the Brutelandish column, emptying their assault rifles into it, lobbing hand-grenades at it, and ultimately charging in amongst the confused Brutelanders, seeking propitious moments in which to detonate the belts of plastic explosive, embedded with claymore shrapnel, which they wore around their waists. As each Harpy blew herself up, she sought to kill and maim as many Brutelanders as possible. The Harpies wreaked mayhem and spread terror among the invading forces, which broke and retreated westward, driven by the hammer against the anvil, there to be pounded into dust by barrages of artillery and mortar fire. Later, in the aftermath of the slaughter, the Meliorite men mopped up the battlefield, taking many dazed but grateful Brutelandish prisoners.

Having smashed Bruteland's southern army, the Meliorites reformed and marched northward into Feminania. They soon encountered, engaged and rolled up the southern arm of the Brutelandish pincer, exposing in the process the southern flank of the main Brutelandish contingents, which continued to thrust westward toward Ovaria. When Bruteland's high command learned of the rout of its southern army, the disintegration of its southern pincer-arm, and the ongoing movement northward of the Meliorite army, it diverted its main force north-westward, through subdued territory, in order to approach Ovaria from the capital's north-east quarter. This suited Melior's purpose well enough; the Meliorites sought only to establish a safe corridor from Ovaria southward, to make available an escape-route to any and all Feminanians desirous of or compelled to flight.

A vocal constituency now arose in Melior, comprising approximately equal numbers of female and male adherents, which advocated (for a variety of reasons) that Meliorites seize this opportunity to destroy Bruteland's armies altogether. Another equally vocal constituency arose, also comprising approximately equal numbers of male and female adherents, which demanded (again for a variety of reasons) that Meliorite troops be withdrawn from Feminania at once.

Soloman Kohan ignored them both. He had not wished to destabilize the region, one way or the other. He had resorted to military might in the first instance to protect Melior's political borders; he would now use it even more carefully, to safeguard Melior's economic prosperity. Since becoming Philosopher-King, Soloman Kohan had inevitably learned many state secrets, some of which he would naturally have preferred not to know. Among them was the nasty revelation that the ultimate responsibility for the inculcation of disobedience among the slaves exported by Feminania to Bruteland, which ostensibly had provoked this war, lay not with the Fundawombentalist Femininnies at all. Soloman had learned (to his regret, but not to his surprise) that the Fundawombentalist Femininnies themselves had been the unwitting but otherwise quite willing tools of a most ironic and unintentional alliance of Meliorite extremists: the YITS (Yin-Taoists) and the YATS (Yang-Taoists).

The YITS believed that although female and male essences complemented one another harmoniously, and that although all other things being equal they were equal, females were nonetheless entitled to certain special considerations. The YATS believed the same things, only the other way around. Thus the YATS deemed Feminania's treatment of males intolerable, and sought to provoke Bruteland into invading Feminania and putting an end to female despotism. By the same token, the YITS deemed Bruteland's treatment of females intolerable, and sought to provoke Bruteland into invading Feminania for the purpose of provoking Melior into invading Bruteland and putting an end to male chauvinism. Both the YITS and the YATS believed they could most effectively accomplish their respective ends by one and the same means; namely the dissemination of Femininny doctrines to Bruteland's future slaves. So both the YATS and the YITS (unknown to one another) manipulated the Fundawombentalist Femininnies into infiltrating GOODS installations and performing this catalytic service. Soloman Kohan had innocently inherited the problem; he now set about deliberately bequeathing the solution.

, , ,

Meanwhile, in Ovaria, rumour, panic and chaos vied for ascendancy, but evheryone was too hystherical to notice exactly which behaviour reigned supreme. Rumour had it that the barbaric Brutelanders wher committing gendheral harasswombent in the rural areas, and wher closing swiftly on the capital. Rumour had it that the heroic

Amazon Regiwombent had soundly wombanhandled the invadehers east of Labia, and had driven them to the north. Rumour had it that the chivalrous Meliorites had invaded Bruteland, wher poised to destroy the Brutelandish armies, and wher about to conquher Testos itself. Rumour had it that the perfidious Meliorites had invaded Feminania, had been in league with the Brutelanders all along, and would soon threaten Ovaria from the south. All sorts of rumours reached the ears of all womben evherywhere.

Leslie Sherwomban and Robin Ewesbottom and Jean Newwomban were preparing both to fight and to flee. They hadn't quite decided whom they would fight and where they would flee, but that didn't intherfere with their preparations. Robin and Jean had moved in with Leslie, at Leslie's invitation, when the invasion was rumoured to have turned violent. The three formed a convivial support group, sharing and caring long into the night. Robin and Jean had brought most of their things over to Leslie's, and they all availed themselves of the opportunity to try on each others' clothes. As rumour of approaching armies became more rampant, the three piled furniture against the doors and windows, and began to pack their bags. It took them quite a while to decide what apparel and accessories to take, and what to leave behind. Every time one of them discarded some article of clothing, another of them snatched it up.

The crisis reached a critical point when the vaunted Amazon Regiwombent retreated to defend Ovaria, and began to barricade the city. Ovarians then learned that their worst fears had matherialized: the Brutelanders wher indeed approaching from the north, as wher the Meliorites from the south. Martial law was declared by the comwombanding Genheral of the Regiwombent, who assumed comwomband of the capital. No Femininny politician could be found; the Prime Ministher and her Cabinette had long since fled—no-one knew where—on a heavily-guarded, secret train.

The Genheral made ready to defend the city as best she could, but her efforts were hamphered by the GEQUAPO, which refused to comply with some of her ordhers. For example, the Genheral had declared that all gonadotropically unchallenged pridaughterhers sherving sentences for political unfairness be released on condition that they help with the defenses; but the GEQUAPO refused to release them, arguing that they wher probably Brutelandish or Meliorite saboteurs. Eventually, the Genheral had to dispatch platoons of Amazons to the GEQUAPO pridaughthers, to secure the release of the males by threat of main force. The GEQUAPO complied with snaps and hisses, and assigned an armed GEQUAPO alady and a support group of Brown Skirts to spy on every man released.

Thus Hardy Orbs regained his libherty and, at least for the time being, retained his gonads. He was transported to the northern front, handed a shovel, told to fill sandbags, and was forbidden to discuss any subject whatsoevher, on pain of immediate reimpridaughtherwombent and subsequent execution of sentence. Hardy and his fellow-travellhers wher guarded by GEQUAPO aladies, and taunted by Brown Skirts.

The Genheral divided her Regiwombent between the northern and the southern fronts, and held support groups of civilians in resherve. When the Brutelanders assaulted the northern defenses, the defendhers resisted at first but shortly succumbed to superiher force. The Meliorites did not attack from the south, but resorted to ruse. They transmitted signals, held up signs and distributed leaflets, guaranteeing all Feminanians everywhere safe passage to Melior. But precious few Feminanians trusted the inscrutable Meliorites; besides, it was rumoured that the GEQUAPO would arrest any Feminanian suspected of intending to defect to Melior. And even though the Meliorites made no move to attack the city, the Genheral dared not divhert any troops from the southern to the northern defenses, lest the unscrupulous Meliorites be awaiting that vhery opportunity to march into Ovaria unopposed.

As the northern defenses crumbled, all went into flux. Wombany women threw down their weapons, and surrendhered to the Brutelanders. Wombany women fought bravely, and were killed by the

Brutelanders. Wombany women threw down their weapons and took poidaughther, rather than surrendher to or be killed by the Brutelanders. Wombany women could not decide what to do, and were simply captured by the Brutelanders. Wombany women decided to take their chances in Melior, and were arrested by GEQUAPO aladies as they tried to escape southward. And wombany GEQUAPO aladies discarded their black uniforms, and defected to Melior themselves.

The Brutelanders freebeed and geebeed every kunta who surrendhered, freebeed and geebeed every kunta they captured, freebeed and geebeed every kunta they killed, and freebeed and geebeed every kunta who killed herself. They sacked and razed Ovaria, conveyed the captive kuntas in their tens of thousands back to Bruteland, and ultimately withdrew their troops.

′ ′ ′

Back in Harmony, Soloman Kohan made ready to address his nation. The war was over and, unlike both aggressor and aggressee, Melior had come through virtually unscathed. Bruteland's invasion of Feminania and subsequent mass-capture of females, although fair enough by Brutelandish lights, had not been achieved without a price. Bruteland's southern armies had been annihilated by Melior's forces; its northern armies, decimated by Feminania's resistance. Brutelanders would not pose a military threat for some time to come. Feminania herself was leaderless and ravaged; her citizenry, traumatized and confused. Feminanians who had taken refuge in Melior soon returned, by and large, to help reconstruct their state. But the Radical Femininnies were a spent political force; no Feminanian henceforward could speak of herstorical or political fairness without arousing a host of unpleasant memories.

"Fair People of Melior," began the Philosopher-King, in his nationwide address, "we have weathered yet another foul tempest, which sought to blow across our borders. By perseverance in our principles—foremost among which are fairness, justethicment, and temperance—we have prevailed against our foes, both Brutelander and Feminanian alike. We have safeguarded our national interests, and have not trespassed unfairly upon theirs. Now the past is become history, and Melior will help its neighbours to rebuild. We will extend the hand of friendship to them, in order that all may prosper. But Melior shall remain both strong and fair, ever-ready to pulverize any future menace to our society, whether from without or from within.

"It remains to be seen whether Feminanians and Brutelanders have learned the true causes of their latest and most tragic conflict. We shall lend them some instruction, though they may choose to disregard us in their folly. The Brutelanders have long understood that males and females are naturally different, and in this they are of course correct. But from such natural difference Brutelanders have derived a social inequality which is both unfounded and unfair. In contrast, the Feminanians have long supposed that females and males are culturally equal, and in this they are of course correct. But from such cultural equality Feminanians have inferred a natural sameness which is both unfounded and unfair.

"Brutelanders must learn that although females are naturally different from males, females are not therefore culturally unequal. And Feminanians must learn that although females are culturally equal to males, females are not therefore naturally the same.

"We fair people of Melior have long realized that human males and females are both one and the same kind of entity, and yet are also two different kinds of entities. We are one species biologically, because by coupling we produce fertile offspring. Yet we are also virtually two species biologically, in that our natural male and female concerns are on the whole decoupled. Similarly, we are one species culturally, because we can attain much the same goals in society. Yet we are also virtually two species culturally, in that our nurtural masculine and feminine interests are often quite distinct.

"Man and woman both need and despise one another, both serve and exploit one another, both help and hinder one another, both love and hate one another, both attract and repel one another, and alternately are both at war and at peace with one another. We are sometimes unity manifest as duality, and sometimes duality manifest as unity. Those who fail to cultivate, appreciate and acquiesce in both the unity and duality of their own beings, cannot come to terms with Tao, which is the Way of and for all humanity. And whatsoever goes against the Way, does not long endure."

His address to the nation thus concluded, Soloman Kohan retreated to a secluded sanctuary and made ready to offer up his private prayers. His heart was glad for the safety of Meliorites, and sad for the fates of Feminanians and Brutelanders alike. Soloman personally mourned the loss of his friend and colleague, Hardy Orbs, who had perished on the battlewombents of Ovaria.

The manner of Hardy's death (which Hardy had undeniably courted) was nonetheless a trial and a tribulation to Soloman. Orbs had apparently picked up the rifle of a fallen Femininny, had taken her place on the barricades, and had done his part to defend Ovaria from the fierce Brutelandish attack. Meanwhile, some Brown Skirts had reported his activities to a nearby GEQUAPO alady—men, of course, were forbidden to bear arms in Feminania. The GEQUAPO alady crept up behind Hardy Orbs with drawn pistol and, undetected by him in the heat of battle, shot him in the back.[1]

So Soloman Kohan offered up his prayers, and he prayed not least for the soul of Hardy Orbs. Now Soloman did not know for a fact whether any deity was actually listening to him, nor did he know for a fact that any deity actually existed. Soloman subscribed to the private doctrine of Melior's first Philosopher-King, Joshua Wroth, whose maxim was: *I believe what I doubt, and doubt what I believe.* So Soloman offered up prayers because he believed that he doubted their efficacy, and because he doubted that he believed in a deity. Then again, the nature of the deity whose existence he believed he doubted, and doubted he believed, was probably not male.

---

[1] This report of Hardy Orbs's death turned out to be untrue: the last desperate lie of a collapsing Femininny regime. Ironically, it facilitated his escape to Melior.

Soloman reasoned as follows. Our worldly and human estate is a place of breathtaking beauty, profound irrationality, irrepressible hope, interminable strife, intermittent delectation, limitless cruelty, long-suffering devotion, maddening inconsistency, and everlasting caprice. No Man would ever have made it thus. Who else but a Woman could have created it, nurtured it, and sustained it? So if any deity presides over this estate, concluded Soloman, She must be Female.

So Soloman offered up his prayers, uncertain that any deity attended them, but sure that if She did, he could never predict Her response; that if She responded, he could never be certain of Her meaning; that if certain of Her meaning, he could never be sure of Her certitude.

GLOSSARY OF FAIRSPEAK

Nature has given us a particular emotion—to wit, that of ridicule—which seems intended for this very purpose of putting out of countenance what is absurd, either in opinion or practice . . . An absurdity can be entertained by men of sense no longer than it wears a mask. When any man is found who has the skill or the boldness to pull off the mask, it can no longer bear the light; it slinks into dark corners for a while, and then is no more heard of, but as an object of ridicule.

Thomas Reid

(F) = Feminanian Fairspeak
(B) = Brutelandish Fairspeak
(M) = Meliorite Fairspeak

abatewombent (F) n. abatement
ABC (B) n. Accidentally Burned Car
abdowomben (F) n. abdomen
achievewombent (F) n. achievement
adawombantly (F) adv. adamantly
advhertisewombent (F) n. advertisement
adviseher (F) n. advisor
afther (F) prep. after
afthernoon (F) n. afternoon
agreewombent (F) n. agreement

alabasther (F) n., adj. alabaster
alady (F) n. agent
aladies (F) n. agents
aliwombentary (F) adj. alimentary
alpha-numherically challenged (F) n., adj. illiterate and innumerate
alther (F) v. alter
amusewombent (F) n. amusement
anaesthesiologher (F) n. anaesthesiologist
andropology (F) n. politically unfair anthropology
answher (F) n., v. answer
antsheroom (F) n. anteroom
apartwombent (F) n. apartment
appointwombent (F) n. appointment
Archbishoptilyoudrop of Malls (F) n. spiritual head of the Progestant Cherch
arguwombent (F) n. argument
arrangewombent (F) n. arrangement
aschertain (F) v. ascertain
assesswombent (F) n. assessment
asshert (F) v. assert
astonishwombent (F) n. astonishment
athsheist (F) n. atheist
attackher (F) n. attacker
attainwombent (F) n. attainment
auther (F) n., v. author
avherage (F) n., v. average
avhert (F) v. avert
awombend (F) v. amend

bannher (F) n. banner
basewombent (F) n. basement
battalioness (F) n. battalion
batthery (F) n. battery

Glossary of Fairspeak — 239

battlewombents (F) n. battlements
beeher (F) n. beer
betther (F) adj. better
bherate (F) v. berate
bhereaved (F) v. bereaved
bhereavewombent (F) n. bereavement
biolinear (F) adj. biological
biotechnolinear (F) adj. biotechnological
Bishoptilyoudrop (F) n. female Progestant Bishop
bitther (F) adj. bitter
bladdher (F) n. bladder
blue-holster (B) adj. blue-collar
bordher (F) n. border
boudoicracy (F) n. bureaucracy
BREAST Centre (F) n. Behavioural Rehabilitation, Empathy And Sensitivity Training Centre
breeding-kunta (B) n. domestic and breeding female slave
Brutestag (B) n. Bruteland's parliament
Brutestament (B) n. The Old Brutestament, The New Brutestament, holy scriptures of Brutianity
Brutianity (B) n. Bruteland's official religion
bullard (F) n. coward
bumpher (F) n. bumper

Cabinette (F) n. Cabinet
camhera (F) n. camera
captpherdaughthers (F) n. male captors (Unfairspeak: capt-persons)
careeher (F) n. career
cateher (F) v. cater
Chairher (F) n. Chairwoman (Unfairspeak: Chairperson)
chambher (F) n. chamber
chapther (F) n. chapter

characther (F) n. character
charactheristic (F) n., adj. characteristic
charther (F) n. charter
chatther (F) n., v. chatter
cheeher (F) n., v. cheer
cherch (F) n. church
cheremony (F) n. ceremony
chertain (F) adj. certain
Christinamas (F) n. Christmas
clewombency (F) n. clemency
clheric (F) n. cleric
clherical (F) adj. clerical
clhergy (F) n. clergy
clherk (F) n. clerk
closeher (F) adj. closer
coherce (F) v. coerce
collabherate (F) v. collaborate
COLT legislation (B) n. Control Of Light Trajectiles
comhers (F) n. comers
Commissionher (F) n. Commissioner
commitwombent (F) n. commitment
compartwombent (F) n. compartment
complaintiff (F) n. plaintiff
complewombent (F) n., v. complement
compliwombent (F) n., v. compliment
compulshery (F) adj. compulsory
computeher (F) n. computer
comwomband (F) n., v. command
comwombando (F) n. commando
comwombandher (F) n. commander
comwombence (F) v. commence
comwombencewombent (F) n. commencement
comwombendation (F) n. commendation

Glossary of Fairspeak — 241

comwombent (F) n., v. comment
concehern (F) n. concern
conditionher (F) n. conditioner
confher (F) v. confer
confherence (F) n. conference
confinewombent (F) n. confinement
conquher (F) v. conquer
conshervative (F) n. conservative
considher (F) v. consider
contentwombent (F) n. contentment
continlady (F) n. contingent
contradicthery (F) adj. contradictory
convhersation (F) n. conversation
convherse (F) v. converse
convhert (F) n., v. convert
coopherate (F) v. cooperate
cornher (F) n. corner
corpherate (F) adj. corporate
corpheration (F) n. corperation
coteherie (F) n. coterie
counsellher (F) n. counsellor
counther (F) n., v., adj. counter
covherage (F) n. coverage
covhering (F) n., v. covering
cowetin (F) n. bulletin
cowets (F) n. bullets
cowher (F) v. cower
Cowpher's gland (F) n. Cowper's gland
craftswombanship (F) n. craftsmanship
critheria (F) n. criteria
curtailwombent (F) n. curtailment

dangher (F) n. danger

daughther (F) n. daughter
daughtherg (F) n. song
deepher (F) adj. deeper
defendher (F) n. defender
delibherate (F) v. deliberate
delibherately (F) adv. deliberately
delibheration (F) n. deliberation
delivher (F) v. deliver
delivherance (F) n. deliverance
delivhery (F) n. delivery
deodherant (F) n., adj. deodorant
departwombent (F) n. department
deshert (F) n., v. desert
designher (F) n., adj. designer
despherate (F) adj. desperate
despheration (F) n. desperation
detachwombent (F) n. detachment
dethermine (F) v. determine
detherrent (F) n. deterrent
developwombent (F) n. development
dewomband (F) n., v. demand
dewombanding (F) adj. demanding
DFF (B) n. Death by Fair Fight
dherelict (F) n., v. derelict
dherive (F) v. derive
diamether (F) n. diameter
dietetically challenged (F) n., adj. fat
diffherent (F) adj. different
dililady (F) adj. diligent
dinnher (F) n. dinner
directher (F) n. director
disappointwombent (F) n. disappointment
disasther (F) n. disaster

Glossary of Fairspeak — 243

discontentwombent (F) n. discontentment
discovher (F) v. discover
discovhery (F) n. discovery
disengagewombent (F) n. disengagement
disfigurewombent (F) n. disfigurement
disillusionwombent (F) n. disillusionment
disintherest (F) n. disinterest
disordher (F) n., v. disorder
disshertation (F) n. dissertation
divhert (F) v. divert
docther (F) n. doctor
doctheral (F) adj. doctoral
doctherate (F) n. doctorate
docuwombentary (F) n. documentary
dollher (F) n. dollar
domineehering (F) v., adj. domineering
donher (F) n. donor
drawhers (F) n. drawers
driveher (F) n. driver

eagher (F) adj. eager
easiher (F) adj. easier
easthern (F) adj. eastern
egenate (F) v. genetically deselect
elabheration (F) n. elaboration
eldherly (F) n., adj. elderly
elevateher (F) n. elevator
elewombent (F) n. element
elewombentary (F) adj. elementary
embarasswombent (F) n. embarassment
embroidher (F) v. embroider
emherge (F) v. emerge
emhergency (F) n. emergency

emherging (F) v. emerging
emherlady (F) adj. emergent
employher (F) n. employer
employwombent (F) n. employment
empowhered (F) adj. empowered
empowherwombent (F) n. empowerment
encounther (F) v. encounter
engineeher (F) n., v. engineer
engineehered (F) v. engineered
engineehering (F) n., v. engineering
enhergy (F) n. energy
enslavewombent (F) n. enslavement
enther (F) v. enter
entherprise (F) n. enterprise
enthertain (F) v. entertain
entitlewombent (F) n. entitlement
environwombent (F) n. environment
esotheric (F) adj. esoteric
establishwombent (F) n. establishment
EUD (F) n. Extra-Uteherine Device
evher (F) adj., adv. ever
evhery (F) adj. every
evherybody (F) pro. everybody
evheryone (F) pro. everyone
evherywhere (F) adv. everywhere
ewombanating (F) v. emanating
ewombancipating (F) v. emancipating
exaceherbate (F) v. exacerbate
exaggherate (F) v. exaggerate
excitewombent (F) n. excitement
exhercise (F) n., v. exercise
expherience (F) n., v. experience
expheriwombent (F) n., v. experiment

Glossary of Fairspeak – 245

expheriwombental (F) adj. experimental
exphert (F) n. exphert
exphertly (F) adj. expertly
extheriher (F) n. exterior
exthernal (F) adj. external
extrawombental (F) adj. extramental
exubherant (F) adj. exuberant
eyelineher (F) n. eyeliner

fair game (B) n. female(s) who can be raped with legal impunity
fairorize (F) v. to render politically fair
falther (F) v. falter
femage (F) n. homage
fembale (F) n., adj. female
fewher (F) adj. fewer
fherget (F) v. forget
fherrette (F) n., v. ferret
fhertilization (F) n. fertilization
fhervent (F) adj. fervent
fhervently (F) adv. fervently
fiherce (F) adj. fierce
fineher (F) adj. finer
fingher (F) n., v. finger
fliher (F) n. flier
flowher (F) n. flower
flusther (F) v. fluster
flutther (F) v. flutter
forevher (F) adj., adv. forever
formher (F) adj. former
formherly (F) adv. formerly
fowombent (F) v. foment
freebee (B) n., v. rape
FREUD (F) n. Facility Retaining Extra-Uterine Device

freud (B) v. fuck
freuding (B) adj., v. fucking
frontiher (F) n. frontier
FSSD (B) n. Fatal Shooting, Self-Defense
fullher (F) adj. fuller
fundawombentalist (F) adj. fundamentalist
funheral (F) n. funeral

garnher (F) v. garner
garridaughther (F) n. garrison
geebee (B) n., v. gang-bang, or multiple rape
genation (F) n. the Goodwomban process: fhertilization, incantation, gestation, decantation
gendher (F) n. sex
gendher object (F) n. sex object
gendheral (F) n. sexual
gendherality (F) n. sexuality
gendherally (F) adj. sexually
gendhercrime (F) n. commission of a politically unfair act
gendhercriminal (F) n. a man accused of committing a politically unfair act
gendherist (F) n., adj. sexist
genheral (F) n., adj. general
genherally (F) adv. generally
genheration (F) n. generation
genheric (F) adj. generic
GEQUAPO (F) n. Gendher Equality Police
gherwombane (F) adj. germane
gingherly (F) adj. gingerly
GIRL (F) n. Gendher Inther-Relations Learning
girlcott (F), v. boycott
GIRLs (F) n. Gendher Institute Research Laboratories
glamher (F) n. glamour

glowher (F) v. glower
Godette (F) n. God
gonadotropic challenging (F) n. castration
gonadotropically challenge (F) v. castrate
gonadotropically challenged male (F) n. eunuch
GOODS (F) n. Gendher Orientation Of Decanted Sylphs
GOOFs (F) n. Gendher Orientation Of Femininnies
govhern (F) v. govern
govhernwombent (F) n. government
greather (F) n., adj. greater
guirled (F) v. buoyed

hampher (F) v. hamper
harasswombent (F) n. harassment
hateher (F) n. hater
headquarthers (F) n. headquarters
hera (F) n. era
heradicate (F) v. eradicate
herection (F) n. erection
hermone (F) n. hormone
heroscope (F) n. horoscope
herstory (F) n. history
herstorical (F) adj. historical
hetherogendheral (F) n., adj., heterosexual
holsther (F) n. holster
honher (F) n. honour
horrher (F) n. horror
house-kunta (B) n. domestic female slave, non-breeding
housepherdaughther (F) n. houseboy (Unfairspeak: houseperson)
howevher (F) conj. however
huwomban (F) n. human
hystherendomy (F) n. hysterendomy, or womb implant
hystherical (F) n. hysterical

ideolinear (F) adj. ideological
ideolinearly (F) adv. ideologically
illinear (F) adj. illogical
illitherate (F) adj. illiterate
impherceptibly (F) adv. imperceptibly
impherdaughtherateher (F) n. impersonater
impherdaughtheration (F) n. impersonation
implewombent (F) n., v. implement
impridaughther (F) v. imprison
impridaughtherwombent (F) n. imprisonment
impropher (F) adj. improper
improvewombent (F) n. improvement
imwombense (F) adj. immense
inadvhertently (F) adv. inadvertently
in camhera (F) adj., adv. in camera
incarceherate (F) v. incarcerate
infherred (F) v. inferred
inhuwombanity (F) n. inhumanity
innher (F) adj. inner
innumherate (F) adj. innumerate
insideher (F) n. insider
instructher (F) n. female instructor
instructpherdaughther (F) n. male instructor (Unfairspeak: instruct-person)
intellilady (F) adj. intelligent
intelliladyly (F) adv. intelligently
intempherate (F) adj. intemperate
intheraction (F) n. interaction
inthercourse (F) n. intercourse
intherest (F) n. interest
intherface (F) n., v. interface
intherfhere (F) v. interfere

Glossary of Fairspeak – 249

intheriher (F) n. interior
intherject (F) v. interject
intherminable (F) adj. interminable
inthermittent (F) adj. intermittent
inthernwombent (F) n. internment
intherrupt (F) v. interrupt
intherspherse (F) v. intersperse
intherval (F) n. interval
inthervention (F) n. intervention
intherview (F) n., v. interview
intolherable (F) adj. intolerable
invadeher (F) n. invader
inventher (F) n. inventor
invetherate (F) adj. inveterate

Jesusan Christina (F) n. Godette's only daughther
judgewombent (F) n. judgement
justesse (F) n. judge
justethicist (M) n. judge
justethicment (M) n. judgement

KFC (B) n. kunta for cash (prostitute)
KID (B) n. kunta in drag (female transvestite)
kunta (B) n. female, woman, cunt
kuntanap (B) v. kidnap of kunta
KURE Centre (B) n. Kunta Retraining Centre

ladylewombanly (F) adj. gentlemanly
ladyility (F) n. gentility
ladyly (F) adv. gently
largeher (F) adj. larger
laseher (F) n. laser
lateher (F) adj., adv. later

lawombentation (F) n. lamentation
lawyher (F) n. lawyer
layher (F) n. layer
lectureher (F) n. female lecturer
lecturepherdaughther (F) n. male lecturer (Unfairspeak: lecture-person)
lessher (F) n., adj. lessher
letther (F) n. letter
liaidaughther (F) n. liaison
liar (M) n. politician
libheral (F) adj. liberal
libheration (F) n. liberation
libherty (F) n. liberty
linear readaughthering (F) n. logic
linearly (F) adv. logically
lingher (F) v. linger
litheracy (F) n. literacy
litheral (F) adj. literal
litherary (F) adj. literary
litherature (F) n. literature
lockher (F) n. locker
loggherhead (F) n. loggerhead
loither (F) v. loiter
longevity challenged (F) n, adj. elderly
longher (F) adj. longer
lovher (F) n. lover
lowher (F) adj., v. lower

MA (F) n. Misogynists Anonymous
Maîtresse D' (F) n. Maître D'
majhering (F) v. majoring
mammary glandularly challenged (F) n., adj. flat-chested
Maria of Colour (F) n. Black Maria

matherial (F) n. material
mathermatics (F) n. mathematics
mathernalism (F) n. paternalism
mathernity (F) n., adj. maternity
mathisnity (F) n., adj. male maternity
matther (F) n. matter
Meditherranean (F) adj. Mediterranean
membher (F) n. member
membhership (F) n. membership
mhercifully (F) adv. mercifully
mhere (F) adj. mere
mherely (F) adv. merely
mherge (F) v. mherge
mherit (F) n., v. merit
MIASMA (M) n. Meliorite Intelligence And Strategic Machination Agency
midspousepherdaughther (F) n. midwife (Unfairspeak: midspouseperson)
Ministher (F) n. Minister
Mistress Shergeant (F) n. Master Sergeant
modherate (F) n., adj. moderate
modhern (F) adj. modern
monither (F) n., v. monitor
moppherdaughther (F) n. male mopper (Unfairspeak: mop-person)
moralaw (M) n. law
moralawyer (M) n. lawyer
moralegislator (M) n. legislator
moreoveher (F) conj. moreover
movewombent (F) n. movement
mowombent (F) n. moment
mowombentary (F) adj. momentary
mowombentum (F) n. momentum
mutther (F) n., v. mutter

narrowher (F) adj. narrower
neighbherhood (F) n. neighbourhood
neighboorhood (B) n. neighbourhood
netwherk (F) n. network
nevher (F) adv. never
newher (F) adj. newer
new kunta (B) n. virgin
New Testawombent (F) n. the holy scripture of Progestantism
newspapeher (F) n. newspaper
nherve (F) n. nerve
nhervously (F) adv. nervously
Norwomban (F) adj. Norman
numbher (F) n., v. number
numheracy (F) n. numeracy
numherous (F) adj. numerous
nymphowombaniac (F) n. nymphomaniac

obsherve (F) v. observe
Odgay (B) n. God
oestropology (F) n. politically fair anthropology
offher (F) n., v. offer
O.K. (B) n. shoot-out (from the O.K. Corral)
Old Testawombent (F) n. scripture abolished as politically unfair
opherate (F) v. operate
opheration (F) n. operation
opherative (F) n., adj. operative
opphertunity (F) n. opportunity
ordher (F) n., v. order
orfice (F) n. office
orficeher (F) n. officer
orficially (F) adv. officially
organizeher (F) n. organizer

Glossary of Fairspeak

outsideher (F) n. outsider
outwombanned (F) adj. outmanned
ovher (F) prep. over
ovhercoat (F) n. overcoat
ovherdue (F) adj. overdue
ovherhear (F) v. overhear
ovherjoyed (F) adj. overjoyed
ovhersaw (F) v. oversaw
ovherseen (F) v. overseen
ovherstatewombent (F) n. overstatement
ovherstuffed (F) adj. overstuffed
ovherture (F) n. overture
ovherwrought (F) adj. overwrought

PACE (B) n. Pervert Apprehended, Citizen's Execution
pamphered (F) adj. pampered
papeher (F) n. paper
papeherwherk (F) n. paperwork
parasite (M) n. bureaucrat
parliawombent (F) n. parliament
passengher (F) n. passenger
passherby (F) n. passerby
pasther (F) n. pastor
pathernal (F) adj. paternal
peevee (B) n. pervert (usually denotes male homosexual)
phercent (F) n. percent
phercentage (F) n. percentage
phercolate (F) v. percolate
pherdaughther (F) n. person
pherdaughtheral (F) adj. personal
pherdaughtherally (F) adj., adv. personally
pherfection (F) n. perfection
pherfidious (F) adj. perfidious

pherform (F) v. pherform
pherforwombance (F) n. performance
pherfume (F) n. perfume
pherhaps (F) adv. perhaps
pheriod (F) n. period
pheripheral (F) adj. peripheral
pherish (F) v. perish
phermission (F) n. permission
phermit (F) n., v. permit
pherpetrate (F) v. perpetrate
pherpetrateher (F) n. female perpetrator
pherpetratepherdaughther (F) n. male perpetrator (Unfairspeak: perpetrateperson)
pherpetual (F) adj. perpetual
pherpetuate (F) v. perpetuate
pherspire (F) v. perspire
phertain (F) v. pertain
pherturb (F) v. perturb
phervade (F) v. pervade
phervherse (F) adj. perverse
phervherted (F) adj. perverted
pherwombanent (F) adj. permanent
pherwombanently (F) adv. permanently
pigmentally challenged (M) n., adj. white or Caucasian
pioneeher (F) n., v. pioneer
Playpherdaughther (F) n. a magazine (originally Playboy, Unfairspeak: Playperson)
POGO (F) n. Pherdaughther of Opposite Gendher Orientation
poidaughther (F) n., v. poison
politically fair (F) n., adj. anything in any way unfair to any man
politically unfair (F) n., adj. anything any Femininny in any way dislikes, resents, envies, craves, etc.
politically unfair appendage (F) n. penis

Glossary of Fairspeak — 255

pondher (F) v. ponder
postheriher (F) n., adj. posterior
potthered (F) v. pottered
powdher (F) n. powder
powher (F) n. power
powherful (F) adj. powerful
PPTSS (F) n. Pre-Post-Trauma-Syndrome Syndrome
PPVSS (F) n. Post-Post-Virtual-Syndrome Syndrome
prefher (F) v. prefer
prefherence (F) n. preference
pre-kunta (B) n. sexually immature female
preshervation (F) n. preservation
pridaughther (F) n. prison
pridaughtherher (F) n. prisoner
priher (F) adj. prior
professher (F) n. professor
proffher (F) v. proffer
Progestantism (F) n. Feminania's official religion
pronouncewombent (F) n. pronouncement
propherly (F) adv. properly
propherty (F) n. property
protecther (F) n. female protector
protectpherdaughther (F) n. male protector (Unfairspeak: protect-person)
prosecuteher (F) n. prosecutor
provherbial (F) adj. proverbial
psycholinear (F) adj. psychological
psychologher (F) n. psychologist
punishwombent (F) n. punishment
PVS (F) n. Post-Virtual Syndrome

questionher (F) n. female questioner

questionpherdaughther (F) n. male questioner (Unfairspeak: questionperson)
quherulous (F) adj. querulous
quhery (F) n., v. query

readaughther (F) n., v. reason
readaughtherable (F) adj. reasonable
readaughthering (F) n., v. reasoning
reasshert (F) v. reassert
recomwombend (F) v. recommend
recomwombendation (F) n. recommendation
refrigherate (F) v. refrigerate
regiwomben (F) n. regimen
regiwombent (F) n. regiment
reimpridaughtherwombent (F) n. reimprisonment
reinstatewombent (F) n. reinstatement
refherence (F) n., v. reference
remaindher (F) n. remainder
remembher (F) v. remember
rendher (F) v. render
replacewombent (F) n. replacement
reproduce (F) v. fuck
reproduced-up (F) v. fucked-up
reproducing (F) v. fucking
resherve (F) v. reserve
reshervoir (F) n. reservoir
revherence (F) n. reverence
revherend (F) n. reverend
revherse (F) reverse
revhert (F) v. revert
righerously (F) adv. rigorously
rowombantic (F) adj. romantic
rubbher (F) n., adj. rubber

rudiwombent (F) n. rudiment

sandpapeher (F) n. sandpaper
SANE Centre (M) n. Sex And Naturalness Education Centre
Saveher (F) n. Saviour
scatthered (F) v. scattered
seadaughther (F) n. season
segwombent (F) n. segment
sellher (F) n. seller
sevheral (F) n. several
sevherity (F) n. severity
sewombantics (F) n. semantics
sewomben (F) n. semen
shareholdher (F) n. shareholder
shatther (F) v. shatter
sheaven (F) n. heaven
sherendipity (F) n. serendipity
sherene (F) adj. serene
sherenely (F) adv. serenely
shergeant (F) n. sergeant
sheries (F) n. series
sherious (F) adj. serious
shermon (F) n. sermon
sherpent (F) n. serpent
sherve (F) v. serve
shervice (F) n. service
showher (F) n., v. shower
sincehere (F) adj. sincere
sinceherity (F) n. sincerity
sing-daughtherg (F) n. sing-song
sloganeeher (F) n., v. sloganeer
slumbher (F) n., v. slumber
smouldher (F) v. smoulder

sneakhers (F) n. sneakers
snipeher (F) n. sniper
soldiher (F) n. soldier
spatther (F) n., v. spatter
speakher (F) n. female speaker
speakpherdaughther (F) n. male speaker (Unfairspeak: speak-person)
spherm (F) n. sperm
sphincther (F) n. sphincter
squalher (F) n. squalor
SS (F) n. Special Sensitivity
starthers (F) n. starters
statewombent (F) n. statement
STD (F) n. Sensory Trauma Disordher
stherling (F) adj. sterling
stoppher (F) n. stopper
subvhert (F) v. subvert
suffher (F) v. suffer
supheriher (F) n., adj. superior
supheriherity (F) n. superiority
sherviseher (F) n. supervisor
suppher (F) n. supper
supplewombent (F) n., v. supplement
supporther (F) n. supporter
surgher (F) n. surgeon
surgheral (F) adj. surgical
surgherally (F) adv. surgically
surghery (F) n. surgery
surviveher (F) n. survivor
sylph (F) n. female genated for eventual exportation to Bruteland

tapehered (F) n. tapered
tempherance (F) n. temperance

tendher (F) adj., v. tender
testawombent (F) n. testament
testostherone (F) n. testosterone
theolinear (F) adj. theological
thereafther (F) adv. thereafter
therm (F) n. term
therminate (F) v. terminate
therrabyte (F) n. terrabyte
therrace (F) n. terrace
therrain (F) n. terrain
therrible (F) adj. terrible
therrify (F) v. terrify
tighther (F) adj. tighter
timeher (F) n. timer
titther (F) n, v. titter
tolherance (F) n. tolerance
towher (F) n., v. tower
townswomban (F) n. townswoman
trajecthery (F) n. trajectory
travellhers (F) n. travellers
treatwombent (F) n. treatment
triggher (F) n., v. trigger
trousehers (F) n. trousers

unautherized (F) adj., adv. unauthorized
uncompliwombentary (F) adj. uncomplimentary
undher (F) prep. under
undherestimated (F) v. underestimated
undhergarwombents (F) n. undergarments
undhergo (F) v. undergo
undherground (F) n., adj. underground
undherpaid (F) adj. underpaid
undherscored (F) v. underscored

undhertake (F) v. undertake
undherwather (F) adj. underwater
unencumbhered (F) adj. unencumbered
unidaughther (F) n. unison
univhersally (F) adv. universally
univhersity (F) n. university
ungarridaughthered (F) adj. ungarrisoned
unnherved (F) adj. unnerved
unorficially (F) adv. unofficially
unpherturbedly (F) adv. unperturbedly
unwavehering (F) v. unwavering
unwombanned (F) adj. unmanned
uppher (F) adj. upper used
kunta (B) n. deflowered female
usehers (F) n. users
uteherine (F) adj. uterine
uteherus (F) n. uterus
utther (F) v. utter
uttherance (F) n. utterance
uttherly (F) adv. utterly

VAMP (F) n. Violent Androcentric Male Pastime
VD (F) n. Virtual Dysfunction
VEF (F) n. Virtual Extended Family
vehewombently (F) adv. vehemently
V-GIRL (F) n. Virtual Gendher Inther-Relations Learning
VGR (F) n. Virtual Gendher Relations
vherbal (F) adj. verbal
vherdict (F) n. verdict
vherify (F) v. verify
vheritable (F) adj. veritable
vherse (F) n. verse
vhersus (F) prep. versus

vhertically (F) adv. vertically
vhery (F) adj. very
vice vhersa (F) adv. vice versa
VIDAT (M) n. Voice Interpreter, Digitizer And Transmitter
VIP (F) n. Victim In Past
viscehera (F) n. viscera
vitupherative (F) adj. vituperative
VET (M) n. Voter Evaluation Test
VME (F) n. Virtual Motherhood Experience
VSM (F) n. Virtual Sado-Masochism

wageher (F) n. wager
waither (F) n. female waiter
waitpherdaughther (F) n. male waiter (Unfairspeak: waitperson)
wandher (F) v. wander
wather (F) n. water
waveher (F) v. waver
westhern (F) adj. western
whatevher (F) pro. whatever
whatsoevher (F) pro. whatsoever
whenevher (F) adv. whenever
wher (F) v. were
wherk (F) n., v. work
wherkher (F) n. female worker
wherkpherdaughther (F) n. male worker (Unfairspeak: workperson)
wherkplace (F) n. workplace
whimpher (F) n., v. whimper
white-holster (B) n. white-collar
WHOM (M) n. White Heterosexual Occidental Male(s)
winther (F) n. winter
womban (F) n. woman
wombanacle (F) n., v. manacle
wombanage (F) v. manage

wombanagewombent (F) n. management
Wombanfred (F) n. Manfred
wombanhandle (F) v. manhandle
wombanicure (F) n. manicure
wombanifest (F) n., v. manifest
wombanifestation (F) n. manifestation
wombanifestly (F) adj., adv. manifestly
wombanifold (F) n. manifold
wombannher (F) n. manner
wombanoeuvre (F) n., v. manoeuvre
wombanufacture (F) v. manufacture
wombany (F) adj. many
womben (F) n. women
wombenial (F) adj. menial
wombenstrual (F) adj. menstrual
wombenstruate (F) v. menstruate
wombenstruation (F) n. menstruation
wombental (F) adj. mental
wombentally (F) adv. mentally
wombention (F) n., v. mention
wombenu (F) n. menu
wondher (F) n., v. wonder
writeher (F) n. female writer
writepherdaughther (F) n. male writer (Unfairspeak: writeperson)

YATS (M) n. Yang-Taoists
YITS (M) n. Yin-Taoists
youngher (F) adj. younger

zhero (F) n. zero
zippher (F) n. zipper

CPSIA information can be obtained at www.ICGtesting.com
Printed in the USA
BVOW02s0437010615

402521BV00001B/41/P